ADVANCE PRAISE
for *The Ugly Truth*

"Jill Orr's comedic capers shine on! The third Riley Ellison mystery *The Ugly Truth* had me in stitches and made me want to visit Tuttle Corner to join Riley on one of her hilarious adventures. Do your funny bone a favor, and pick this book up now."

—**Hannah Mary McKinnon**, author of *The Neighbors* and *Her Secret Son*

"Jill Orr hits an almost impossible combo with *The Ugly Truth*; page-turning suspense, laugh-out-loud humor, and a delightfully complex mystery you just can't put down. If you like smart criminals, smarter women sleuths, and endearing side characters you care about, Orr delivers with the third book in her charming Riley Ellison series."

—**Libby Kirsch**, Emmy Award–winning journalist and author of the Stella Reynolds Mystery Series and the Janet Black Mystery Series

PRAISE
for the Riley Ellison Mysteries

"A ray of sunshine cloaked in a mystery. Jill Orr is the best humorous mystery writer around, with a voice all her own."

—**Laura McHugh**, best-selling author of *The Weight of Blood* and *Arrowood*

"Fresh and funny, romantic and sunny, Orr's book checked three genre boxes for me: a smart cozy series, a Southern small-town setting, and, my favorite, a newspaper mystery.... I loved the hilarious emails the author interjects into the narrative."

—**Carole Barrowman**, *Milwaukee Journal Sentinel*

"The laughs keep coming."

—*Kirkus Reviews*

"I loved this fresh page-turner—it's fun, funny, and moves like lightning."

—**Lian Dolan**, Satellite Sister and author of the best-selling novels *Helen of Pasadena* and *Elizabeth the First Wife*

"Crime novels are one of the most popular fiction genres, so it is difficult for writers to keep it fresh and explore new twists on the traditional whodunit. Author Jill Orr is successfully among those who have [a] niche all of her own.... By actually capturing the unique voice of a generation, Orr brings something out of the ordinary and elusive to so many."

—*BookTrib*

"Fans of comic light mysteries will be rewarded."

—*Publishers Weekly*

"The small-town nature of this mystery, with the requisite fishbowl local politics, relationships, and grudges, makes it perfect for cozy lovers who want something more modern."

—*Booklist*

The Ugly Truth

By Jill Orr

Prospect Park Books

Published by Prospect Park Books
2359 Lincoln Avenue
Altadena, California 91001
www.prospectparkbooks.com

Distributed by Consortium Book Sales & Distribution
www.cbsd.com

Library of Congress Cataloging-in-Publication Data is on file with the Library of Congress. The following is for reference only:

Names: Orr, Jill, author
Title: The ugly truth: a Riley Ellison mystery / Jill Orr.
Identifiers: ISBNs 9781945551468 (hardcover); 9781945551444 (softcover); 9781945551451 (ebook)
Subjects: | GSAFD: Mystery fiction

Cover design by Susan Olinsky
Cover illustration by Nancy Nimoy
Book layout and design by Amy Inouye
Printed in the United States of America

To Jimmy
forever and ever, amen

Dear Miss Ellison,

Thank you for updating your Click.com profile and uploading a current profile picture. A photo that puts you in the best possible light (both literally and figuratively) is an important first step in snagging the interest of that special someone! #knowyourangles #shootfromabove #noduckface

I see you've also updated some of your personal information. Well done! At Click.com we are big proponents of keeping things fresh. However, I believe there are a few areas we might be able to improve with some positive reframing to get you #fromnottohot in no time! For example, you say that you are "really focused on your career right now." To a potential suitor it could look as if you don't have the time to invest in a new relationship. Consider instead saying simply, "I love my job!" #moneymoves

Also, I understand you find reading the obituary section "very life-affirming," but to the average person that might sound ghoulish. Consider reframing this as, "I'm an avid reader of nonfiction!"

Finally, you mention that you are "recently out of a relationship." #disaster! Highlighting your recent breakup is the last thing you want to do when trying to attract a new man. Consider omitting any mention of past relationships and instead focus on your future. #blankslate #likeavirgin

If you'd like some assistance attracting the high-quality matches you deserve, please be aware that for a onetime fee of $49.99 our experts at Click.

com will craft an original and authentic profile just for you (photo retouching available for an additional $14.99). Let me know if you are interested in adding this service to your current plan! #investinyourself #youreworthit

Sincerely,

Regina H,
Personal Romance Concierge™
Click.com

TWO WEEKS LATER

Dear Miss Ellison,

I wouldn't be worth the paper my Click.com Personal Romance Concierge™ certificate is printed on, if I didn't notice that you might not *quite* be ready to move on after your painful breakup with Jay.

Over the past couple of weeks, I've detected a certain level of cynicism not typical of the Riley Ellison I've come to know. For example, when I told you about Chase, the gentleman whose profile said he likes to "work hard/play hard," you wrote back, "Overgrown man-child. Pass." And when I came to you with Aidan, who mentioned his family is very important to him, you wrote back, "Momma's boy. Pass." And perhaps most dishearteningly, when I presented Spencer, who said he loves to laugh but also has a serious side, you responded with, "Bipolar, unmedicated. Pass." #savage #thatmeansharsh

Maybe it's time we took a step back from searching for love and focused on you?

I'd like to make you aware of a new opportunity available from Click.com designed to meet the needs of our more challenging clients like yourself. Our new program, **Sugar, How'd You Get So F.L.Y.™ (Fiercely Love Yourself)** is an intense initiative focused on the important practice of self-care!

Are you ready for the most exciting part? #drumrollplease

As a part of my training to become a F.L.Y. Guy™ Concierge, I have been authorized to offer you a **FREE** seven-day trial of Sugar, How'd You Get So F.L.Y.™ #keepyourmindonyourmoney#andyourmoneyon-yourmind

To redeem this offer simply fill out the attached Self-Care Inventory, use activation code: **GOLOVE YOURSELF**, and I will have the program materials overnighted directly to you. You will receive a subscription box full of F.L.Y.™ approved self-care essentials to help you fall in love with the most important person of all...YOU! Keep what you like, return what you don't. #extrachargesapply #selfcareaintcheap

I look forward to taking this journey together!

Sincerely,

Regina H,
Personal Romance Concierge™ and F.L.Y. Guy™-in-training
Click.com

CHAPTER 1

MONDAY

Southerners will go to great lengths to avoid speaking ill of the dead, no matter how much they hated a person's guts while they were alive. *"He sure loved his mama." "There was nobody who knew more about NASCAR." "I'll bet he was a real good flosser."* In my experience as an obituary writer in Tuttle Corner, VA, people dug deep to find any bright spot in an otherwise dim and detestable life—or at least that had been my experience until I was assigned to write about Justin Balzichek.

Justin Balzichek was thirty-one years old when he was brutally murdered, and no one I talked to had anything remotely nice to say about him. I'd interviewed several of his school classmates, two former employers, even his childhood pastor—and not one of them could find a single positive thing to say. Justin had been a bad seed from the very beginning, according to Doris Johnson, his third-grade teacher. Tricia, the woman who worked at the Kwikee Stop where he bought his chewing tobacco, said she got the heebie-jeebies every time he looked at her. And Justin's landlord, upon hearing the news of his death, said simply, "He's the devil's problem now." From what I could tell, it came as a surprise to exactly no one that Justin had met a sticky end, and it was even less shocking that he'd left a trail of violence and destruction in his wake.

I was on my way to the Campbell & Sons funeral home to see if they had had any luck finding his next of kin. It had been almost two weeks since Justin's body was found, and so far there'd been no takers. I was writing a piece on him for the *Tuttle Times*, and I thought if I could talk to a relative, I could get a broader perspective on who Justin had been—or perhaps more interestingly, why he had been that way. I wasn't trying to glorify who he was or what he'd done, but I didn't believe that anybody outside of a Bond villain could be so one-dimensionally bad.

There were no services scheduled for that day, so I figured Franklin wouldn't mind me popping in. Over the past few months, I'd gotten to know Franklin Campbell fairly well. When someone died in Tuttle County, the families would often work with the funeral home to submit death notices to the *Times*, and it was part of my job to help edit and format the pieces for publication. It was, unfortunately, what passed for an obituary section in most newspapers these days due to declining budgets, although the *Times* had recently decided to allow space for one editorial obit each week. Justin Balzichek, however, would not be our featured obit this week; I was writing his story for the Crime section.

Franklin Campbell was an older man, probably the same age my granddad would have been if he were still alive. Old-school through and through, Franklin favored the Victorian approach to death notices. That is to say, no one Franklin wrote about ever *died*. They "went to be with the Lord," or "were called home," or my personal favorite, could be found "gathering the angels for a rousing game of canasta." Franklin was a quiet man who always spoke in hushed tones and gentle metaphors, even when he wasn't at work. The years of restrained sympathy had seeped into his bones, and when you came upon him walking through Memorial Park or eating dinner at the Shack, he'd clasp your shoulder gently and say, "How are you?" And even when you were having a perfectly lovely day, the reflex was always to respond with, "I'm hanging in there."

When I walked into the building, I saw that all the lights were off except for one coming from Franklin's office in the back hallway. This was unusual. Franklin often had his staff dusting the pews or polishing the brass fixtures when services weren't going on. He took great pride in Campbell & Sons, a family-owned funeral parlor serving Tuttle Corner since 1877.

"Hello?" I called into the empty space. "Franklin, you here? It's Riley."

When I didn't get an answer, I walked back toward his office. The door was cracked slightly. "Knock, knock," I said, hesitating for a minute before peeking my head inside. But instead of seeing Franklin, I saw a much younger man sitting in his chair. He was leaning over, holding his head in his hands as if he'd been crying.

"Oh, I'm sorry—"

The man wiped at his eyes and stood up quickly. "We're closed today. There's a sign out front."

"Sorry...I didn't see it." I swiveled my eyes to the floor. This man, whoever he was, was clearly embarrassed. "I'm here to see Franklin. I'm from the *Times*."

"Franklin isn't in."

I looked up. The man was dressed in a plaid shirt in reds and blues untucked over worn-in jeans. His eyes were moist, his cheeks ruddy from wiping away the tears. He looked like the whole world had just crashed around his shoulders. I took a half step closer. "Are you okay?"

He looked down for a split second, and when he raised

his eyes it was as if he'd put a little suit of armor on each one. "I'm fine."

I blanched at his harsh tone. "Okay, um, do you know when Franklin will be back?"

"No."

I was starting to get the feeling this guy didn't want to talk. But, as my mother always said, being upset is no excuse for rudeness. Besides, I knew most of Campbell's employees and I'd never seen this guy before. It was strange that none of the regulars were here. "Do you mind me asking who you are?" I said, careful to keep my tone conversational.

"As a matter of fact, I do."

So much for keeping things conversational. "Well," I said, crossing my arms in front of my chest. "I really need to speak with Franklin, so if you don't mind, I think I'll wait."

"Suit yourself." He grabbed keys off the desk, turned off the lights in the office, and walked past me, nearly knocking my shoulder with his.

"Hey!" I called after him as he moved down the dark hallway. "Where're you going?"

"I told you. We're closed. I'm going home."

"And you're just going to leave me here?"

He let out an impatient sigh. "You said you wanted to wait."

I sped down the hall to catch up to him. He opened the front door, but I came up behind him and slammed it closed. "You've got a lot of nerve, whoever you are! I don't appreciate being treated like this."

"Look, honey, you're going to have to—"

"—Oh no, I am *not* your honey—"

He rolled his eyes. "Fine. Whatever—your honor, your majesty, your eminence—whatever your name is, I gotta go.

I don't have time for this."

Now that I was up close, I could see that this guy wasn't much older than me, despite his condescending tone. It gave me a boost of confidence. "I'm not going anywhere until you tell me where Franklin is and—"

"Fine," he said, and with that he walked out the door, leaving me inside. I heard the key go in the lock from the outside.

I was stunned silent for a second. "Hey!" I shouted once I recovered. I banged on the door a few times. "Let me out!" It took a good thirty seconds of shouting and pounding on the door before I realized I could just twist the deadbolt and let myself out.

I swung it open to find the mystery man standing there, an amused grin tugging up one corner of his mouth. He reached around me to close the door, pulling on the handle to make sure it was locked. "Figured it out, did you?"

"There is something seriously wrong with you," I grumbled. "I'm going to talk to Franklin about this. Just who the hell do you think you are?"

The man was halfway down the front steps when he turned around to face me, the sunlight bouncing off of his tawny eyes. "I think I'm Ashley Franklin Campbell," he said, pausing to watch the surprise register on my face. "And I think you're trespassing on private property, *honey*."

CHAPTER 2

I found out after a couple of phone calls—one to my mother and one to Eudora Winterthorne, the grande dame of Tuttle Corner—that Franklin Campbell had suffered a stroke two days earlier. He was in pretty bad shape and if he made it at all, according to Eudora, it would be some time until he could go back to work. I was sorry to hear it. Franklin had always been kind to me, and I knew how important his business was to him. I asked Mom to add me to the meal train for Franklin's wife, Patricia. She'd be exhausted caring for him, as she had some health problems of her own, which, according to Mrs. Winterthorne, meant she "wore out quick." The Campbells had a lot of friends who would no doubt pitch in, though they were in their seventies, and they didn't have family in town, or at least not until recently.

Franklin and Patricia Campbell had raised two sons, neither of whom was involved in the family business. Their youngest son, Martin, died suddenly from an undetected heart condition at the age of seventeen during a high school basketball game. The whole town was shocked by the unspeakable tragedy, and many claimed that the Campbell family never truly recovered.

I knew little about their other son, Thomas, except that he lived out of state and had been estranged from his parents for some time. Whenever anyone around town mentioned him, it was always in a whisper, like how people say "cancer" or "herpes" or, in some circles, "liberal." Mom told me she had actually known Thomas Campbell back in school and said that while he was smart and charming, he'd made a series of bad decisions that had landed him in various rehab centers for various addictions that always seemed to result in various relapses. He was currently serving a three-year sentence in Dillwyn Correctional Center for "credit card fraud."

This Ashley character—or Ash, as Eudora said was common parlance—was Thomas's son, and although he was born in Tuttle, his mother moved the family to Texas after the divorce some twenty-odd years ago. That would explain why I'd never seen him before. He was just a couple of years older than me and had recently graduated from law school. Mrs. Winterthorne said Patricia had begged her only grandson to come help run the business until Franklin was back on his feet. As hard as it was for me to believe the guy I'd met could do anything nice for anybody, I guess he had agreed.

I plunked myself down in the chair across from Will Holman, my co-worker and mentor at the paper, and told him the new information about Franklin and his heir apparent.

"So you didn't ask him if anyone had come to claim Balzichek's body yet?"

"Didn't you hear my story?" I said. "He wouldn't talk to me."

"BZZT!" A brash sound erupted from Holman's lips.

I flinched. "What was that?"

"BZ—"

"—I heard you," I said, stopping him. "I was just wondering why on earth you would make that sound."

"Oh." He blinked. "I was simulating the sound of a game show buzzer to illustrate your answer was incorrect."

"It was not incorrect. Ash wouldn't talk to me."

"BZZT!" Holman did it again. "He talked to you quite a bit. He said that they were closed, that he was fine, that you were trespassing..."

"You know what I meant."

Holman gave me one of his blank stares that indicated he did not, in fact, know any such thing.

"He tried to lock me inside a funeral home!"

I saw him start to curl his lips inward again, and I held up my hand. "So help me if you make that sound again, Will Holman, I will get up and leave this office."

He shrugged, looking mildly offended. "I thought you said you got out by simply turning the deadbolt?"

"I did, but—"

"Then he didn't lock you in."

At times Holman's logical brain was simply maddening. "*Anyway,*" I said. "He's difficult. I'll have to try to talk to someone else at Campbell & Sons later. Carl said that if they can't locate Balzichek's next of kin or get anyone to claim the body in the next couple of days, he'll likely be cremated and his remains kept in a four-by-six-inch box on a shelf in the sheriff's office basement. Seems so bleak, even for a guy like Balzichek."

"Ironic." Holman typed something into his laptop and twisted it around to show me. "Greer Mountbatten got quite a different farewell. This was in the *Washington Journal* yesterday."

On the screen was a picture of a large crowd of mourners, an understated sea of black, navy, and camel-colored wool coats, streaming out of a grand-looking church I recognized from TV. The headline read, "Hundreds Gather to

Mourn Shocking Death of Socialite." I scanned the article and saw all the sordid details were there....

Two weeks ago the car of Greer Mountbatten, wife of prominent Washington, DC, lobbyist Dale Mountbatten, was found abandoned and covered in blood just inside Tuttle County. The next day, a jogger discovered Greer's body lying facedown in the tall grass of Riverside Park along the bank of the James River. She had been killed by a blow to the head. It was a shockingly brutal crime against a woman of Greer's blue blood pedigree, and made even more shocking by the surrounding circumstances.

About two weeks before Greer's body was found, someone had thrown a sledgehammer through the window of Rosalee's Tavern in downtown Tuttle Corner. I know this because the sledgehammer in question almost killed me. I'd been in Rosalee's at the time with my (regrettably) ex-boyfriend, Jay. Justin Balzichek was eventually arrested for the vandalism, but he swore up and down that he'd been hired to do it by Greer Mountbatten. There were rumors around town that Rosalee, who used to be the Mountbattens' au pair, had been having a years-long affair with Dale. In exchange for a lighter sentence, Balzichek agreed to testify that Greer hired him in order to send a message to Rosalee to leave her husband alone.

However, before anyone could question Greer, she went missing—and later was found dead. And then in a twist right out of an episode of *Law & Order*, two days after that, Justin Balzichek was also found dead, his body lying facedown at the entrance of Sterns cemetery in Tuttle Corner. The sheriff's department has not released how Balzichek died, but the running bet in the newsroom was that he had been hit over the head just like Greer had.

The weird part is that no one had been able to find

Rosalee since then. And while many of us worried for her safety—after all, Greer Mountbatten was dead, Justin Balzichek was dead, it wouldn't be crazy to think that Rosalee might have met the same fate—Rosalee was being treated by the press more like a potential suspect than a potential victim. Her enigmatic air and good looks, combined with the juicy story about an affair with a powerful man, had elevated her to femme fatale status, and the press couldn't get enough of the story.

"If we could just find Rosalee, maybe she could shed some light on all of this..." I twisted a strand of my hair between my index and middle fingers. "Do you think she's okay?"

Holman and I had had this conversation at least half a dozen times in the days since Rosalee disappeared, and my mind was split between two bad options: Either Rosalee was in danger, or she was the cause of it. A third option was that she was scared for her life and simply decided to go on the run. But if that were the case, why not go to the sheriff? No one had seen or talked to her since Balzichek's body was discovered, and even I had to admit that it looked a teensy bit more like she ran away than like she was in trouble. For starters, she'd left her cats in a crate outside of her café manager/cook Melvin's front door with a note saying, "Please take care of them while I'm gone." For another thing, when the sheriff went to talk to her at the Tavern the morning they found Balzichek, he found the door locked up tight with a note addressed to the staff letting them know about the schedule of deliveries and specials for the upcoming week. Planning out Wednesday's Quiche Lorraine with leafy green salad didn't sound like the act of a woman afraid for her life.

"My gut tells me Rosalee is okay," Holman said,

bouncing slightly on his ergonomic exercise ball chair. "She's obviously mixed up in all of this somehow, but it's too early to know exactly how. We need more information. I'm working a couple of sources and hoping they'll give me something we can use."

"Any more on Dale Mountbatten?" I asked, nodding to the article still up on Holman's laptop.

When a woman is violently murdered for no apparent reason, all eyes turn to the husband. This case had been no exception, but so far Greer's husband seemed as shocked and distraught as you'd expect an innocent husband to be. Friends and family who'd been interviewed said as far as they knew the couple was happily married. Plus, Dale had an airtight alibi for the time his wife was killed: He was giving an interview in the studio at the NPR affiliate in Manhattan.

Holman shook his head. "Nothing new. He admits to the affair but says it ended a long time ago," he read off the screen.

"What about her family? Doesn't she come from money?" If love gone wrong was the number one motive for murder, money had to be number two.

"Yes," Holman said. "Her father has made a fortune in oil and gas, but according to his lawyer, Dale signed a prenuptial agreement stipulating he is not entitled to any of her family money."

"Does she have any siblings? Could there be bad blood there?"

"One sister, Hadley Lawrence of Charleston, South Carolina." Holman scanned the article. "She's quoted saying she is heartbroken and that 'Greer had the perfect life.' She says she can't understand why anyone would have wanted to hurt her."

I checked the time on my phone. "The press briefing starts at ten, do you want to come with?" I said, standing to leave.

"No thanks."

"Are you working on your Sterns book?" I asked. Holman had started research for a book he planned to write about a local historical site called the Sterns Smallpox Graveyard. Back in the late 1700s, a medical doctor by the name of Josiah Sterns bought a plot of land to bury all of his patients who died of smallpox. He claimed it would help stop the spread of the pox, which had wiped out half the town. Eventually, the Campbell family bought the graveyard and expanded it. However, the good people of Tuttle Corner didn't want to be buried in a smallpox cemetery, so someone had come up with the bright idea to cordon off the victims of smallpox with a copper fence to separate the contaminated dead from the uncontaminated dead. It was actually listed on the historic register of Tuttle County. I'm not sure when people started joking about it, but it was an oft-used threat by parents to their misbehaving kids or wives to their misbehaving husbands that if they didn't straighten up, they'd have them buried "in the Sterns Copper." Strange, because it wasn't even a good threat. Obviously, you can't get smallpox if you're already dead. But anyway, it was one of those Tuttle colloquialisms that was braided into the fabric of our town. And Holman was fascinated by all things historical.

"No, Kay gave me a new investigative piece to look into."

"Oh yeah?" I asked, surprised I hadn't heard about it.

"Stormer Windows. They have a couple hundred complaints through the BBB for shoddy workmanship, bait-and-switch selling tactics, and possible tax fraud."

"Sounds like a real *pane*," I said with a wink. When Holman didn't react, I added, "Get it? A *pane*—like a windowpane?"

Holman raised his eyes, which looked about three times larger than normal through his thick lenses. His face was an implacable façade of stony indifference. "I got it. It was a pun." Then he blinked at me, owl-like, and went back to what he was doing.

I thought about arguing that my joke was at least worthy of a chuckle, but thought better of it. I knew Holman was nothing if not literal; besides, I had never seen him chuckle before. He often smiled and occasionally laughed, but a chuckle just wasn't in Holman's wheelhouse.

"All right, well, good luck with the window people!"

He made a noncommittal noise as I left his office. I grabbed my bag off the back of my chair and started toward the front door of the newsroom. Before I walked out, however, I ditched into Flick's office to see if he was in yet.

Hal Flick was in his early seventies and was the obituaries editor for the *Times*, which meant he didn't work a full-time schedule. He'd earned the right, as back in the day he'd been a hard-hitting reporter, covering everything from foreign wars to Watergate to the Iran-Contra scandal. That was how he met and became rivals, then later best friends, with my beloved granddaddy. They'd worked at the same paper up in Washington, DC, for years and then both settled into the downslope of their careers here in Tuttle Corner.

It had been almost six years since Granddad died under what I believed were suspicious circumstances, and not a day went by that I didn't think of him. At first, Flick refused to listen to my theory that Granddaddy hadn't committed suicide like the police report said, but since I'd started working at the paper with him, it seemed like he was finally coming around. In fact, he had recently been looking into some things about Granddaddy's death but kept saying he wasn't quite ready to share the information with me yet. I'd hoped that today (like I did every day) might be the day he decided to let me in on it. I texted him to let him know about the press conference and asked him to meet me there as I headed for the door.

"Where are you off to in such a hurry?" Gerlach Spencer, my least favorite colleague at the paper, said as I walked past his desk. "Is there a shoe sale somewhere?" He laughed and reached over to high-five his cubicle-mate, Bruce Henderson.

I looked down at my red Chuck Taylors, the same shoes I'd worn nearly every day since I started working at the *Times*, and then back up at each of them. "Seriously? A shoe sale? That's the best you could come up with?"

"Oh relax," Spencer said. "I'm just giving you shit, kiddo."

"Actually, I think what you were trying to do was to degrade me by suggesting that as a young woman the only thing that could possibly motivate me would be some sort of trivial retail event. And furthermore, I think you tacked on the 'kiddo' to the end of your quasi-misogynist insult to seal the deal."

With anyone else I might have let the comment slide, but I'd had enough of these sorts of interactions with stupid Spencer over the past few months to know calling him out was the only way I'd ever get him to stop. My usual policy of polite-or-die just did not get it done with Gerlach Spencer.

His fleshy face reddened as his eyes slid over to see Henderson's reaction, which basically was restrained laughter. At least Henderson was an equal-opportunity douchebag.

"Geez, who peed in your Cheerios?" Spencer sniped at me—or rather to my back—as I walked out the door with a little extra spring in my step.

CHAPTER 3

I was halfway to the courthouse when my mom called. "Honey? Is that you?"

This was how ninety percent of my conversations with my mother started. "Yeah, it's me, Mom. You called my phone, who else would it be?"

"Oh right," she said with a laugh. "Okay, well I just wanted to report that I finally did it!"

"Did what?" I could see the crowd of reporters gathering up ahead.

"I took your advice and signed up for that Uber thingy you were telling me about. I thought it'd be good for when we're out on the road and don't want to take the tour bus around locally. It can be so hard to park, you know."

My mom and dad made up the two-person band The Rainbow Connection and traveled regionally playing for kids at libraries, schools, churches, state fairs, etc. As the quintessential aging hippies that they were, they'd bought a VW van a few years back and referred to it as their "tour bus."

"Good for you." I'd been trying to get Mom and Dad into the twenty-first century with technology and thought Uber would be an easy way to start. Plus, it'd cut down on the number of notes my dad had to leave on people's windshields apologizing for tapping their bumpers.

"I just downloaded the app, like you said—but boy howdy, did they want a lot of information! My credit card number, my birth date, my address, my social security number, my driver's license number, whether or not I've ever been convicted of a felony—"

Uh-oh.

"—they even needed to know the make and model of my vehicle! It took forever to fill out that sign-up thingy, and all from my phone, too. You know I have trouble sometimes toggling between the number keyboard and the letter one—"

"Mom—" I said, trying to get a word in.

"—they asked about past speeding tickets, moving violations, driving under the influence, for the love of Pete—and then there was the background check!"

"Um, Mom?"

"—I mean, I understand you can't be too careful these days, but a background check seemed a bridge too far, if you know what I mean. Then again, I know I need to get with the times, so I did it and—"

I couldn't stand it anymore. "Mom," I said, stopping her. "I think you might have signed up to be an Uber *driver*."

"Oh." She paused. "Well, now that you say that, that actually makes sense. I thought it was a little strange that the next day I got a notification from some lady who needed a ride to the Piggly Wiggly over in West Bay."

That did it; I busted out laughing.

"What's so funny?"

"Nothing," I said, trying to get control of myself. "Sorry. Whatd'you do?"

"What did I do?" she asked as if I was insane. "I gave her a ride, of course!"

"You did not—" I was laughing so hard, people around

me were starting to stare.

"I just thought it was like a co-op or something. Give a ride, get a ride," she continued, sounding somewhere between confused and resigned. "I don't know why you think this is so funny, Riley."

"No reason." I forced myself to gain control. I didn't want to offend the poor woman. "It's just that most people sign up to *get* rides, not to be drivers, that's all. I should have mentioned that. I'll come by the house later and fix it for you."

"Fix what?"

"Fix it so you're not a driver."

There was another pause. "Oh, that's okay."

"No really, it'll take two seconds."

"I think I'll just leave it."

"But people are going to keep bugging you for rides."

"I really don't mind," she said. "It actually kind of reminds me of when you were little and needed me to drive you all over creation...and I've already met several interesting people!"

My mother had fallen ass-backward into a career as an Uber driver. I was dying. *Dying*. "How many rides have you given?"

"Oh, I don't know, maybe eight? And I have a perfect five-star rating, I'll have you know."

When I was finally able to stop laughing, I said, "I wouldn't expect anything less, Mom."

CHAPTER 4

The front steps of the courthouse were already packed with reporters. Since I worked for the only local newspaper in Tuttle County, I knew that everyone there was from someplace else. Then again, I could tell that just by looking at them. As I scanned the hordes of people buzzing around, holding camera equipment, phones, and notebooks, I didn't see a single familiar face. That simply didn't happen in Tuttle. If there was a gathering of more than five people in one spot in town, it was a guarantee I'd know at least two of them—if not by name, then certainly by sight. I was born and raised here, as were my parents and my grandparents, and while I didn't know everyone in town personally, there weren't that many faces I hadn't seen before. Besides, the preponderance of coffee cups from McDonald's was a dead giveaway, as the closest McDonald's was seven miles up I-95. The locals got their coffee at Landry's.

The big tell, however, was the need for a press conference at all. Normally, the sheriff would just talk to someone from the paper on the phone or have us come by the station. The fact that Greer Mountbatten was a big deal from the city, combined with the salacious details of the case, had attracted the attention of the national media. I'll admit I wasn't loving it.

"Excuse me," I said as I attempted to push my way up to the front of the crowd. "I just need to get in here..."

"Nuh-uh. No preferential treatment, little lady." I heard a whiny nasal voice cut through the din of the crowd. Toby Lancett, the mayor's nephew, stood in front of the steps like a bouncer.

"Hey, Toby," I said, forcing a laugh to indicate I knew he was joking—or to warn him that he'd better be. "Your aunt has you doing crowd control, huh?"

"*Mayor* Lancett asked me to make sure things remain orderly." He lifted his chin into the air. "So yes, in a manner of speaking, I suppose so." Toby, barely topping out at five-foot-seven, suffered from a severe case of short-man's syndrome, which manifested itself in part through his holier-than-thou attitude and in part through his policy of wearing athletic clothing exclusively, no matter where he was or what he was doing. He must have thought this made him seem macho somehow, like he might have to dash to the gym on a moment's notice to pump some iron. The problem was that Toby didn't actually work out, a fact that was painfully obvious by looking at him. Especially in spandex.

He stood before the crowd of reporters in gray sweats and a navy blue long-sleeved technical T-shirt stretched tight across the expanse of his belly emblazoned with the phrase "My game is sick. Too bad it ain't contagious." He had not one but two fitness trackers on his right wrist, and donned bright neon green high-top basketball shoes that I would have bet good money had been fitted with lifts. The whole thing would have been laughable if Toby wasn't such an unpleasant little fellow.

"Do you know if Carl's planning on giving out any new information today?" I asked, looking around.

Toby ignored me and pulled out his mini-bullhorn and pointed it toward a leather-jacketed reporter who had placed his foot up on the third step to tie his shoe. "PLEASE STAY OFF OF THE COURTHOUSE STEPS!"

The reporter didn't so much as turn his head in Toby's direction.

"Hey, have you seen Flick around?"

This seemed to distract Toby from the shoe-tier for a moment. He pointed a stubby finger toward the large Bower Glory tree at the far side of the courthouse. "I saw him skulking over there about ten minutes ago." He looked in the direction of the tree. "Don't know where he got to now...."

I followed Toby's gaze but didn't see any sign of Flick.

"PLEASE DISPERSE! I REPEAT, PLEASE DISPERSE. THIS AREA IS FOR OFFICIAL PERSONNEL ONLY!" Toby was now pointing the bullhorn directly at the poor reporter, who stumbled backward, causing a domino effect. The woman behind him wobbled and spilled her coffee down the front of her jacket.

"What's your problem, man?" the guy said as he stood up.

"Yeah, who are you anyway?" the coffee-stained woman snapped.

"I'll leave you to deal with your adoring fans," I whispered and walked off to look for Flick.

Five minutes later, there was still no sign of him, so I texted again. No response. Sheriff Carl Haight was walking out of the courthouse flanked by Deputy Chip Churner (whom everyone just called Butter) and Deputy Ted Wilmore. Carl was an old friend of mine who had been promoted to acting-sheriff a few months ago after Holman and I busted the then-sheriff, Joe Tackett, for corruption and conspiracy to commit murder. Carl was a good guy, as honest as they come, but maybe in a bit over his head. I felt a pang of empathy thinking of him having to give a press briefing to all these big-city reporters.

Carl approached the makeshift podium and turned on the mic. A crackling sound curled out from the speakers, alerting the crowd that the show was about to begin. He cleared his throat before speaking. "Thank y'all for coming out today. We have a few updates on the Mountbatten investigation, but first I'd like to thank the men and women of the Tuttle County Sheriff's Department for their hard work on these investigations. We're a small office, and this level of criminal activity means all hands on deck. These folks," he gestured to Butter and Ted, "and all the rest of the employees back at the office have really risen to the occasion."

I had moved up closer, just off to the left of the steps. I held up my phone and opened the recording app so I'd be sure to get it right. Knowing that several other newspapers would be running this story made me even more freaked out than usual about accuracy.

Carl's eyes scanned the crowd from under the brim of his hat, and he paused for a millisecond when they landed on me. I was probably the only friendly face out here.

After a beat he continued. "I'm going to read a brief statement that will bring y'all up to date with where we are in the investigation. After the statement, I'll take questions.

"As you know, the Tuttle County Sheriff's Department responded to a call at Riverside Park on November seventh at 6:14 a.m. from a jogger who had found the body of a deceased female who was later positively identified as Greer Mountbatten of McLean, VA. Initial findings of the forensic autopsy conducted by Dr. Mendez of the Richmond, Virginia, Medical Office show Ms. Mountbatten died after being struck several times in the back of the head with a heavy object. We believe this was most certainly a homicide and are investigating it as such. We further believe Ms. Mountbatten had been dead for several hours before her body was discovered. It was clear from our findings at the scene that Ms. Mountbatten had not been killed at Riverside Park. We believe her body was brought to that location after she died."

This was new information, and you could hear the indistinct sounds of surprise ripple through the crowd.

"Prior to the discovery of Ms. Mountbatten's body, a Mercedes S Class registered to Greer Mountbatten was found abandoned on the side of Interstate 95. The interior of the car was covered in blood, and while it is still undergoing extensive testing, we know that at least some of the blood found in the car matches Ms. Mountbatten's blood type. Further testing will be needed to make a positive identification, but we believe there is a high degree of probability that Ms. Mountbatten may have been killed inside that automobile."

Another titter of anonymous chatter and the click of photos being taken fluttered through the pack of reporters. Carl waited before continuing. "A second homicide victim was discovered at the entrance to the Sterns cemetery on November ninth at 7:30 a.m. The victim was later positively identified as thirty-one-year-old Justin Fenwick Balzichek of West Bay. We are asking for the public's help with any information about anyone seen in the area, anything out of place, anything at all that might provide us with some additional insight into this crime."

Reporters began shouting out questions.

"How was Balzichek killed?"

"Was his body found in the same condition as Greer's?"

"Is Dale Mountbatten a suspect?"

Carl decided to address only the last question. "Dale Mountbatten is cooperating fully with the authorities and is not considered a suspect at this time."

"How about Rosalee Belanger? Was she having an affair with Greer's husband? Would that be considered motive for murder?"

Carl's face darkened, which might have gone unnoticed by anyone other than someone who'd known him his whole life. His voice was calm and even when he said, "Ms. Belanger is considered a person of interest at this point. I want to be clear, she is not an official suspect. We haven't been able to locate Ms. Belanger, and we'd very much like to speak with her." He paused and cleared his throat before continuing. "If you're out there, Rosalee, please call or come in as soon as you can. We just want to talk."

CHAPTER 5

The event wrapped up after several more questions from reporters that mostly went unanswered. Carl stayed on message with "Rosalee is a person of interest" and "we just want to talk to her." Eventually he cut off the questions and said he'd give another briefing as soon as there was new information he could share with the press. I turned off my recorder once he walked away and scanned the crowd again for Flick. I caught sight of him on a bench just down from where the conference had been held.

"Hey," I said as I approached him.

"Hay is for horses," he answered. At seventy-one years old, Flick was of another generation, one that viewed the ever-increasing informality of youth as a marker of the decline of Western civilization.

I looked back at the crowd of reporters that was slowly starting to break up. "What've you been up to?"

"Working on the Klondike obit. Should have a draft soon," he said without looking at me. I'd known Hal Flick my entire life and was used to his gruff manner, but I couldn't help but notice there was more edge to his voice than usual today.

I sat down beside him on the bench. "Everything okay?"

"Yeah. Fine." Now he appeared to be aggressively avoiding eye contact.

"You sure about that?"

When he didn't answer, I knew better than to push. I waited quietly until he was ready to talk.

"You know I went away for a couple of days to look into some things regarding Albert, right?"

About a month ago, Flick told me he was going to Washington, DC, to follow a lead, something to do with my granddad's death. He wouldn't elaborate because he said he'd promised Granddaddy he'd keep me safe. Apparently, telling me what he was looking into somehow threatened to break that promise.

"Of course."

"Well, Albert had been working on a project when he... when he..."

"Was murdered," I finished the sentence.

Flick looked up sharply but didn't correct me. He paused before continuing. "Most of his files were confiscated by the police, along with his hard drives and notes, so it's been nearly impossible to know exactly what he was working on. But I think I might have found out."

I stilled. I'd been desperate to find out what story my granddad's last days had been spent on, convinced it must have had something to do with why he was killed.

"I don't know if there's any significance to this story and what happened, but I think there might be something there."

Flick was choosing his words so carefully that he was barely saying anything at all, a skill usually reserved for politicians and press secretaries.

"What was it? Is that what's in the file in Kay's office?"

Before leaving town last month, Flick warned me that if anything were to happen to him, our editor Kay Jackson had a folder in her office under lock and key that I was to receive. I'd thought about what could be in that folder nearly every day since. And if I wasn't sure I'd be fired on the spot, I might have tried to steal it out from under her.

"No, not exactly." Flick looked down. "He was working on a series of obituaries for an anthology he was calling, 'The Dead Alone.' It was about people who have died and been buried without any family or friends to mourn them."

I couldn't help but think of Justin Balzichek's remains sitting unclaimed at Campbell & Sons.

"Albert identified subjects who died and were buried or cremated with no mourners. He tried to track down people who knew them so that he could not only examine the question of why these folks died alone but also so he could tell their untold stories. He believed strongly that every life has a tale worth telling."

I let this sink in. Granddaddy had been writing a book of obituaries for people who didn't have anyone else to write them. He was giving a voice to their memories, making sure their lives, no matter how ordinary, weren't forgotten. It was beautiful. Tears sprang to my eyes at the same time that a smile crawled across my face—the bittersweet push/pull of grief and memory. "That's so like him."

Flick looked down at his hands. "It sure is."

We sat quietly for a moment, each of us sharing a private moment with the Albert Ellison we loved and missed. "And you think something he wrote about in one of those obits is the reason he's dead?"

"I'm not sure, but it sure looks as if someone went to great lengths to get rid of his notes, files, records—everything that had any trace of this project."

There had been so many shady things about my grandfather's death, not the least of which was how the now-imprisoned Sheriff Joe Tackett handled the investigation.

I'd tried to call foul on it years earlier, but no one would listen to me. They all just thought I was a young girl overcome with grief about her granddaddy.

"But why? Everyone he was writing about was already dead...why would anyone care?"

"That's what I intend to find out."

"Let me help!" I blurted out.

"No," Flick said automatically. When I started to protest, he added a softer, "Not yet."

I'd been round and round with him on this particular subject too many times before. I knew there was no chance I'd get him to budge an inch. I folded my arms across my chest in silent protest.

"You know I can't let you anywhere near this. Not until I know what we're dealing with. The last promise I ever made to Albert was to keep you safe. And I intend to keep it."

"I'm not a child anymore, you know," I said, sounding exactly like a spoiled child.

"I know." Flick laughed his wheezy old-man laugh. "You're shaping up to be a good journalist with good instincts."

I rolled my eyes. "Don't think flattering me will make me any less mad about being shut out here."

"I'm not flattering you, and I'm not shutting you out either," he said. "Quite the opposite, actually."

I looked over at him, surprised.

"What I was trying to say before you bit my head off is that when the time comes I hope you'll partner with me on this investigation."

I leaped off the bench. "Really?" All I'd ever wanted since the moment I'd found out my grandfather died was to know what really happened to him. Now, not only was Flick offering me a chance to find out, he was offering me a role in uncovering the truth. It felt like being called up to the Majors.

"When the time comes." He nodded to make sure I understood. "Not until I say."

"Yes! Okay! Thank you...Flick, I can't tell you how much—"

"Yeah, yeah..." He stood up and looked at his watch, uncomfortable with my emotion.

I didn't want to torture the poor guy with sentiment, so I simply reached for his hand and said with as much meaning as I could, "Thank you."

He met my eyes for a brief second, then squeezed my hand. "We're going to find out what happened to Albert, Riley. That's a promise."

After Flick left, I felt the hum of cautious adrenaline in my veins. We were so close and yet so far from finding out the truth. It wouldn't do to get in a hurry; we were playing the long game here and the stakes were high. But it was the first time in a long time that I allowed myself to feel hopeful about eventually bringing those responsible for my grandfather's death to justice. This drive was a part of everything I had done over the past six years, particularly my decision to become a reporter. In some ways, it felt like Granddaddy was guiding me toward the answers, especially in moments like these.

Too amped up to go back to the office, I decided to head over to the sheriff's department to see if I could get any additional information. On my way there, I saw Ash Campbell walking along the path on the west side of Memorial Park toward the bank. I still needed to ask him if anyone had come to claim Balzichek's remains, so I jogged to catch up with him.

"We meet again," I said when I was about two feet behind him.

Without breaking stride, he gave a half-turn to see who it was. I couldn't be sure, but I thought I saw him roll his eyes. "If you want to call this a meeting."

"What are you up to?"

"I was under the impression this was a public park. Am I not allowed to be here?" He walked at a brisk clip, and because he was well over six feet tall, it was a challenge to stay on pace with him. Every few steps I had to throw in a sort of skip-step just to keep up.

"Were you listening to the sheriff's press conference?" I asked, quickening my pace till I was beside him.

"I don't see how that's any of your business."

"I'm a reporter. Everything is my business."

He snort-laughed. "Geez, you people never quit until you get what you're after, do you?"

"You people?" I said. "What is that supposed to mean?"

At this, he stopped and turned to face me. He wasn't wearing sunglasses, and I could see those lion-eyes of his glinting in the sunlight. "Listen, Riley is it?" He was standing close to me, and I was suddenly very aware of his tall frame, broad shoulders, and strong jaw. And even though it made me hate myself just a little bit, I felt my cheeks heat up.

"Yes."

"I'm in a hurry here...what is it you want from me?"

"Um, well..." My mind went blank. I was thrown off by how much he seemed not to want to talk to me. I wasn't used to getting that sort of response in Tuttle. Just before the silence got too awkward I said, "I just wanted to tell you I was sorry to hear about your grandfather's stroke."

"Oh, thanks." Ash's face softened, and for a second he

looked like a different person. He rubbed the back of his neck with one hand and looked down.

"How's he doing?"

"Not great. The doctors don't sound optimistic."

"I'm sorry," I said again, and I meant it.

Ash looked over my head into the distance and blew out a breath. "Yeah, me too." And then in an instant, the hard shell was back in place. "Is that all?"

"No, actually," I said, trying to recalibrate as quickly as he had, "I wanted to know if anyone has come in to claim the remains of Justin Balzichek?"

"Not that I'm aware of."

"But you're running the funeral home now while Franklin is..."

"It would appear so."

"So then you'd know whether someone had come in to claim the body."

"I guess I would."

"Okay..." I said. This was like trying to squeeze blood from a stone. "So just to be clear, you're telling me, on the record, that there has been no one in to claim the remains of Justin Balzichek?"

"How many different ways do you want me to say it?"

I stiffened. "And what will Campbell & Sons do if nobody shows up to claim the body?"

"Well, Miss Ellison, I imagine Campbell & Sons will work in compliance with Virginia state legislature code 32.1-309.2, which says that if a body remains unclaimed after fourteen days, a funeral service establishment as chosen by the county in which the death occurred will handle disposition of the body and the reasonable expenses shall be paid by the locality in which the decedent resided at the time of his death—which, as you know, is Tuttle County."

Damn. I had forgotten Ash was a lawyer.

"But you already knew that, didn't you?"

"Just checking my facts, Mr. Campbell."

"There's a first time for everything, isn't there?"

"I don't know what your problem with me is, but I'm just doing my job here."

"If you say so," he said, looking away.

My thermometer-face had evolved from the pink-cheeked blush of attraction to the nuclear red of indignity. "You know, you're awfully unpleasant for a guy who's supposed to be in the business of comforting people during their most difficult moments."

An expression rolled across his face that almost made him seem vulnerable. "I'm sorry," he said and looked directly at me, this time without challenge in his eyes. "It's just that—well, it's just complicated and I'm not exactly—" he broke off. "I've got a lot going on, and I'm just not myself right now. Sorry if I was rude."

His apology and the pained look on his face took some of the sizzle out of my steak. I wasn't sure how to respond. "It's okay," I said finally.

"Can we start over?" He held his hand out toward me. "Nice to meet you, Riley. I'm Ash."

I tentatively took his hand, but as I shook it, I couldn't help but wonder which guy I'd met that day was the real Ash Campbell.

CHAPTER 6

As I walked into the sheriff's office, I hoped my lifelong local status might convert to some additional information on the case that they weren't going to release to the general media.

"Sorry, honey," said Gail, who was my ex-boyfriend Ryan's cousin, after I asked her for more details. "We've all been warned: no leaks." Gail Stratham had been working at the front desk at the Tuttle Corner Sheriff's Department for more than fifteen years. She'd survived through three different sheriffs partially because she knew when to keep her mouth shut.

"Can you at least tell me if Carl has spoken to Dale Mountbatten again?"

"Girl, you know I can't."

"Any leads on Rosalee's whereabouts?"

She shook her head and lowered her voice. "If that isn't the craziest thing! You live near someone for years and think you know them...I don't know if she's behind any of this, but she sure is making herself look bad by skipping town."

"*If* she skipped town, you mean."

Gail raised her eyebrows and lowered her chin. "I think it's a pretty safe bet. People who are kidnapped—or worse—don't plan for their disappearance. I'd say Rosalee has gone missing very much on purpose."

"Can I quote you on that?"

"Not if you expect me to ever speak to you again. Carl would have my head."

"Have you been able to confirm if Rosalee and Dale were still in touch?"

Before Gail could answer, or not answer, Carl walked out of his office. "Riley, I just gave all the information I'm going to share in the press briefing. You're all set for now."

"C'mon, Carl. I know you know more than you're letting on. Just give me a little something—something for the hometown paper that'll show these city folks they're not better than us."

"I'm not interested in showing anybody anything except for who committed these atrocious crimes in our backyard. Go on now. I'll let you know when we have more to share."

"Fine." I resisted my urge to stick my tongue out at him.

I thanked Gail, went back to the office, and filed the story on the press conference after checking it four times for accuracy. I wanted to be sure that the reporting coming out of the *Times* was as good as or better than the reporting by the larger outlets. Editor in Chief Kay Jackson gave it a once-over before publishing it in our online edition.

By then it was almost 1 p.m. and Holman was out of the office. I was hungry and didn't feel like eating the salad I'd brought from home, so I nipped out to Landry's to grab something less lettucey. Lunch in downtown Tuttle was almost always Rosalee's Tavern or Landry's General Store, and since Melvin wasn't comfortable running it on his own, Rosalee's remained closed. Landry's, on the other hand, was bustling.

"Pretty hectic around here," I said to Joe Landry when I

finally got to the front of the line.

"I'm busier than a one-legged man in an ass-kicking contest," he said with his easy laugh. "That'll be nine forty-six."

I handed him my debit card. "Well, I guess that's the silver lining of all this stuff."

"I guess so." He shrugged. "Wonder when Rosalee'll be back...if she'll come back?"

"Have you heard anything?"

"Nope, but I sure hope she's okay."

I took back my card and signed the pin pad. "Did she ever mention any family or friends in the area?"

He shook his head. "You know Rosalee—she didn't say much. I talked to her most every week for the past five years and I couldn't tell you much more than her last name and where she grew up. Dijon, France. I remember that 'cause I used to joke and call her Miss Grey Poupon."

I smiled. "Well, good luck! Hope you get to catch your breath before too long!"

I was on my way back to the office when I spied a very tall, very blond, very look-how-quickly-I-bounced-back-from-my-pregnancy woman pushing a stroller toward me. I might have turned the other way if the stroller in question had not contained Rosie Elizabeth Sanford, otherwise known as Lizzie, otherwise known as the cutest little ladybug you've ever seen, otherwise known as my goddaughter.

"There you are!" called out Ridley, who was Lizzie's mom and the baby mama of my ex, Ryan. "I was hoping I'd find you."

Ridley was ridiculously beautiful, charming, and confident. Naturally, there was a part of me that wanted to hate her, but she was also generous, smart, and loyal—which made hating her much harder. Originally from Sweden, Ridley had dated Ryan briefly while they were living in Colorado right after he'd unceremoniously ended our seven-year relationship with a middle-of-the-night phone call. The relationship between them hadn't lasted, but Ridley got pregnant and rather than move back to Sweden, she moved here to Tuttle Corner to raise the baby around Ryan's family. Ridley and Ryan were not together, though they were set to move into the house directly behind mine in just a few weeks. As for Ridley and me, we were not exactly friends but not exactly not-friends either. Our relationship existed in a strange space, full of closeness and distance, fondness and jealousy.

"Is everything okay?" I asked, already peering down into the stroller to get a look at Lizzie. She was sound asleep, bundled in a light pink fuzzy blanket.

"Yes, of course," Ridley said. *Of course*, like how could I ever think the fabulous Ridley would have a problem. "I just wanted to see how you're doing."

"I'm fine, just a little residual pain, but other than that I'm good," I said. About a month ago, I'd been shot in the leg by a psycho who wasn't too happy when I figured out he had murdered a local cardiologist and tried to pin it on my friend Thad. But I was healing well, walking without crutches, and trying to put the whole thing in the rearview mirror. "How are you?" I asked.

"Great! I don't know why everyone says having a newborn is so exhausting. Lizzie sleeps at least eight hours every night."

Of course she does.

"Anyway," Ridley said, tucking her long blond hair behind her ear, "I wanted you to be one of the first to know: I am going back to work soon!"

"You are?" My complicated feelings about Ridley had prevented me from trying to get to know her too well. The truth was, other than knowing she'd been a former junior Olympian snowboarder, I had no idea what she did for a living.

She nodded, a huge, life-altering smile lighting up her face. "I'm going to be the new Rosalee!"

Of all the things I thought she might say, that was not one of them. "Um...huh?"

"I'm going to take over Rosalee's Tavern!"

"Take over the Tavern?" I asked, more confused than ever. "Is that...I mean, do you even..."

"I know a little something about the restaurant business." She threw back her head with a devious laugh, which I knew meant *How silly of you to question my skills.*

"But...how would that even work? I mean, we have no idea where Rosalee is, if she's coming back, if she's even okay?"

Ridley looked suddenly contrite. "Yes, well..."

"What?" I eyed her suspiciously.

"Nothing, it's just that...well, let's just say I have Rosalee's permission."

I sucked in a quick breath. "Ohmygod, do you know where she is? Has she been in touch with you?"

Ridley took a step closer and lowered her voice. "Look, I don't know where she is, I only know that she's safe."

"Ridley!" I squeaked. "This is a big deal. You have to tell Sheriff Haight. Everyone's looking for her!"

"I don't want to get involved." Ridley shrugged like the investigation was either beneath or beyond her. "All I know is that the people of Tuttle Corner deserve to have choices about where to dine, and I think I can help out with that. Besides, what else am I doing?"

As if on cue, Lizzie made a soft gurgling sigh as she adjusted herself. Ridley looked down at her daughter with an adoring glance. "Lizzie can hang out at the Tavern with me—can you imagine all the people who will want to hold her while I work? It'll be fun!"

Fun? Only Ridley could think something like this would be fun. Rushing in to take over for Rosalee felt like a leap. There were just so many unanswered questions. Plus, and I was not necessarily proud of this, the thought of Ridley becoming so enmeshed in my beloved Tuttle Corner as a purveyor in one of our central businesses felt vaguely threatening. It shouldn't, and while I knew that intellectually, emotionally it felt like one more way Ridley was living a life that should have been mine.

"What does Ryan think?"

"He is in full support."

I sighed and looked toward Rosalee's Tavern sitting empty on the main square. I had to admit, it did leave a void in our town. But why did Ridley have to be the person to fill it?

"What happens if—*when*—Rosalee comes back to town?" I asked, my voice already dripping with the tepid blessing we both knew I'd give.

Ridley shrugged. "I'm sure it will all work out!"

Of course it would. Things had a way of always working out where Ridley was concerned.

Chapter 7

When I got back to the paper, I went directly to Holman's office to tell him the news that Roslaee was alive and well enough to be making plans for her restaurant to reopen. *Damn.* He was still out. I really needed to process this information with someone, but I wasn't ready to go to Carl or Kay with it yet. What did I really know for certain anyway? Only that Rosalee had been in touch with Ridley at some point. It wasn't like I knew where she was or anything. At least not yet. Plus, it felt wrong to implicate Ridley if she didn't want to get involved. Besides, if Ridley did end up opening the Tavern, Carl would be there in a hot second to talk to her about the how and why.

I tapped my pencil against the edge of my desk, a habit I had when I was deep in thought. (I knew this because sometimes when I did this, stupid Spencer would yell across the newsroom, "Ellison! Quit it!") If Rosalee was out there communicating with people in Tuttle, I wanted to be one of them. And I needed to figure out how. I'd already interviewed her cook Melvin, who predictably said nothing. No surprise there. I knew he would never rat out his boss and old friend even if he did know something. But if Rosalee had been in touch with Ridley, maybe Ryan knew something? I started to formulate a plan. If there was anyone in this town I had a chance of sweet-talking into giving me information, Ryan Sanford was it. He'd made no secret of the fact that he still had feelings for me and hoped we might be able to get back together someday.

I put down my pencil and texted Ryan to see if he wanted to meet up for a drink later. I said I had something I wanted to talk to him about. I suggested we meet at five o'clock at James Madison's Fish Shack, home of Tuttle's best happy hour. When he replied with: "It's a date," I squashed the protest from my internal ethics department. Even though Ryan and I had a long history, and even though he and Ridley were no longer romantically involved, my burgeoning friendship with her made for conflicting loyalties.

I spent the rest of the afternoon working on a story about the new softball fields planned in West Bay and the recent vote by the town council to approve a change in recycling bins. At about 4:30, Kay Jackson called out from her office, "Ellison, can you come in here a sec?"

This prompted jeers from stupid Spencer as I walked, heart-in-throat, to see what she needed. Historically, when Kay called you into her office like this, it was not to praise you for a job well done.

"Close the door," Kay said without looking up from her laptop. After a few more silent seconds while Kay's focus remained on something she was reading off her screen, she looked up. "There's been a development. In the Mountbatten story."

"What is it?"

"It wasn't us who reported it."

I felt my face heat up.

"The *Daily Reporter* out of Fairfax is reporting that Justin Balzichek was poisoned."

"*What?* How the hell did they get that information?"

"An unnamed source with knowledge of the investigation says, 'Mr. Balzichek died from respiratory failure thought to have been caused by a chemical agent introduced into his bloodstream,'" Kay read from her computer screen.

Not only was I surprised, I was angry. How could Carl have given this to another reporter? We'd worked together on two high-profile cases over the past few months and he knew I was trying to establish myself in my field—just like he was. This felt like a betrayal.

"Listen, Kay," I said, noting the whine of desperation in my own voice. "I've been over at the sheriff's office every day. I was just there, but no one would talk to me. I don't know how this reporter got this info, but I'll find out. I promise."

"Better yet, get some new information." Kay didn't sound mad, but she didn't sound happy either. "Find out who they're looking at—is it just Rosalee, or is it the husband too? Anyone else? Dig into possible motives, alibis. Anything new."

I nodded. "I've asked about all these things, of course, but all I get is 'No comment.' "

"Find someone who will comment." Kay nodded toward the door. "I don't like being scooped in my own backyard."

"Trust me, Kay," I said on my way out, "neither do I."

CHAPTER 8

I left Kay's office seething with the kind of irrational anger that's made up of fifty percent humiliation and fifty percent hurt feelings and fifty percent envy. (Math was never my strong suit.) But the truth was that I had no one to blame but myself for not having gotten the same information as the *Reporter*. Obviously, I hadn't asked the right questions of the right people. I had put too much weight on the fact that I was the local girl and assumed, incorrectly, that if there was any information to leak, it would be leaked to me. I decided that first thing in the morning, I'd head back over to the sheriff's office. I had a bone to pick. If they were going to be talking to the press, the decent thing to do would at least be to talk to me.

I zipped home to change and take Coltrane, my spoiled-rotten German shepherd, for a quick walk before I was due to meet Ryan for drinks. And after my meeting with Kay, his enthusiastic you-are-the-sun-and-the-moon greeting was just what I needed. The walk did me some good too, and I left Coltrane with a big bowl of kibble and promises to come home again soon.

Despite its name, the Shack was Tuttle Corner's nicest restaurant by a mile. It sat close to the James River in an old house that had been converted into a restaurant. On any given day in the spring, summer, or fall people would sit outside on the large deck overlooking the river, but tonight the crowd was mostly inside. The main floor housed the bar and dining room, and the upstairs was a lounge space filled with comfy furniture, low tables, and intimate lighting. I walked in and was on my way upstairs when I caught a glimpse of Ash Campbell's red-and-blue-plaid shirt. He was sitting at the bar with a beer and a shot glass in front of him. I walked over to him in the spirit of our "new start."

"You okay there, chief?"

Given his Jekyll and Hyde personality, I braced myself for some rude comeback, but he just turned his head slowly and looked at me through glassy eyes. "No. Not really."

Oh no. Franklin, I thought. "What's going on?"

"Um," he started to say, but then stopped himself. "Uh... well, I think this is the end of Campbell & Sons after 142 years." He held up a finger to the bartender, who nodded and grabbed the bottle of Wild Turkey.

"Did something happen to your grandfather?"

He shook his head.

"Then what's going on?" I asked, relieved.

"I just can't do it," he said, and knocked back the shot of bourbon. "I'm just not cut out for it."

"What? The funeral home?"

"Yup. Dead bodies, grieving families...it's all so..."

I understood what he was trying to say. I didn't imagine being a funeral home director was an ideal career for everyone.

"And I know I'm letting them all down, all of them!" He made a wide gesture toward invisible members of the Campbell family from generations gone by. "Worst of all, PopPop." He paused for at least five seconds before swiveling his stool toward mine. "I have a job all lined up at

Strauss & Shapiro. I bet you didn't know that, did you?"

I was pretty sure this was a rhetorical question because why in the world would I know that—but he seemed a little too fragile for banter, so I kept my mouth closed.

"They're one of the top firms in Austin for criminal defense. I beat out seven other candidates in three rounds of interviews to get the position. Was supposed to start this week, in fact. I told them I had a family emergency, and they agreed to push my start date a couple of weeks."

His frustration was unmistakable, and I thought I detected a hint of resentment as well. I could understand that, though. He had a plan for his life and then circumstances beyond his control cropped up and changed everything. I'd been faced with a similar about-face in my own life a few months earlier and remembered that feeling of helplessness and uncertainty.

After another moment of silence he raised his eyes to meet mine. "He isn't going to make it back from this, is he?"

"It doesn't sound like it," I said gently. From what I had heard, there was little hope Franklin would recover—and even if he did, the chances of him being healthy enough to run the funeral home were slim.

Ash took a deep breath in. "Grams isn't well enough to take over, Dad's in prison for Christ's sake, Emily lives in California and just had her third kid, so either I step up and run things or my family not only loses our patriarch but our entire legacy as well." His sadness, grief, and crushing sense of obligation were palpable.

"I'm so sorry." It was all I could think to say. I'm not even sure he heard me.

"PopPop was basically like a father to us growing up. After it became clear my dad wasn't going to be much use, Franklin stepped in and essentially took over that role. He sent my mom money, he sent Emily and me cards, called every week, and made sure to visit four times a year—extra, if one of us was in a play or graduating or something like that. He was always there for us. No matter how hard it must have been."

His words brought back vivid memories of my own special relationship with my grandfather. Although both of my parents were very much involved in my life, I knew how powerful a close relationship with a grandparent could be. And I knew the pain of losing that relationship.

"Have you tried talking to Patricia? Does she know about your job offer?"

"I can't," he said, shaking his head. "She's so stressed right now...and if PopPop finds out about this it would kill him. *Literally.*"

He was right, the last thing the Campbells needed was to worry about their business.

"I'm sorry," he said, sitting up a little straighter and looking at me as if he just realized I was there. "Can I get you something? Do you want a drink?"

"Oh, no. That's okay. I'm actually meeting someone upstairs," I said feeling slightly guilty, though I didn't know why.

"Right," he mumbled. "Shoulda known." All of a sudden, he sounded like the first Ash I'd met that day, the one who was combative and temperamental. He held up his hand to the bartender again.

I put a hand on his shoulder as I stood to leave. "Take it easy, okay."

He swiveled his bar stool back around to face me, the tops of his knees brushing against my legs. When he raised his amber eyes to mine, gone was any trace of his earlier vulnerability. He'd put his armor back on. "Aye-aye, honey."

Ash may have been upset, half-crocked, and undeniably frustratingly attractive, but I wasn't going to let him off the hook for being a chauvinist. "I told you: I don't like it when you call me 'honey.'"

He continued to stare at me for an unsettling amount of time, and then a slow, cocky smile slid across his face. "You sure about that?"

CHAPTER 9

Ryan was already upstairs with two drinks in front of him, a Coors Light for him and by the looks of it, a Revolutionary Rum Runner for me. He must have either gotten there early or snuck in while I was talking to Ash.

"Hey," I said, picking up the drink and taking a sip before I even sat down.

Ryan stood up so quickly, he knocked his knee on the table. "Ow, shit—um, I mean, shoot. Sorry." He laughed and leaned over to give me a hug hello, an intimate habit we'd never quite gotten out of. I let him hug me, momentarily enjoying the firm feel of his arms around me and his clean, soapy smell.

"You okay?" he asked. "You look flushed."

Stupid Ash and his stupid comments. I pushed all thoughts of him from my mind and took another sip of my drink. "I'm fine."

"Good." Ryan gestured to the glass in my hand. "I ordered your favorite—I mean, at least what used to be your favorite. Looks like it still is," he said.

"Sorry. It's been one of those days."

"You never know, your day might still turn around." He flashed his dimples at me and raised his beer toward my glass. "To the day not being over yet."

I hesitantly clinked glasses, an uneasy guilt creeping up on me. Did Ridley know we were meeting tonight? What would she think if she did?

"Hey listen, Riles," he started to say. "I wanted to talk to you about something."

"Okay..."

"You and I have been through a ton," he said. "I mean, that's an understatement, right?"

I nodded. It was more than just an understatement. All of my firsts had been with Ryan—my first boyfriend, my first love, my first heartbreak. And then seven years of firsts had abruptly come to end when Ryan broke up with me and moved away without so much as an explanation.

"And I know everything's different now, Ridley's living here and we've got Lizzie and you've got your new career and all. But even though so much has changed, there's so much that hasn't, you know?" He looked up at me from underneath his swath of thick lashes. "You're so smart and you're still my best friend, Riles, and I—I—"

I didn't like where this was heading. There were lots of reasons why Ryan and I would never get back together—Ridley and Lizzie were two of them—but also, getting over the breakup with Ryan had been one of the hardest things I'd ever done, and there was no way I was going to put myself through that again. I'd been clear with him that while there was a part of me who would always love him, we were just going to be friends. True to form, Ryan thought my opinions were merely a jumping-off point for negotiation.

Could that be what he was working up to say? To make another push for us to try again? It had been a while since he'd brought it up, but maybe because he knew I was no longer with Jay he thought my answer would be different now. As flattering as it was to be pined for, Ryan and I made no sense as a couple. He might not know it, but I was sure enough for the both of us.

"Funny you should mention Ridley," I said, cutting off whatever he was trying to say. "That's why I asked you here tonight."

He looked thrown off. "It is?"

"I wanted to ask you about something she said yesterday. She said she's going to take over Rosalee's Tavern." I took out my notebook and poised my pen over it. "What's that all about?"

"So this is an interview?" I watched as Ryan began to understand that tonight was never going to be about us; I simply wanted information.

"Of course," I said, like that was obvious. "So, what about Rosalee's..."

Ryan picked up his beer and took a long sip. When he lowered it, he shook his head, a bewildered expression on his face. "Um, yeah, well, we've been talking about it and Ridley really wants to do it, so yeah."

"How did this all come about?"

"When she first moved to town, Ridley talked to Rosalee about working at the Tavern," he said, then added, "Ridley really knows her way around a kitchen."

"Of course she does," I said, unable to control myself.

"Rosalee seemed really interested. She said she was planning to do more traveling soon and was ready to 'move on' from having such a demanding schedule with the restaurant and all. Obviously, Ridley was super-pregnant at the time and couldn't commit to anything. But a couple of weeks ago Rosalee came into the store and she asked if Ridley would still be interested."

Ryan worked at his family's business, Sanford Farm & Home. "I gave her Ridley's number, and later that week she texted saying she was going away and asked if Ridley would want to run things while she was gone."

"Didn't you think that was weird?" I asked.

"I don't know, I guess not," he said, taking another swig of his beer. "Rosalee was always a little mysterious, and I just figured she was going back home to France to see her family or something. Besides, Ridley was super-excited, so I didn't think too much about it."

That seemed dense, even for Ryan. "Even with all of the stuff about Greer Mountbatten and Justin Balzichek going on?"

He shook his head. "Oh no, this was before any of that."

"Wait, what?" I got a tingle on the back of my neck.

"She was in on November fourth," Ryan said. "I remember because it was the same day that we got in a huge shipment of ice melt we'd been waiting on. I'm pretty sure that was before any of this crazy stuff happened."

I mentally ticked through the timeline in my head. Greer's body hadn't been found until November seventh. And Justin's not until the ninth. Rosalee had planned to be gone before that? Why? I was no expert, but that sounded like premeditation to me. And then a dark thought started circling around my brain like a vulture.

"Ryan, what did Rosalee buy that day she came into the store?"

He thought for a minute and then his face drained of color. I honestly don't think he made the connection until that very moment.

"Don't tell me," I said, reading his expression. "A sledgehammer?"

He nodded, words escaping him. He ran a hand through his sandy brown hair and left it on top of his head. "She said she was planning to do some remodeling, something about needing more storage in the basement or something...I can't remember exactly. I never in a million years pegged Rosalee for a killer. I really thought this would all be cleared up any day now and she'd come back and run the Tavern like always."

I knew how he felt. There was a part of me that thought the same thing. "I think you need to tell Carl what you just told me."

"Yeah," he said, downing the last of his beer. "I'll stop by the sheriff's office on my way home."

"You know what?" I said, standing up and holding a hand out to him. "I'll go with you."

"Thanks, Riles." He sounded so happy, I didn't have the heart to tell him I had my own reasons for wanting to see Carl Haight that had nothing to do with him.

CHAPTER 10

While Ryan was giving his statement to Butter, I knocked on Carl's office door and asked if he had a minute.

"Not really, Riley." Carl sounded just plain worn out. He'd basically been living down here since Greer's body had been found, and it was starting to show on his face. He looked far older than his twenty-six years.

"Can I bother you anyway? It'll only take a second."

He made a gesture that I took to mean come in and sit down. It's possible it was intended to say go away and don't come back, but I was an optimist, so I took a seat.

"The *Daily Reporter* out of Fairfax is saying Justin Balzichek's cause of death was poisoning. Can you confirm that?"

Carl looked up, surprised. "You know we're not discussing that with the press. I said as much at the press conference this morning. We're wanting to hold back certain details until we're able to collect more evidence."

"How did the *Reporter* get it then?"

He furrowed his brow. "That's what I'd like to know."

"You didn't leak it?"

"Hell no, Riley. I'm not going to start leaking things to the press in this case. Are you crazy? Not with all the scrutiny I'm under. This case is getting national attention, in case you hadn't noticed. I'm going to stay well inside the lines on this one, you can be sure of that."

I nodded. That was the Carl Haight I'd known since preschool—the rule follower, the one who wanted to prove to everyone that he was up to the job. Carl and I had a unique understanding of each other as Tuttle Corner's next generation. We were both starting out in our careers, both had a lot of responsibility, and both felt slightly in over our heads. Though we never talked openly about it, I felt our shared bouts of deep professional insecurity bonded us together in some way. As a result, there was a level of trust there that allowed us to talk candidly.

"Is it true?"

He looked at me a long moment before nodding slowly.

"How?"

"You can't print any of this—not yet."

"Understood."

"Cyanide." Carl sighed. "The M.E. found lethal levels in his blood."

"Hmm," I said, trying to think what the implications of that were. "Any cyanide used to kill Greer?"

"Not a trace. It's very strange. We have two victims who were clearly connected—Balzichek was set to testify that Greer hired him to vandalize Rosalee's Tavern—but who were killed in two very different ways." He sighed again. "It's possible we're dealing with more than one perpetrator."

That was something I hadn't considered. I'd always assumed Justin and Greer were killed by the same person. I think most people did.

"Have you tried talking to Greer's sister?" I asked, trying to think of anyone who might be able to shed some light on things. "Maybe Greer had enemies from a past life or something?" I knew it was a long shot, but still. Sometimes people had hidden pasts, even oil heiresses.

"We spoke to her a couple of days ago. She's staying with Dale and the boys and helping with the funeral arrangements and such." Carl frowned.

"What?"

"I don't know," he said. "She's a little off. I can't exactly put my finger on what it is with her...just something a little weird, for lack of a better word."

I leaned forward, interested. "Do you think she could have had something to do with Greer's death?"

He shook his head. "Doubt it. It was a pretty brutal crime, doesn't fit the profile of a female perp. Besides, what's the motivation?"

"Money?"

"Their father's estate is set to be divided equally among them when he dies," Carl said.

"Who will inherit Greer's half now?"

"Her boys. It's in a trust that they can't touch for a few years, but eventually they'll get it all," Carl said.

"So Dale doesn't get anything?"

Carl shook his head.

I looked over my notes and sighed. "Can you give me anything I can print? Kay's mad as a hornet that the other paper got the scoop about the poison."

He thought for a moment. "You can quote me saying that we are exploring the possibility that the murders were committed by more than one person—nothing about the cyanide though, okay?"

I wrote the words down exactly as he had said them. "Thanks, Carl."

He nodded. "Thanks for sending Ryan in," he said. "His testimony about Rosalee buying that sledgehammer and her plans to leave town may become important."

"Do you think Rosalee is really...involved in all of this?" I tried to convey with my voice that I was asking what he thought personally, more neighbor-to-neighbor than reporter to sheriff.

"She's definitely involved, that much we know for sure. Whether or not she's behind either of these deaths...well, that's what we don't know. I sure wish she'd come to her senses and talk to us."

I thanked him for talking with me and told him he ought to go home and get some sleep. Then I went home and took my own advice.

Self-Care Assignment #1:
A Better You Through Sensory Awareness

Light a scented massage candle such as our free-trade Rose-de-mai coconut oil massage candle ($51.99). Breathe in the clean, centering aroma that is completely free of toxins, endocrine disruptors, and chakra-imbalancing free radicals. Pay attention to how focused and aligned you feel after just a few breaths. #deepbreathingisthenewblack

Once you feel sufficiently transformed, pour the warm wax onto your body directly from the ceramic vessel, allowing the hot liquid to completely coat your skin, creating a barrier to lock out energy-destroying microtoxins. #waxon #waxoff

Do not be afraid: the prickling, burning sensation you feel is just trapped negative energy trying to work its way out.

Spend at least fifteen minutes journaling about how this activity made you feel, noting reactions from all five of your senses (F.L.Y.™ journal made from recycled paper, $27.99).

✳

Dear Miss Ellison,

Thank you for your email. I apologize for the first-degree burn that resulted from the sensory self-care exercise. I should have specified that using old birthday candles would not provide the same healing effect as the Rose-de-mai coconut oil massage candle, though I certainly understand that the cost of our candle is "a little steep." #aspirationalproductline

We will try again tomorrow with Self-Care Exercise #2 that will focus on packing up your emotional baggage and hope for a better outcome. #bonvoyage #hastalavistapsychictrauma

Yours in Loving Alignment,

Regina H,
Personal Romance Concierge™ and F.L.Y.
Guy™-in-training
Click.com

CHAPTER 11

TUESDAY

Our editorial obituary for Sunday's paper was for a man named Jonathan Klondike, the founder of the local chapter of the Kiwanis Club. He'd died from complications of a staph infection he'd contracted after going on a church mission to help flood victims. He'd lived an admirable life and touched many in our community. I was excited to read Flick's obit as both another set of eyes and his protégée. I always learned something when I read Flick's writing. He started writing obituaries later in his career, like Granddaddy, and maybe because of that, his read more like profile pieces than tributes. It was a true talent to make readers forget the subject they were reading about had recently died, something Flick did quite well. He'd often receive letters from friends and families thanking him for bringing their loved ones to life again on the page.

I went by Flick's office to see if he was in yet, but the lights were off, door closed. I walked down the hall to Holman's office, same deal there. He hadn't texted or called since yesterday, which wasn't totally unusual, but radio silence from him was never a good sign. I knocked on the door to Kay's office.

"Have you heard from Holman today?"

"Mmm," she said, distracted. "No, I don't think so."

"Me neither. Maybe the Stormer Window investigation is heating up?"

"What Stormer Window investigation?" she asked without taking her eyes off her laptop screen.

"You know, the piece he's working on about the complaints to the BBB and possible tax fraud?"

Kay looked up at me, blank. "First I'm hearing of it."

Holman had told me specifically that Kay had given him that story. Why would he lie about that? I didn't want to throw Holman under the bus if he was working on something privately. "Oh, well," I said, "maybe I got it wrong."

Kay nodded and went back to reading whatever was on her computer screen, which was clearly more important to her than Holman's current whereabouts. I left her to her work and went back to my cubicle to call Holman. He picked up on the second ring.

"So what's on your agenda today?" I asked, trying to keep my voice casual. I didn't want to tip him off that I was on to him.

"I've got some sensitive sources to follow up with, so I'm making calls from home."

"On the Stormer piece?"

A brief pause. "Yes."

"How's it going? You getting anywhere?"

"Um, yes," he said, suddenly sounding less sure of himself. "It's a complex story."

"BZZT!" I blurted out. Several heads in the newsroom turned. I pressed the phone to my ear and lowered my voice. "I just talked to Kay. I know there's no Stormer investigation!"

Another brief pause. "Good work, Riley. I am actually very impressed—"

"Don't even try to change the subject by complimenting

me!" I whisper-hissed. "What are you working on? And why are you lying to me about it?"

Holman sighed. "I take no pleasure in lying to you, believe me, so you have to know that the only reason I would is if I thought it was in your best interest."

"What does that even mean? Does this have something to do with Flick?" I said, thinking that was exactly the same kind of overly protective rationale Flick was using to keep me in the dark about Granddaddy.

"Flick? No, why?"

The surprise in his voice was enough to convince me his behavior and Flick's were unrelated. "Never mind," I snapped. "Tell me what you're working on that's so important you have to lie to me about it!"

"I can't do that," he said softly. "I'm sorry."

"I can't believe you don't trust me, Holman. After everything we've been through."

"It's not that...it's just...complicated."

I was about to launch into a rant about how that is the lamest excuse ever when my phone bleeped, alerting me I had another call. I checked the screen: Hal Flick. Of course *now* he calls. I growled into the phone, "I have to go, but make no mistake: This isn't over." And before I even waited for his goodbye, I clicked over.

"Riley?" I could barely hear Flick's voice over the noise in the background. It sounded like he was standing on a runway or something, a combination of high-pitched whining and the deeper whooshing sound of air being displaced. "Can you hear me?"

"Barely," I said. "Where are you?"

"Riley, if you can hear me, I want you to know I'm going on another trip, but I'll be back in a couple of days. The Klondike obit is done. I just need you to give it a final proof.

I'll email it to you. Can you do that?"

The machinery sounds were getting louder. I could hear the beeping sound of a truck backing up along with some shouting between anonymous personnel in the background. I pushed the phone closer to my ear. "Yeah sure, but...is everything all right?"

"I'm sorry," Flick was practically screaming now. "I can't hear you real well, but everything's fine. I don't want you to worry. I'm following a lead over on Chincoteague Island."

"Chincoteague?" I felt a few people look over. I was talking too loud for the relatively quiet newsroom, but I didn't care.

"They're telling me I have to go," Flick shouted. The repetitive thump-woosh-thump-woosh sound was quickening. It sounded like a helicopter getting ready for takeoff. "Don't worry. I'll be in touch as soon as I can."

And then the line went dead.

CHAPTER 12

I spent the next forty-five minutes going through the Klondike piece Flick sent and trying not to perseverate over what he was looking into on Chincoteague Island. He'd promised I could be his partner on this investigation when "the time was right"—whatever that meant—so there was no point obsessing about it until he decided to share.

It was a chilly, gray day, typical of Virginia in November, and I'd chosen to drive to work that morning instead of braving the ten-minute walk. I had parked my green Nissan Cube, which I'd affectionately named Oscar, around back of the *Times* office in the shared parking lot for a few of the businesses on our side of the square. I glanced over to the spot where Rosalee would normally be parked, expecting it would be empty as it had been every day since she disappeared. But it wasn't. Ryan's massive truck was there. I knocked on the back door of the Tavern.

"Hi!" A fresh-faced Ridley beamed at me as she opened the door. She wore no makeup but looked like she had just walked out of one of those commercials for face wash—bright-eyed and smooth-skinned—and when she leaned in to kiss me on both cheeks, I noticed her long blond hair felt even thicker and silkier than normal. Motherhood definitely agreed with her.

"So happy you came by! Come in, come in!" She looked

down at my bandaged pinky finger. "What happened to your hand?"

"Collateral damage from self-care."

She crinkled her brows together, still smiling widely like she wasn't sure if I was joking or not.

"Just a minor burn. It's nothing."

"I have the perfect salve for burns! It's an old family recipe—my mother taught me never to be in a kitchen without it. I have some in my purse, c'mon."

I followed her through the narrow hallway toward the kitchen. She had on a black-and-white-striped three-quarter sleeve T-shirt with faded (pre-pregnancy) jeans and tall black Hunter boots. She wore Lizzie, the perfect accessory, against her chest in one of those brightly colored baby slings.

Ryan, who was moving boxes around the cramped kitchen, looked up when I walked in. "Hey, Riles. What're you doing here?" I couldn't help but notice his voice didn't have its usual warmth. And that there was no hug hello this time.

"Just passing by and saw your truck, " I said. "So you guys are really doing this?"

"We are going to open for business tomorrow!" Ridley practically squealed with delight.

"Where do you want these?" Ryan asked Ridley, holding up two large cardboard file boxes.

"Um," Ridley said, looking around the small space, "put them in the office for now. I'll try to find a better place later."

Ridley and I flattened ourselves against the walls while Ryan scooted past us to put the boxes away.

"I don't know how Rosalee functioned in here—it's tiny," Ridley said.

"So," I said, looking around the chaotic kitchen.

"Tomorrow? Really?"

She nodded and went back to stacking cans on the wire shelves against the back wall. "Yes. Melvin will cook, Maddie will come over and work the lunch shift like always, I'll keep everything moving along—it'll be great! We're just going to do breakfast and lunch at first while we figure out what we're doing, but isn't it exciting?"

Exciting wasn't exactly the word I would have chosen. Rosalee was missing and suspected of some very serious criminal activity—not the least of which was murder—and Ridley and Ryan were just moving right on into her restaurant and taking over. It was kind of unbelievable.

"So Rosalee is really okay with this?"

"I told you," Ryan said, sounding slightly irritated. "She said she was fine with Ridley running things for her while she's gone."

"Yeah, but..." I wasn't sure exactly how to articulate my concerns. They were both acting so blasé about the whole thing. "Is she even planning to come back? She's in a lot of trouble, you know."

"She actually seemed really concerned about her customers. I think she feels a real responsibility to the people of Tuttle Corner," Ridley said.

I thought that was a little dramatic. It wasn't like the people of Tuttle Corner were going to starve if Rosalee's Tavern remained closed. Why would a woman on the run, wanted for questioning in the deaths of two people, be so concerned with keeping her business open? But both Ryan and Ridley didn't see it as strange, or they didn't want to talk about it, so I changed the subject. "Hey, did Rosalee buy anything else when she was in your store that day?" I asked Ryan.

"Yeah," Ryan said. "Carl asked me the same thing. She

had a key made."

"Like a house key?"

"Nah," he said, relocating a large cardboard box to the other side of the stainless-steel island. "I don't think so, it was shorter and thinner than that. Cash had a helluva time finding a blank that would match it."

"Do you know what it was for?"

He shook his head. "You know Rosalee. She didn't say a whole lot, and it wasn't my business to ask."

"Ridley," I said, turning my attention to her. "You said you didn't know where Rosalee was contacting you from, only that she was safe. What did she say exactly when she called you?"

"She didn't call, she texted."

"What did the text say?"

She took out her phone, scrolled through, and then handed it to me. The text read: Had to leave sooner than I thought. Melvin has keys, deliveries made after close on M,W,F. Thank u.

"Hmm," I said. "Not much there."

Ryan took a step closer to Ridley and said, "Remember you're talking to the press here, babe."

Babe?

"Riley isn't the press," Ridley said, flashing a warm smile my way. "Well, she isn't *only* the press—she's our friend. And she's Rosalee's friend too."

"He's right," I said, still a little thrown off at Ryan's use of the word *babe*. "I mean, I am your friend, but I'm also a reporter working on this story. I'm trying to find out the truth."

"Of course," Ridley said.

Just then Lizzie started crying.

"Oh *min älskling*, are you hungry?" Ridley looked down

at the fussing baby. “Does it bother you if I feed her?” She already had her hand down her shirt. Of course I didn’t mind, but in another second or two I’d be confronted with what was undoubtedly the most perfect breast since Aphrodite roamed the planet. I didn’t think my ego could take that.

“Go right ahead,” I said, turning away. “I’ll give you some privacy. I’ve got to get going anyway. I’ll call you later, though, okay?”

“Okay,” Ryan and Ridley said in unison.

We all stopped for half a second as the oddity of the interaction set in. Two months ago, that comment could only have been meant for Ryan, but now...now we had this three-headed monster of a friendship going on. It was strange, new territory for us all.

“I meant Ridley,” I said awkwardly.

“I win,” Ridley winked at Ryan, who turned away, annoyed, and I made a beeline for the back door, ready to leave Ryan and Ridley (and her perfect breasts) behind.

CHAPTER 13

While I was out, I decided to check in with the mysterious Mr. Holman. Or maybe check up on him was a better way to put it. I pulled into the parking lot of Holman's apartment complex and saw his car. *Sweet*, I thought, *he's home*.

I had only been to Holman's apartment a couple of times before. If we hung out away from the office, it was usually at my house or a coffee shop. His place was a first-floor, two-bedroom unit and typical of a single guy's—kind of messy and not a lot of emphasis on décor. Unless you count Lego sets as décor. Holman had put up IKEA shelving units on three of the four walls in his living room for the sole purpose of showcasing his Lego sets. He had the Millennium Falcon, the Hogwarts Castle, and all of the Lord of the Rings sets. I estimated that over the course of his lifetime, Will Holman had probably spent the GDP of a small country on Legos.

Holman finally came to the door after I knocked a second time. "Riley." He did not sound happy to see me. That was definitely unusual.

"Hey," I said, "just thought I'd come by and make sure you're doing okay." I tried to peek around him.

"That is very kind of you," he said without moving or inviting me inside. "I'm fine. Just busy."

"Busy with what?"

"Work."

"The story you can't tell me about?"

His eyes darted to the side. "Yes. And I actually have an appointment, so I really have to get goin—"

Holman was an interesting guy for a lot of reasons, but one of them was that he had certain peculiarities. He ate the same thing for lunch every day for the past three years (a peanut butter and jelly sandwich on whole-grain white Bunny bread). He wore only light khaki pants from American Eagle, size 32 x 36. And he was almost incapable of lying. And yet he stood before me, for the second time in as many days, and lied right to my face.

"What are you hiding from me, Will Holman?"

He blinked. Then he blinked again. And again.

"Don't bother denying it. Your nervous blinking is a dead giveaway." I pushed on the door and moved past him into the living room, expecting to see something shocking. I was ready to let out a triumphant "aha!" but when I got into the room, there was nothing there. His laptop sat open on the ottoman across from his ugly brown cloth sofa, a can of ginger ale on the side table next to him.

"Riley," Holman said as he walked over to his laptop and closed it, "I told you. I'm working on something that I'm just not ready to share with you yet."

I looked around his place like a jealous girlfriend. I glanced into the kitchen, peered down the hallway, peeked behind the curtains. I was looking for any evidence that might explain his strange behavior but didn't see anything suspicious. I did, however, smell something.

I sniffed the air. "What is that?"

Holman blinked rapidly three times. "What is what?"

"That smell." I moved closer to the kitchen. "It smells

buttery and toasty..." It was too late for lunch and too early for dinner, and besides, this didn't smell like Holman-food. It smelled *heavenly*. And vaguely familiar, but I couldn't put my finger on what it was.

"Are you cooking something?" I stepped past him to get closer to the kitchen and was hit with another scent. "And are you wearing cologne?"

"Riley, I'm really going to have to ask you to lea—" Holman was now blinking like a toad in a hailstorm.

And then things started to lock into place. The secrecy. The cooking. The blinking. The cologne. Maybe Holman wasn't hiding something work-related from me. Maybe he was hiding something of a more personal nature.

"Holman," I said, a grin sliding across my face. "Do you have a date?"

For a moment he looked so uncomfortable that he might spontaneously combust, but an instant later his face changed. "Yes, that is it. You've figured it out." He put two long-fingered hands on each of my shoulders and led me toward the door. "I have a date. And she'll be here soon, so you understand why I'm in such a hurry."

Holman had a date? I couldn't believe it. I had never heard him say anything remotely resembling a romantic interest in a woman—or man, for that matter—in all the months I'd known him. I was shocked. "Who is she?" I asked. "Anyone I know?"

"No." Holman had the door open and me halfway out. "She's new to the area, and I don't want her to get the wrong idea if she gets here and sees me pushing a pretty girl out the door..."

Aw, he said I was pretty. "Okay, okay, I'll go," I said, smiling. "But text me later and tell me how it went. Promise?"

Holman's face was fifty shades of red. "Fine. Okay."

I walked down the concrete path toward the parking lot, but before I got far I turned back around. "And Holman, maybe don't analyze the symmetry of her face. Or comment on the size of her feet. Or guess her IQ."

"Thank you for the advice," Holman said in a tone that, had it come from anyone else, I would have sworn was sarcastic.

Chapter 14

The rest of the day passed uneventfully. I called Flick on my way home from work. No answer. I left a message for him to call me back. I was worried about him, but I'd have been lying if I said I wasn't glad he was out there chasing down leads. Ever since he'd admitted he also thought Granddaddy had been murdered, it seemed we were getting closer to the truth. And the closer we got, the more risk we were both willing to accept. It felt like being high up in a tree, inching out bit by bit to grab the fruit at the end of the branch. Risky but worth it.

Flick wasn't much of a texter, but I tried anyway, just in case: This is Riley. All ok?

No response.

When the doorbell rang, even though the logical part of my brain knew it wouldn't be Flick, the breath hitched in my throat. I rushed to the door, but Coltrane's longing whines told me it could only be one person. *Ridley*. My dog, like males of all species, got inappropriately excited to see her.

"Um, hi." Ridley stood on my front porch and looked over her left shoulder. "I forgot to give you that stuff for your burn earlier, so I thought I'd bring it by."

"Oh, you didn't have to do that," I said, embarrassed just thinking about what Ridley would say if she knew I was enrolled in a self-care program. "It's really nothing."

I opened the door wider to let her in, Coltrane eagerly circling her as she walked into my living room. She handed me a small tin. "Use a small amount at bedtime. It'll really help."

I couldn't help but notice she wasn't making eye contact. Or smiling at me like she usually did. "Thanks," I said. "You okay?"

My question must have been the invitation she'd been waiting for. She looked down at her feet, then up at me. "Um, could I ask you a question? In confidence?"

My expression froze for a second. Was this going to be about Ryan? It made me deeply uncomfortable to talk about Ryan with Ridley. "Sure," I said, trying to sound breezy. "Of course."

"Can we sit?"

I did not like the direction this conversation was going. An anxious cloud loomed over us as we settled on the couch. I offered her something to drink, which she declined. When it became clear she wasn't going to be the one to start the conversation, I did. "So what's up?"

Ridley leaned forward and lowered her voice to a whisper even though the only one listening was Coltrane (who sat at her feet waiting for a scrap of attention, the mutinous beast). "Um, what if someone had information about a certain other someone and that first someone thought perhaps the second someone might be involved in certain activities that might be, shall we say, not strictly speaking, legal?"

I gave her a look that said, *Huh?*

She widened her crystal blue eyes and tried again, this time in an even lower voice. "I mean, what is a person's ethical responsibility in terms of reporting something to the authorities that might shed light on an ongoing criminal investigation?"

This obviously had to do with Rosalee, not Ryan. My relief gave way to the electric tingle of anticipation. "I'm no lawyer, but I think there are laws against withholding information about a crime." I paused. "Do you know something about a crime?"

Ridley looked down. "No—I mean, maybe." She tucked a long, shiny section of hair behind one ear. "I came across some information at the restaurant this afternoon, and it raised some concerns about Rosalee's involvement in all the stuff that has been going on."

"The murders, you mean?"

Ridley nodded. "I'm not even sure it's anything, but—"

"Why don't you tell me and maybe I can help you figure it out?" Something had happened in the past few hours, and whatever it was, I had a feeling it was most certainly newsworthy.

"I don't want to get her in trouble, especially since I'm not even sure it means anything."

This was big. I could sense it. I wanted it so badly, I was practically salivating, but I needed to play it cool so I didn't scare Ridley off.

"Maybe I can help?" I said again, feeling like the old crone tempting Snow White to take a bite of the poison apple. Not that telling the truth was a poison apple or anything—telling the truth was good—but telling the truth to a reporter could be complicated, and I wasn't sure Ridley understood that.

"My parents own a restaurant in Sälen, did you know that?"

I shook my head.

"I grew up working for them, so I know a little something

about how the industry works."

That explained Ridley's enthusiasm for taking over while Rosalee was indisposed. Despite my best intentions, I felt a swell of empathy for Ridley. She had just had a baby and was living thousands of miles from her family, her home. Ridley got so much attention everywhere she went, it never occurred to me that she might be lonely. Maybe running Rosalee's Tavern was a cure for homesickness as much as anything else.

She continued. "In preparation to open, I had to look through the books to see how she handles her accounting and to check on how she orders supplies. At first glance, everything looked pretty standard. She keeps the financials in notebooks—handwritten—with the daily total sales marked, subdivided by cash and credit card purchases. Most use computers, but some still do it old-school. That was not so unusual."

I waited quietly to hear what was.

"I also found her file containing invoices from suppliers. It appears she pays some of them in cash, which could be a way to avoid paying taxes, but again, not completely out of the ordinary in the restaurant business."

"So what's the problem?" I held my breath in anticipation.

Ridley heaved out a big sigh. "It's the butter."

"The butter?" That was not what I was expecting to hear.

"Her expenditures on butter are astronomical."

I didn't know much about the restaurant business, but I would think a French café would spend a fair amount on butter. And I'd had Rosalee's pastries—they were buttery works of culinary art.

"Could that just be because of her recipes?"

"It isn't the amount of butter that concerns me," she clarified. "It's what she's paying for it."

"Like, what are we talking?"

"According to her invoices, she orders about six thousand pounds of butter per month."

"Is that a lot?" Without context I had no idea.

"More than most, but that's not the strange part. For those six thousand pounds, she's paying over sixteen thousand dollars, which even with the recent *'crise du beurre' c'est très coûteux.*"

Freaking Ridley and her multilinguality, I thought. "English, please."

"The great butter crisis in France."

I gave her another blank stare. Blank stares were becoming a theme in this conversation.

"The French butter crisis. Surely you have heard about it?"

I had not. A butter crisis? This had to be some sort of joke. I leaned back against the chair and laughed. "You're messing with me, aren't you?"

"No," Ridley said, her eyes widening. "You can look it up! There is a shortage of butter in France, and it has caused the price to skyrocket."

"Really?" This sounded very strange. How could the French run out of butter? That's like Italy running out of pasta or Mexico having an avocado shortage or America running out of Twinkies.

"Anyway," Ridley continued her story. "Those numbers just seemed odd to me, so I did some research, and even with the increasing prices, I wouldn't expect her to pay more than twelve thousand for the amount she's using. But Rosalee has been paying so much more for years now—practically since she opened."

I had to think about this for a minute. What were the implications of Rosalee overpaying for butter? "Do you think she's, like, getting a kickback from the butter supplier or something?"

"That is definitely possible," Ridley said. "I have seen this before back in Sweden. An acquaintance of my parents was shut down by the government for a hazelnut payola scandal in 2006. It was ugly."

"Okaaayyyyy...." I held up my hand. Hazelnut payola? Butter crisis? I just couldn't.... I shook my head trying to think through the absurdity. "Even if something is up with her butter, what does that have to do with the murders?"

"Her files indicate she orders butter through a company called Colonel Mustard Enterprises. I scoured the internet looking for information on them and found nothing. There is a website, but it has no information. I couldn't have ordered butter from there if I'd wanted to."

"I still don't see what any of this has to do with—"

"On a piece of scrap paper in one of her files, I found a phone number next to the initials CME, so I thought maybe that was it. I called the number and it just rang and rang. No one picked up and there was no voicemail. But about a minute after I hung up, the number called me back. I asked if this was Colonel Mustard Enterprises and a woman demanded to know who I was and where I got this number. When I refused to say, she told me the company had gone out of business and told me never to call again."

I was beginning to see why this was troubling to Ridley.

"One other strange thing," Ridley continued. "I've been going into the restaurant pretty much every day for the past few days...and maybe I'm crazy, but I swear that butter is slowly disappearing from the refrigerator."

Of all the unbelievable things Ridley had told me

during this conversation, this may have been the most unbelievable. "Someone's *stealing butter*?"

"At this rate, I'm going to have to order more soon—and of course now I don't even know where I will get it from."

I was still trying to work out how Rosalee's expensive and possibly suspicious butter dealer was involved with the recent murders in our town, so I could hardly focus on someone stealing a nip of butter here or there. Maybe Ridley had calculated the inventory incorrectly? Or maybe she was imagining it? Or maybe, even more likely, Ryan had developed a taste for French butter.

"Listen, I'm sure no one is after your butter—" I started to say, but as soon as the word was across my lips, a thought came to me: *butter*. That smell at Holman's apartment. It was butter. And not just any butter—it was the deep, rich, buttery smell of decadence. I stood up. "I have to go!"

Ridley flinched "Are you all right?"

"Yeah, I'm fine," I said, grabbing her by her perfect elbow and hurrying her toward the door. "I just remembered something I have to do tonight."

"Oh, okay..." she said.

"We'll talk later—I'll come by the café tomorrow, I promise!"

After I shooed a baffled Ridley out the door, I grabbed my keys and headed out, for the second time that night, to Will Holman's apartment.

"Where is she?" I demanded as soon as he opened the door.

"What? Riley, I—"

"Save it." I pushed past him into his apartment, and the familiar luscious aroma hit my nose. This time it took me less than two seconds to figure out where it was coming from. Atop Holman's drab, builder-grade, Formica breakfast bar was a wire rack containing six of the most perfectly formed almond croissants I'd ever seen. I knew those croissants—I'd been eating them twice a week for nearly a year.

Holman saw me look at the pastries, and his eyes, already almost perfect circles, widened to anime effect. He said nothing; his silence told me everything I needed to know.

I glared at him hard, then said loudly toward the back bedroom, "Rosalee, you can come out now."

CHAPTER 15

B*onjour*, Riley." Rosalee walked out and leaned against the arched wall separating Holman's living room from the back hallway. She wore a plain white button-down shirt, dark skinny jeans, and red ballet flats. Her dark brown hair fell to just below her shoulders and was parted deep on the left side so that it swooped across her smooth, pale forehead in one clean diagonal line. Even in hiding, she looked stylish.

"Someone better tell me what the hell is going on around here. *Now*." I looked from Rosalee to Holman and back to Rosalee.

"Let's sit down," Holman said, gesturing to his living room. "Riley, first you need to know that Rosalee didn't kill anyone."

I'll admit I felt a tiny bit relieved to hear Holman say that. Holman was more precise with his words than most, and he was rarely so definitive about things.

"She came to me two days ago afraid for her life and asked me for help."

"Why you?"

He thought for a moment before answering. "She didn't think the sheriff could keep her safe."

"From who?" I looked at Rosalee. It was time she spoke for herself.

“Dale Mountbatten wants me dead.” The words were incongruous with her tone, which was somewhere between uninterested and bored.

“We don’t know that for sure,” Holman jumped in. “He might just want you locked up in prison.”

A harsh laugh erupted from Rosalee’s red-lipped mouth. “Where I will have an unfortunate ‘accident,’ no doubt.”

There was so much information being thrown out, and I didn’t have context for any of it. “Rosalee,” I said as patiently as I could manage. “Can you start from the beginning?”

“Yes, but first,” she said and walked toward the kitchen, “croissants.”

The story came out over the course of one hour and four croissants (only two of which were mine). Rosalee came to America nine years ago at the age of twenty-two as an au pair. She worked for a reputable agency and was given her first assignment the summer after she finished university: the Mountbattens of northern Virginia. While working for the family, she lived in guest quarters over the garage, doing all the usual things an au pair does. She looked after the children, drove carpool, supervised playdates, arranged meals for the kids with their personal chef, and occasionally ran a non-kid-related errand for Greer. She said Greer was nice but aloof and made it clear that Rosalee was there in service to—not as an extension of—the family. Dale was friendlier. And about five months into Rosalee’s tenure on the job, he became friendlier still.

“It was completely consensual,” Rosalee said without the slightest hint of self-consciousness. “He was unlike any man I’d known before—of course, until then I had only dated boys.” She shrugged. “Dale was different. He was ambitious and driven, he knew what he wanted, and, I suppose as a young woman, I felt flattered that what he wanted was me." Rosalee's green-gray eyes seemed to spark at the memory. "We became consumed with each other, stealing time away from the kids whenever we could, our desire for each other leading us both to make stupid decisions—" she broke off, "—and ultimately Greer found out."

"How?"

Rosalee shrugged again. "I think there was a part of Dale that wanted to be found out...at least that's the only explanation that makes sense to me looking back. Dale told me—told both Greer and me together—that he loved me and was planning to leave her."

Interesting. This was new information. "I assume she did not take that well?" I asked.

"No, she did not." Rosalee took a long sip of tea before continuing the story. "She threatened to call my agency and have me sent back to France. I was in clear violation of the terms of my employment agreement and would have been sent home immediately. But over the course of a few days, Dale made a deal with her: He would stay with them if I was allowed to remain in the country."

"Why would she agree to that?" I furrowed my brow. "Why would you?"

"Dale was very charming."

"Did you keep seeing each other? And what happened with your posting with the au pair agency? And why Tuttle Corner?" There were mile-wide holes in the story she was telling me.

"The arrangement was that the Mountbattens would keep providing the appropriate payment and updates to my agency for the length of my contract, and I would 'go away.' Dale said he would make sure I was taken care of. Tuttle Corner was his idea. He asked what kind of work I would like to do, and I said I had been a waitress in a café back in Dijon. The next week he formed a new company, Colonel Mustard Enterprises, and bought me a restaurant."

Colonel Mustard Enterprises. The butter distributor. Things were getting interesting now.

I had heard versions of Rosalee's origin story in the form of rumors about a young French woman suddenly moving, alone, to Tuttle and opening a restaurant. But as far as I knew, Rosalee hadn't ever confirmed or denied the gossip. She was not the sort of woman to offer more information than was asked of her—and sometimes not even that. Plus, people in Tuttle Corner never asked directly. Why risk ruining juicy gossip with the truth?

"So the relationship continued?"

"Yes."

I waited for her to elaborate, but apparently that was all she had to say about that. I pressed. "Like, for how long?"

Holman, who had been listening quietly up until this point, jumped in. "Their relationship persisted until very recently, but it had...evolved."

"Evolved how?" I asked. Both Rosalee and Holman were being cagey about something. If Rosalee had essentially been Dale Mountbatten's sidepiece for seven or eight years, did Greer know about it? And perhaps more importantly, didn't that provide Rosalee with a pretty strong motive for murder?

As if she read my mind, Rosalee offered an explanation. "We saw each other as often as we could get away with it. He'd say he was traveling for work, and I'd join him in a hotel for a weekend here, an evening there. And for a long while, it seemed that there might be a future for us somewhere down the road, once the children got older. But given the constraints," she said, "our relationship was primarily a sexual one."

She was so matter-of-fact, I could see how she and Holman would get along. I, on the other hand, felt uncomfortable talking about such intimate things with a woman whom, until now, I had spoken to mostly about breakfast pastries.

"And this was okay with you?" I asked.

"It was," she said, "until a few months ago. I decided that perhaps it was time to move on and find a love of my own. I had begun to feel lonely." Her eyes flitted over to Holman when she said that. And although he pretended not to notice, his cheeks burned pink.

"And what—you told Dale?"

"Yes. He got angry and tried to persuade me to stay with him, but eventually he accepted my choice."

"What changed his mind?"

She held my gaze for a few seconds, perhaps trying to decide if she was going to answer me honestly. "Let's just say that Dale did not want to upset me."

"Why not?" She didn't respond. "Listen, I can't help you if I don't know the truth."

A look passed between Holman and Rosalee, then he gave her an encouraging nod.

She said, "Dale uses the Tavern to launder money."

And there it was. "Let me guess," I said as the pieces fell into place. "He used a fake French butter supplier to funnel the money?"

"How did you know?" Rosalee seemed honestly surprised.

Holman too. "Riley, I'm very impressed—"

"Don't even." I gave him a death glare. I was still annoyed that he'd left me in the dark about Rosalee. "Never mind how I found out." I didn't want to drag Ridley into this mess if I could help it. Besides, I had more pressing questions. "Why is he laundering money in the first place, and what does all of this have to do with the murders?"

"That's what we're trying to figure out," Holman said. "And I want to be clear that we do not have any concrete answers yet. But our working theory is that Greer must have found out about Dale and Rosalee—and possibly even about the money laundering. So she hires local thug Justin Balzichek to vandalize the Tavern."

"But why? What was the goal there?"

"Greer had a terrible temper," Rosalee said, "but she wasn't stupid. She would know that if the Tavern was damaged or destroyed, the authorities would be all over it during the insurance investigation. They would no doubt uncover the financial discrepancies. It was only because your Jay was inside that the investigation took another turn."

My mind flashed back to the day that that hammer came hurtling through the large plate glass window, narrowly missing me. The panic. The confusion. Jay sprung into action and called in the authorities, who swarmed the place, certain that the attack had been intended for the DEA agent, of course. After all, there was no shortage of criminals who wanted Jaidev Burman dead.

"I think she intended it as retribution on me and Dale."

"Women have been known to act irrationally upon finding out their partner has been unfaithful. Fun fact," Holman said as he lifted one bony finger into the air, "the popular expression 'Hell hath no fury like a woman scorned' is from the play, a tragedy naturally, called *The Mourning Bride* written by the late William Congreve that premiered in 1697—"

Both Rosalee and I stared at him. He blinked. "What?"

"The murders?" I said, trying to steer him back on track.

"Oh, right." He paused for a fraction of a second, and I

could tell he wanted to finish his *Mourning Bride* story, but fortunately he let it go. "Well, if Greer had indeed discovered Dale was being both financially and sexually unfaithful, it could be that he had Greer and Balzichek killed to protect himself."

"How much money are we talking about here?"

"Over the years? Millions," Rosalee answered.

"Millions?" I gaped. "Was he selling heroin or something?" Whenever I heard about someone laundering that kind of money, my mind immediately went to drugs. I blame Jay for that. And Netflix.

"No." She shook her head. "Nothing like that. He did some work for a client who preferred to pay him in cash. He chose not to report that income." She said this as if not paying taxes was a legitimate option and not a federal crime. "I am the only one left who could expose him. I think he had Greer killed to silence her, and now he's trying to set me up to take the blame."

If any of this were true, it would make sense that Rosalee was in hiding. Dale Mountbatten was a powerful man with deep pockets. If he had already killed twice to protect his secrets, there's no telling what he might be willing to do. And desperate, violent men are never to be taken lightly.

I picked up Rosalee's train of thought. "So if Dale did set this whole thing up, that would do two things for him: One, in addition to neutralizing the threat from his wife, it would get you effectively out of the picture. I mean—you could potentially be given the death penalty for double homicide." Rosalee winced at the words. "Sorry, but it's true. It would also completely discredit any accusations you made against him, because it would look like you were just trying to save yourself."

"Exactly," Rosalee said. "Now you understand."

For a brief moment I did, but then I remembered that two days before Greer was killed, Rosalee had sauntered into Sanford Farm & Home and bought a sledgehammer. I debated whether or not to tell her I had this piece of information, but ultimately my eagerness to hear her explanation superseded my self-control. "Sheriff Haight says he has records proving you bought a sledgehammer just prior to Greer's death."

Holman turned his head sharply to look at Rosalee. Clearly, she hadn't mentioned this to him.

"Yes, so? I have been planning to do some work at the Tavern for months, years, actually. Ask Melvin. He will tell you. There is an old root cellar that's full of half-walls and strange angles. I want to knock out the walls in order to gain more storage."

"You were going to knock out the walls yourself?" I asked, giving her my best *yeah right* look.

"I was!" Rosalee seemed offended for the first time in the conversation. Apparently the insinuation she was weak was more offensive to her than the insinuation she was a murderer. "It was going to cost me over three thousand dollars to hire someone. I am not going to pay those prices when I am perfectly capable of doing the work myself!"

"All right, all right," I said, holding my hands up. I decided to leave it alone for now. "But you have to admit, that looks bad."

"I don't care what it looks like. The truth is the truth." She squared her shoulders and raised her chin. If she was lying, she was damn good at it. "Listen, Riley. I'm scared for my life. Do you know what that feels like? Every minute, I'm terrified Dale Mountbatten is going to find me and do to me what he did to his wife and Balzichek." Her big green-gray eyes seemed to get even bigger and greener and grayer with every word. She was mesmerizing. "The only place I feel safe is here with Will," she said and looked at Holman, who looked back at her like she was a combination of Princess Leia, Jessica Jones, and Daenerys Targaryen.

I asked the obvious question: "Why not go to the police? I know you're scared, but you're also holding all the cards in a way. You could tell Sheriff Haight everything you know, and the authorities would crawl all over Dale Mountbatten."

Rosalee looked down at her half-eaten croissant and picked a toasted almond off its top.

"Or are you afraid that you'd be implicated in the money laundering? You could explain that you were just a pawn," I said. "The authorities would have to realize you had no control over that—"

Rosalee looked down and to the left, refusing to meet my eyes. Then the realization hit me. "You're not living here legally, are you, Rosalee?"

When she raised her eyes to mine, they were not filled with the sort of misty-eyed emotion I might have expected, and they were certainly not filled with fear. Her face was hard, unyielding, and defiant when she said, "No. I am not."

"What the hell are you thinking?" I whisper-shouted at Holman as he walked me out of his apartment.

"Right now?" He blinked. "I was actually thinking how curious it was that a woman your size ate twice as many croissants as the rest of—"

"*Holman!*" I cut him off. "I mean, why would you agree to hide her? You could get in a lot of trouble for this!"

"I didn't plan it. I was doing some research at Sterns for my book the other night, late, and I saw her hiding behind one of the mausoleums. She said she needed help. What was I supposed to do?" A deep pink hue spread across Holman's cheeks.

"*Ohmygod*," I said. "You like her!"

"No, I...I—" The rapid-fire blinking was back in action.

"Please." I rolled my eyes. "And promise me you'll never play poker for money. You are possibly the worst liar I've ever met."

He furrowed his brow. "I don't enjoy games of chance, Riley. I would think you'd know that."

I ignored him and lowered my voice another notch. "What if she's guilty? The evidence doesn't look good..."

"I don't think Rosalee is guilty."

"What we need to do is go straight to the police."

"Then she will get deported—if Dale doesn't get to her first."

"Maybe not. Carl can help her."

"We only need a little more time," Holman said, almost pleading. "We just need proof that Dale Mountbatten was behind Greer's death."

We were standing outside Holman's apartment, and I was aware Rosalee was probably listening to every word through the open window. "Let's talk tomorrow," I whispered. "At the office."

"Would you like some tea, Will?" Rosalee's question drifted outside like a siren song.

The two pink splotches darkened on Holman's cheeks as he tried, unsuccessfully, to hide his smile. "I'll see you tomorrow."

For a guy who didn't like games of chance, Holman was certainly taking a big one on Rosalee. And I didn't like his odds one bit.

Self-Care Assignment #2:
A Better You Through Guided Meditation

Find a comfortable spot on the floor, grass, or other foundational surface. Configure your legs into a W position with your knees touching the floor in front of you and your feet extending behind you diagonally. Do not be alarmed if you feel a tight pulling sensation under your kneecaps or a numbing, pins-and-needles sensation in your lower extremities. This is just trapped negative energy trying to work its way out.

Imagine that you are in a field of green grass high on a mountaintop. Blue sky surrounds you, white fluffy clouds dot the horizon. The air is clear and crisp. In the distance, you see a child walking toward you. You look into her eyes and recognize them as your own. You realize this child is your younger self. She looks sad. When you are near enough to reach her, grab her by her narrow shoulders and hurl her off the side of the mountain. Listen to her screams as she falls deeper, deeper, deeper, down toward the earth below. Be aware of the dull thud her body makes as it hits the ground. #wileecoyote

We are what we think and become what we thought. Feel all of your negative beliefs, fears, and emotional trauma evaporate as your inner child gasps for air in the valley below. She was holding onto these damaging beliefs because she didn't know any better. By snuffing out her infantile ignorance, you are now free to heal and move forward without the drain of these memories and experiences. #byebyelittledemon

Spend at least fifteen minutes journaling about how

this guided meditation made you feel, noting how luminous and unencumbered your conscious mind now feels. Go forth into the world a blank slate, determined not to allow the many psychic vampires you encounter access to your newly tranquilated state of being.

Essential Products for
Optimal Guided Meditation Practice,
all available at Click.com/F.L.Y.™Store

Adaptogenic Charcoal Imagination Dust, $16.99

Alchemized specifically to untether your most creative and innovative thinking. Sprinkle a microspoonful* into a glass of distilled water and drink before meditation.

*Microspoon available for an additional $4.99 on Click.com/F.L.Y™Store

Clear Your Mind Headband, $329.99

Using proprietary biofeedback technology, the Clear Your Mind Headband trains your brain for optimal mindfulness using sound cues of your brain's electrical impulses in real time.

Psychic Vampire Repellent, $34.99

Aromatic protective mist designed to drive a stake through the heart of those thoughts that drain the lifeblood out of you. Spritz your physical surroundings before meditation and say goodbye to emotional anemia!

*

Dear Miss Ellison,

Thank you for your email. To answer your question, a psychic vampire is a person who *drains* others emotionally. They can do this literally by draining your auric life force or metaphorically by continually taking without giving anything back to their victims. Psychic vampires are not to be confused with actual blood-sucking vampires who appear in folklore and the *Twilight* series. #noneedforgarlic #teamedward

Additionally, I have checked with my supervisor and he says "tranquilated" is indeed a word, despite it not appearing in Merriam-Webster's. (Click.com is considering trademarking it.)

Yours in Loving Alignment,

Regina H,
Personal Romance Concierge™ and F.L.Y.
Guy™-in-training
Click.com

Chapter 16

WEDNESDAY

I woke up the next morning exhausted. Probably because I hadn't been able to sleep for more than a couple of hours and the sleep I did get was punctuated with dark dreams about corpses, bloody sledgehammers, almond croissants, and the wild ponies of Chincoteague. It did not make for a restful night. I checked my phone before even getting out of bed. No call from Flick. *Damn.*

Over my morning coffee, I tried to sift through all the information that had come in over the past twenty-four hours on the Mountbatten case. Rosalee and Dale Mountbatten's longtime affair. Rosalee's accusation that Dale was laundering money through the restaurant. Greer's murder. Balzichek's murder. The attack on the café. Rosalee's illegal status. Obviously, it was all connected, but I was having trouble figuring out how.

If I believed Rosalee's story, like Holman seemed to, Dale Mountbatten hired a hit man to kill his wife, tried to pin it on his lover, then had the hit man killed to close the loop. But why? Money was the obvious answer...but the money was already his. Why would he go to such drastic measures? Rosalee said it was revenge for her wanting to move on from him, and I suppose that was possible, but something about that didn't ring true.

I was mulling over these thoughts on my walk into work when I almost ran smack-dab into Dr. Hershel Harbinger, my former boss at the Tuttle Corner Library.

"You certainly look lost in thought, my dear," he said with the ever-present twinkle in his eyes. "Mentally writing the next front-page scoop for the *Times*, I trust?"

I smiled, my automatic response to seeing Dr. H. "Something like that," I said. "What are you up to?"

A sad look crossed his face. "I'm afraid I'm heading over to see my dear friend Franklin—you heard he had a stroke, right?"

I nodded.

"I thought I'd bring Patricia a breakfast pastry from Rosalee's. Poor dear hasn't eaten much lately. I remember those long days at Louisa's bedside. It's easy to forget to take care of yourself during a time like this." Dr. H had lost his wife years ago to a long battle with cancer. I rarely had a conversation with him in which he didn't mention her name.

"I've been working with Ash, their grandson, over at the funeral home."

He nodded. "I know Patricia is so glad to have him here to help out with everything. He seems like a nice young man."

I wasn't exactly sure I agreed with that assessment, but it was hardly the time, place, or audience with whom to get into that, so I decided to go with a diplomatic, "He's been very upset about his grandpa."

"That boy certainly has been through a lot." Dr. H sighed. "What with his mother passing so suddenly last year..."

"Oh, I didn't realize." Eudora Winterthorne hadn't mentioned anything about Ash's mother dying.

"Yes, Franklin and Patricia have been so upset over the whole affair. Suzanne, Ash's mother, died in a car accident last year just before Christmas."

"I had no idea," I said.

"Ash was driving at the time."

My hand flew up to my throat.

Dr. H nodded. "A semi coming the opposite direction on the highway was going too fast and lost control. It was raining, Ash swerved to avoid a head-on collision and..." he trailed off. "Suzanne didn't survive. It wasn't his fault, of course, but Franklin said the boy has been consumed with guilt and grief ever since."

Poor Ash. I couldn't imagine living with that kind of guilt. It put some of his strange behavior into perspective. I knew shame could get inside a person's heart and lead them to some dark places.

"That's awful," I said. "I had a conversation with Mrs. Winterthorne about him and she didn't mention anything." I knew I didn't need to say it; Dr. H would get the implied question about why Eudora Winterthorne wouldn't know about something like this.

"Franklin and Patricia probably didn't mention it to her. I'm sure they were just trying to protect the boy." He lowered his voice and looked around. "Eudora can be a bit of a gossip, you know."

I nodded, the irony of the situation completely lost on him. "Thanks for letting me know."

I heard a car pull up behind me and I saw Dr. H hold a hand up to the driver. "That'll be my ride! Take care, my dear," he said and gave me a cheery wave goodbye.

I turned to watch him go.

"Mom?" I should not have been surprised, yet I was. There was my mom sitting in her car, Uber beacon proudly displayed on the windshield.

"Riley? Is that you?" she called out through the passenger-side window as Dr. H climbed into the back of her Camry.

"Yeah, Mom, of course it's me," I said. "You can see me, right?"

"Can't talk with the meter running! I'll call you later!"

I started to say that isn't how Uber worked, but stopped myself. There were some things you just couldn't explain to a person over the age of fifty.

CHAPTER 17

When I got to the office, I debated whether or not to tell Kay Jackson any of the revelations I'd become privy to over the past twenty-four hours. Ultimately, I decided to keep them to myself a while longer. I wanted to dig deeper into Dale Mountbatten's life to see if I could trace the thread of money laundering to its source. Plus, Holman had agreed to come in this morning to talk to me, and I wanted to run all of this past him again. He and I needed to map out a strategy for moving forward on this story.

I did a quick perusal of the other outlets' websites, starting with the *Daily Reporter*, to make sure none had written yet about Dale's dirty financial deeds. Not a word. So far. But with all the media attention on this story, I knew it was only a matter of time.

I called the number Ridley had given me for Colonel Mustard Enterprises and got no response. No voicemail either. It hadn't been disconnected, but clearly no one was answering. While I let the phone ring and ring, I Googled the company and it was just as Ridley had said, a dummy webpage with vague language about who they were and what they did. No clickable links. Whoever and whatever this company was, they were going out of their way to be under the radar, which was the opposite aim of most small businesses.

Hitting a dead end there, I decided to read up on Dale Mountbatten. I learned little beyond what I already knew. Born and raised in Washington, DC, Dale Mountbatten came from a long line of lawyers. Both his parents worked in the Bush forty-one White House and later opened their own firm specializing in public policy law. Dale distinguished himself academically, and as an undergraduate at Princeton majored in finance. After that, he went to work for a hedge fund on Wall Street for a few years before deciding to go back to school, this time for a law degree.

He graduated at the top of his class from NYU School of Law, and it was during this time that he met Greer Lawrence, also a law student at NYU. They started dating in their second year, and were married within a month of graduation. The couple then moved back to the Washington, DC, area, where Dale opened MB Ideals, and Greer gave birth to their first child.

Being fairly well connected and having the kind of natural confidence that bordered on arrogance, Mountbatten quickly gained several blue-chip clients. His firm represented the interests of more than a few Fortune 500 companies and he was listed as a political consultant on the rolls of many more. The Mountbattens had homes in DC, Miami, and Park City, UT. They were invited to parties at the homes of senators and socialites, and his number was on speed dial by lots of companies looking to carry sway with important legislators. Simply put, Dale Mountbatten was a political baller. If he was laundering money through a café he bought for his mistress, he could face jail time if caught. It didn't take a huge stretch of the imagination to see a person in that position feeling desperate enough to kill. Another tick in the motive box for old Dale.

I saw Holman enter the newsroom, and I was up and out of my cubicle before he'd even passed reception. "We need to talk."

"Oh look," stupid Spencer called out from his desk, "the award-winning journalist has decided to grace us with his presence."

It was no secret that Spencer was jealous of Holman's status at the *Times*. Spencer had been an up-and-comer when Holman moved to town and started working for the paper as a grunt. But Holman's hard work, dedication, and laser-like focus quickly became evident, and before long he was being assigned the most high-profile stories.

"Aw that's sweet, Spencer," I said. "You missed him."

"Hello, Gerlach," Holman said, and it was impossible to tell from his tone whether he had caught the sarcasm, or if he thought that Spencer had actually missed him.

"What's been keeping you so busy these days?"

Before Holman's blink reflex got tripped, I jumped in to save him from lying. "Wouldn't you like to know?"

Holman looked at me, confused. "I think that's why he asked, Riley."

Spencer continued to ignore me. "On some big story, are you?"

"You'll just have to wait to read about it like everyone else." I steered Holman by his elbow down the hall toward his office. Once we were inside, I closed the door and leaned against it.

"You seem nervous," Holman said, taking off his cross-body bag and laying it on the desk. "Is something the matter?"

I stared at him slack-jawed.

"What?"

"How could you ask me that?"

Holman blinked. "I don't understand."

"I mean, how could you ask me if anything is the matter?"

He raised a single eyebrow. "Are you asking me literally how I formulated the question or..."

I sank into the chair opposite his desk and let out a deep sigh. "If I seem nervous, Holman, it's because you are currently aiding and abetting a person of interest in an ongoing criminal investigation who may or may not have played a role in the murders of two people and who may or may not have some very dangerous people looking for her!"

Holman then also took a seat. He bobbled gently up and down for a moment before saying, "You're worried about me."

"Yes. Among other things, I am worried about you."

"I appreciate your concern," Holman said with uncharacteristic tenderness. "Actually, it's been a long time since anyone has worried about me and I...well, it feels nice to be worthy of your distress."

The majority of the time, my conversations with Will Holman left me frustrated or confused—or both—but every now and then he'd say something so sweet and sincere, it would nearly overwhelm me. This was one of those times. I put a hand to my chest. "Of course I'm worr—"

"—then again you do tend to be high-strung, don't you? Sometimes you remind me of...of..." he started snapping his fingers in rapid succession. "Oh, what's that little guy's name? You know, he's small and pink and friends with Winnie the Pooh..."

I narrowed my eyes at him. "Piglet?" I was not happy with the direction this conversation was taking.

"Yes. That's it—Piglet! Sometimes you remind me of Piglet."

"Are you seriously comparing me to a nervous baby pig?"

"I don't think Piglet is technically a baby, though I understand your confusion due to his name and small stature. However, if you listen to the sophistication of his sentence structu—"

"*Holman!*"

"What?"

"What are we going to do about Rosalee? She has to turn herself in!"

"I agree."

"Wait—what?"

"I agree with you. We talked it through last night. Actually, she suggested we should go to Carl today and tell him everything."

I'll admit I was surprised, and pleasantly so. "Isn't she concerned about being sent back to France?"

"I know an immigration lawyer up in DC. I told her I'd see if he can help figure out a way she could stay." There was something a little too hopeful in his voice.

"Okay, good," I said. "So, what's the plan?"

Holman fished a file out of his bag and handed it to me. "Here is what we have on Dale so far. It isn't much, but I could use your help. If we can prove his financial crimes, we'll have something concrete to tell the authorities. Plus, a story like that will be picked up by the AP and appear in every newspaper on the East Coast."

"Do you think the police are already investigating him?"

"My impression is that his alibi checked out, and without any motive, right now they're more focused on Rosalee."

"Speaking of," I said, "I take it she doesn't have an alibi for the night Greer was murdered? Or Balzichek?"

Holman shook his head. “She was home alone, both times.”

“Okay,” I said, irked at his blanket-defense of Rosalee. “I’ll get to work on this as soon as I can. I have a few other things I need to get done first.”

He looked at his watch. “I am supposed to go home and get Rosalee at four o’clock and take her to the sheriff’s office.”

“Meet you there?”

He nodded and I left.

CHAPTER 18

Working as a reporter at a small-town newspaper meant that there was never a shortage of things to do. We all pitched in to make sure any and all stories were covered, plus there was the ongoing challenge of updating the online edition. Even when you had a big story to work on, it wasn't like you could just push all of your other stories aside. So I spent the next couple of hours checking in on the other stories that were, admittedly, not as sexy as a double murder, but probably more relevant to the bulk of our readership. I needed to follow up with the den mother of local Cub Scout Pack 787 about their upcoming food drive, check in on the lineup for the Thanksgiving Day parade, and I wanted a quote from Mayor Lancett on the most recent stunt from local legend "Batty Betty" Grimes, who had decided last Monday to paint herself purple and sit at the intersection of Main and Park holding a sign that read "Shaylene Lancett Colluded with Russia to Get Elected."

It wasn't until I heard Henderson and Spencer talk about wanting to go to Rosalee's for lunch because "that hot chick's running it now" that I remembered I'd promised to look in on Ridley.

Holman had already eaten his peanut butter and jelly sandwich at his desk, so I walked over to Rosalee's alone a little later than I'd planned, around two-thirty. About half the tables were still full, and by the looks of things, they'd been busy.

"How's it going?" I asked Ryan, who was functioning as host for the moment.

"It's been crazy," he said, leading me to a small table by the window. "I'm surprised how many people knew we were opening back up today."

"You know you can't keep a secret in this town," I said. "How's Ridley doing?"

"Cool as a cucumber," Ryan said. "She's in the back, but I'll tell her you're here. She asked if you were gonna come by."

On the surface, Ryan looked and sounded fine, but I knew better. I'd spent seven years of my life analyzing his every expression, posture, and tone of voice—and I could tell something was bothering him. I wondered if he still felt hurt from the other night.

"Listen, Ryan," I said. "I'm sorry if you were expecting to talk about something else at the Shack and I cut you off." I didn't want to embarrass him, but I felt I needed to address this weirdness between us. Tuttle Corner was too small and our lives too enmeshed for us not to be able to have a normal conversation.

"Thanks for saying something," he said as he sat down and leaned forward. He looked directly into my eyes the way he used to years ago, and I felt an unwelcome stirring from somewhere within the depths. "I know I screwed everything up for us. I know it was my fault, and I take full responsibility for that. I let you go, and that was one of the worst mistakes I ever made."

The stirring turned to a churning feeling in my gut. I knew where this was going. *Again*. "Ryan, I—"

"No." He cut me off. "I tried the other night and it didn't work out, but there's something I *need* to ask you."

Okay. I guess we were going to do this. I'd have to find a way to explain that we made no sense as a couple anymore. It was true I'd been feeling a little lonely ever since Jay left, and in so many ways it'd be easy to fall back with Ryan, but ultimately it would be a disaster. I'd just have to be strong enough for both of us. I took in a deep breath and steeled myself for his declaration of love.

"How can I keep from losing Ridley the way I lost you?"

I felt like I'd been slapped in the face.

Ryan's eyes were moist with emotion as he lowered his voice. "I think if she'd just give me a chance, she'd see that we could be happy together—you know, as a family."

I stared back at him, my mind blank, and my mouth dry as dust. I was so certain that Ryan was going to tell me he loved *me*, say that he couldn't live without *me*, that he wanted a future with *me*—and even though I didn't want those things, him not wanting them knocked me off balance. And not in a good way.

"Wow," I finally forced myself to say. "I didn't know you had those kind of feelings for her."

"I didn't either, I guess. I mean, we always had heat—jeez, just freaking look at her."

My jaw tightened.

"After our fling in Colorado, I was so focused on getting you back that I just shut her out. And when she told me she was in love with me, I turned her down and told her I belonged with you."

I knew Ryan had delusions of us getting back together a few months ago, but he never told me the extent of it. Ridley and I certainly never talked about our respective relationships with Ryan. Hearing that she was in love with him—at least at one point—added to my growing nausea over this situation.

Ryan continued to talk, words flowing out of him like a faucet that wouldn't shut off. "And then she found out she was pregnant. I brought her back here out of a sense of responsibility and because that's what's best for the baby—but the whole time I was really hoping you and I would find our way back to each other. Obviously, I know that's never gonna happen now."

"Ryan, I never meant—" I broke off. I didn't know how to finish that sentence. *I never meant to hurt you. I never meant for you to give up so easily. I never meant for you to end up with Ridley.* It was a complicated stew of guilt, longing, jealousy, and insecurity. And I hated how it made me feel.

"Then she had Lizzie and it was like, I don't know—magic or something. It's like Ridley became a whole new woman to me, like I was seeing her for the first time."

Even though I was looking down at my hands, I could tell Ryan was smiling by the sound of his voice. I felt a stinging sensation behind my eyes, and I took a deep breath to stop emotion from taking over.

Ryan, bless his self-absorbed heart, didn't even notice. "She's amazing. The way she takes care of the baby and just holds everything together—she's pretty much the most capable woman I've ever met."

"What does she think?" I asked, trying not to feel insulted.

He looked back toward the kitchen to make sure Ridley wasn't on her way out front. "She's still technically dating David Davenport," he said, surprisingly without any rancor. "But between having Lizzie and David's crazy schedule, they hardly see each other. I don't see it working out."

I had unwittingly introduced Ridley to David Davenport,

a resident at Tuttle General Hospital, a few weeks earlier, and the two hit it off. That was approximately ten days before she had the baby, though, so I could see it being hard to cultivate a new relationship after just giving birth to another man's child.

"Does she know how you feel?"

He shook his head. "I don't think so. That's why I wanted to talk to you. I wanted your advice on when and how to tell her I'm serious, that I want us to be a real family."

"Riley!" Ridley's voice rang out from behind the counter and she made her way toward us, her cheeks glowing from the busy day she was having. Or the incandescent light that shone within her perfect soul. Whichever.

"Congratulations," I said as brightly as I could manage. "Looks like your opening day has been a success."

"Thanks." Ridley looked around at the restaurant. "I think it all went really well."

Ryan stood up. "Why don't I take Lizzie home for a nap while you finish things up here?"

I watched them work together to free the baby from the sling. Ryan gently hoisted a sleeping Lizzie into his arms as Ridley tucked a soft lilac blanket around the baby and gently kissed the top of her head. With her eyes cast down, Ridley couldn't have seen the look of utter infatuation on Ryan's face. But I could.

Not really sure where it was coming from, I swallowed the newly formed lump in my throat. "Ridley, do you have a minute? There's something I want to talk to you about."

Ryan's eyes snapped to mine, a look of panic reflecting fear that I was going to campaign for him right there and then. I gave him an almost imperceptible shake of the head as Ridley handed off the diaper bag like they were a tag team in a relay, which I suppose they sort of were.

“Let’s talk in the back,” Ridley said to me once she’d freed herself of the baby gear. “Ryan, I’ll see you at home in an hour or so, ’kay?”

“I’ll be counting the minutes,” he said in a lighthearted tone that belied the fact that he probably would be doing just that.

CHAPTER 19

Back in the kitchen, Melvin was busy prepping and cooking. The kitchen was going to stop serving soon, and from the looks of the cooktop, he was at the tail end of new orders.

"Hey there, Miss Riley. You come in to get one of those croissants you love so much?"

"Am I that predictable?"

"You are indeed." Melvin smiled. "How's your sweet mama doing?"

Melvin and my mother had gone to high school together, and while they weren't close friends, they had a deep fondness for each other.

"She's become an Uber driver."

Melvin laughed. "Sounds about right. That woman is like the Energizer Bunny. Tell her I say hi, okay?"

I assured him that I would and followed Ridley into Rosalee's tiny broom closet of an office at the rear of the kitchen. "What's up?" Ridley asked once we were sitting down.

"I wanted to ask a few more questions about what you told me last night—about the funky butter expenditures."

Ridley gave me what could only be described as a cat-that-ate-the-canary look. She reached into the bottom file drawer of Rosalee's desk and pulled out a thick manila folder that was double wrapped with rubber bands. She handed it to me. "I thought you might."

"What's this?"

"Those are the invoices from Colonel Mustard Enterprises for the past several years. Every bit of paper I could find that had anything to do with them, I put in there."

My mouth hung slightly open.

"What?" she asked. "Not good?"

"No, this is great," I said, trying to push aside my astonishment. "I'm just surprised is all." When did she have time to do this? Not only did she open a restaurant today but she had a newborn baby at home and was moving in three weeks. I came to the only logical conclusion there was: Ridley must be a robot. Or a vampire. Or an alien. Whatever she was, she was definitely superhuman. No wonder Ryan was infatuated with her.

"I just figured you were going to ask, so I came in a little early this morning and pulled it together." Ridley beamed at me the way a child would for her teacher. She looked like she was waiting for a gold star.

"Thanks." I opened the file and thumbed through a few sheets of paper. "Have you noticed anything else odd or out of place in her records?"

"Not really."

"What about the cellar? Have you ever been down there?"

"Cellar?" Ridley said, her brows knitting together. "I didn't even know this place had a cellar."

Well, that was interesting. Rosalee said she'd bought the sledgehammer to do renovations on the cellar. Then I remembered she mentioned Melvin could back up her story. "Do you mind if I ask Melvin something real quick?"

Ridley stood and up and followed me out of the office. I asked Melvin if the Tavern had a basement.

"It does indeed," he said, flipping a chicken breast on the griddle. "It's basically a dungeon, though. There's all kinds of walls and piles of bricks and stuff down there. Rosalee always wanted to make it into a true root cellar for storing food and such, but we never got to it."

"Was she planning to remodel?"

"Rosalee always had some kind of plan," he said with a wink.

"I've never seen a cellar," Ridley said. "Where is it?"

"You're standing on it."

"It's in the floor?"

He nodded. "This building is *old*. As in old-ass old. Kitchens used to be underground before refrigeration, did you know that? This here—where we're standing—used to be the butler's pantry, and the food was brought up a staircase right there under that table. Kind of hard to access, but when this stuff is all moved out of the way, you can open up a door right there in a floor. Rosalee used to have me move the stuff for her sometimes so she could get down there and sketch out the plans for remodeling it into a storage area. It's kinda tight in here, case you haven't noticed."

I bent down and looked under the stainless-steel prep table. Sure enough, there was a rectangular outline of a door cut into the floor. "Have you ever been down there?" I asked Melvin, who had turned his attention back to his grill.

"Me? Nah," he said. "I don't do small, enclosed spaces. Or spiders. Or snakes—which I am sure are having themselves a big ol' party down there. Butter came and checked it out a few days ago and said it was like a scene outta *Indiana Jones* or something, couldn't wait to get back up here." He shuddered. "I told Rosalee I'd go down there once she got it all fixed up. Till then, I'm staying aboveground."

I left the Tavern and got into my car, ignoring the alarming wheezing sound that seemed to happen every time I started it. Poor Oscar. I didn't have the money or time to deal with his problems at the moment. And besides, if something was really wrong—wouldn't some sort of light come on on the dash? Surely Oscar would give me a warning before he conked out completely. That's just the decent thing to do.

Comfortable with my irrational rationale, I drove over to Campbell & Sons to check on Ash before I went back to the newsroom. He was pretty upset last night, and after what Dr. H told me this morning about his mother, I felt a new kind of empathy for him. He really had more than his share lately. I thought he might be able to use a friend.

"Hey there." When he opened the door, Ash looked more like he could use IV fluids, a cheeseburger, and a good long nap. He also looked like someone who'd recently drank his body weight in bourbon.

"Hey," I said, taking in his rumpled jeans and T-shirt that looked like it had recently been picked up off the floor. That, combined with his hair that was mussed up (in a not altogether unpleasant way), led me to ask him, "You feeling okay?"

He smiled and looked down at his feet. "Uh, yeah. Sorry about last night. I was slightly overserved."

"At least it doesn't look like you're too busy today."

"Nah, not too bad," he said, scratching at the stubble on his chin. "What are you doing here?"

"Um," I said, suddenly uncomfortable telling him I came to check on him. It wasn't like we knew each other that well or anything. And I didn't want him to get the wrong impression. "I was just...um, going to see if you'd heard anything else about Balzichek's next of kin?"

"Actually, funny you should ask. I just did."

"You did?" I said, surprised. "You found them?"

"Follow me," he said and led me back to Franklin's office. He sat down in his grandfather's chair and gestured for me to take the one opposite. He picked up a piece of paper and read off of it: "A woman named Sofia Scheiner called. She said Sheriff Haight's office tracked her down in northwest Arkansas. She's the deceased's paternal aunt. Said she doesn't have any money for a funeral but will take the ashes once he's been cremated on the State's tab."

I wrote down this information and got the phone number from him as well. "Did she say anything else?"

"Not really," Ash said. "Just asked if he had left behind any valuable personal effects."

I rolled my eyes. "Wow, how caring."

"She said she hadn't seen him in a few years. Last time was when he borrowed money from her to get his car out of the impound lot. She wanted to know if she could get her three hundred bucks back." Ash let out a soft laugh. "I told her not unless she could sell two dimes, a nickel, three pennies, and a ginormous rosary for three hundred dollars."

"If it's okay with you, I'll give her a call later today," I said. "I'm writing a piece on him for the paper, and she'd be the perfect person to answer some of my questions."

"Sure," he said and smiled. "Happy I could help."

I realized that might be the first genuine smile I'd ever seen out of him. All the others had been sarcastic or gloating or caustic in some way. Being nice suited him—even with the slightly bloodshot eyes and scruffy day-old beard, he looked good. I felt the flush of attraction creeping into my cheeks again.

"Listen," I said, standing up to leave. "I know you're in a

tough spot with your family business and everything, and I just want you to know that if you ever want to talk to someone, I'm a pretty good listener."

"Talk to a reporter?" His nice smile morphed into his more familiar evil grin. "I may look dumb, but I ain't stupid."

I laughed. "Can I ask why you hate reporters so much?"

"Let's just say I've had a bad experience."

"What kind of bad experience?"

"A really bad one."

"What—were you misquoted? Libeled? Did someone refer to you in print as Miss Ashley Campbell?" I joked.

"In short, yes."

"Wow. Must have been some story."

"Oh, it was."

"But you can't judge all reporters by the actions of one. That'd be like saying *all* lawyers are greedy sons of bitches." It was my turn to give him an evil grin.

"Right. And no one would ever say that."

"I'm just saying maybe the person who interviewed you was just a bad reporter. Maybe he or she had a bias on the story or something?"

"There was no maybe about it. She was definitely biased."

"What—did you call her 'honey' one too many times?" I raised an eyebrow.

"Not exactly," Ash said opening the front door to let me out. "I left her at the altar."

CHAPTER 20

Before Ash could explain the whole I-left-a-girl-at-the-altar thing, Flick called. If it had been anyone else, I would have let it go to voicemail, but I really, *really* needed to hear that Flick was okay. I'd been so worried since our last call. After a hasty goodbye to Ash, I scrambled out to the sidewalk. "Where in the world have you been? Are you okay?"

"I'm okay, but I don't have a lot of time to talk." Flick spoke in an urgent whisper. "I'm going to tell you a few things and I don't want you to write any of this down, but you will need to remember them."

"You're scaring me," I said, climbing inside my car where it was quieter.

"I've found out a little more about what Albert was researching when he was killed."

It still gratified me to hear Flick say Granddaddy was murdered and not refer to his death as a suicide. I'd known that was wrong from the very start, and even though no one believed me initially, I never doubted it. It was nice to finally have someone on my side.

Flick continued. "Back many years ago, an entire family was tragically killed in a plane crash outside their home state of—" His phone cut out and I missed what he said.

"Wait—I missed that—what?"

Either he couldn't hear me or he didn't have time to repeat himself because he kept talking. "The youngest daughter was only four years old at the time. Her name was Shannon Miller. Remember, Riley, don't write any of this down, particularly not on your phone, okay?"

"Okay," I said, repeating the name Shannon Miller over and over and over in my mind.

"I came over here to Chincoteague because this is where their plane went down—" there was more crackling on the line. It sounded more like he was in Afghanistan than on Chincoteague Island. I waited for him to come back.

"Riley? You there?"

"I'm here—where are you? I can't hear you very well..."

"I'm sorry, reception's bad in here—"

I was picking up on something in the tenor of Flick's voice, a sort of worry or fear. My protective instinct kicked in. "Maybe you should just come back. We can work on this together from Tuttle?"

Flick let out a wheezy laugh. "Don't worry about me, kid. I've confronted worse than a pack of professional liars. Besides, I'm doing this for Albert. I'm onto 'em now. We're going to get justice for him, Riley. You'll see."

Tears sprang to my eyes and I nodded, even though I knew he couldn't see me.

"Listen," Flick said, lowering his voice to just barely above a whisper. "I've got to go. They're here. I'll call you back later tonight, okay?"

It was not okay, but I guess it would have to be. He hung up and I felt both hope and fear, in equal parts. I reminded myself that Hal Flick had been embedded with troops in the first Gulf War and had covered difficult and dangerous stories all over the globe. Talking to some folks on a small island off the coast of Virginia was well within his capabilities. At least I hoped so.

I went back to the office and called Sofia Scheiner, who confirmed she was coming to Tuttle Corner on Saturday to pick up "what's left of that sorry excuse for a man." I asked her if she'd be willing to sit down for an interview with me when she got into town and she said yes. I quickly logged the update on Balzichek's body being claimed by his next of kin and turned it into Kay Jackson, who said it'd go up later that afternoon.

I was still all keyed up from Flick's phone call and I didn't feel like hanging around the newsroom doing busywork, so I made a last-minute decision triggered, in part, by Flick. He was such an intrepid reporter—even at his age—and watching him go outside his comfort zone to track down a story inspired me. I got back into my car, coaxed poor Oscar to start up, and headed for I-95. It was time I obeyed the first rule of any investigation: Follow the money. In this case, the money was in Washington, DC, specifically with Dale Mountbatten.

Traffic was light until I hit the mixing bowl with its inevitable slowdown, but even then I made the trip to McLean, VA, in just over two hours. Holman and Rosalee would be going in to meet with Carl at that very moment. I had texted Holman earlier to let him know I wouldn't be there. As much as I would have liked to be there for that meeting, I'd already heard Rosalee's side of the story. Now I wanted to hear Dale's. I knew it was a little risky going there unannounced, but with Rosalee planning to turn herself in, I also knew I had a very limited window before the story was made public, and every reporter east of the Mississippi would be on it. Today I had the element of surprise in my favor.

I pulled up to the stately home in Langley Forest, a prestigious neighborhood in the already prestigious suburb of McLean. I'd gotten the Mountbattens' address from Holman's notebook that just happened to be lying open on his desk while he was in the bathroom. I'd called Dale's office posing as an old friend of Greer's, and the receptionist had been more than happy to tell me that Dale was taking some time at home "in light of what just happened," so I thought it was a safe bet he'd be home even though it was a Wednesday afternoon. I pulled in the circle drive with my heart beating at the top of my throat. I wasn't sure that what I was doing was smart or safe; I only knew that if I was going to get the scoop on this story before it broke wide open, I'd have to talk to Dale Mountbatten face-to-face.

I rang the bell and waited. About fifteen seconds went by and I was about to ring again when a woman opened the door. I'd never met Greer in person but had seen enough pictures to know that whoever stood in front of me was a blood relation. She had the same jet-black hair, the same blue irises rimmed in charcoal. She wasn't as pretty as Greer despite the obvious Botox and fillers, her hair wasn't quite as shiny, her physique not as fit—but the resemblance was striking. This had to be her sister.

"Yes?" The woman seemed cold, suspicious.

"Hi." I smiled, hoping to disarm her with my youthful charm. "My name is Riley Ellison and I was wondering if I could speak with Dale Mountbatten?"

She narrowed her eyes at me like a cat. "What is this in regard to?" So much for my youthful charm.

"Butter," I said. "It's in regard to butter."

The woman looked blank, but I felt sure that had the toxins not prevented it, her brow would have crinkled in confusion.

"He'll know what that means," I added with a confidence I didn't feel.

She continued to look at me for a few moments and then said, "Wait here." She closed the door. It was less than a minute before it opened back up.

Dale Mountbatten, who I recognized from his photos in the paper, opened the door. He was tall, tan, and had a thick head of hair. He exuded a relaxed sort of confidence that I could see would be attractive to a young woman in his employ. "Miss Ellison?"

"Riley, please."

"Come on in." Dale stepped back, swinging the door wide open to let me into the foyer. "Let's talk in my office."

The Mountbatten home was stunning, decorated in all whites and grays, with opulent touches in every corner. It did not show evidence of anyone actually living there, however. I thought of the home I grew up in and how different this was. Our house had art projects on the fridge and pictures of family vacations lining the wall up the staircase. The Mountbatten home was devoid of any personal touches that I could see. The art on display was created by professionals, certainly not their children, and every knick-knack seemed perfectly placed by a decorator. The house emanated a sense of aggressive perfection. It was definitely not my cup of tea, but I was nothing if not a good Southern girl. "You have a beautiful home," I said.

"This was Greer's turf," he said in a wistful tone. He was in front of me, so I couldn't see his face to judge whether or not the "wist" was sincere.

"Please, sit down." Dale's office was equally as beautiful, done in the same neutral-color palette. He settled into a black leather chair behind a large metal desk, and I took one of the two smaller upholstered chairs opposite. Neither of us said anything for a few moments.

"I'm sorry about your wife," I said, finally breaking the silence.

"Thank you," he said, closing his eyes briefly. "It's been hell."

In spite of my suspicions and everything Rosalee had told me, I found myself believing him. His grief, at least in that moment, seemed genuine.

"What can I do for you? My sister-in-law tells me you want to talk to me about butter?"

"Yes." I looked across the desk at him, trying to gauge his reaction to the strange topic.

After a beat he smiled and leaned back in his chair, a move that I expect was meant to disarm me, to make me feel like we were two old friends just having a visit. "Okay. What's your question?"

"I was wondering if you've been using a fake butter importer to launder money through Rosalee's Tavern in Tuttle Corner, and if that might have something to do with the death of your wife. And that of Justin Balzichek, of course." It was a risky move, but I'd watched enough press conferences to know that sometimes you ask the questions you know you won't get an answer to just to let the interviewee know that you know. It made people uneasy, threw them off balance, especially if they're hiding something. Sometimes you can get lucky and they'll slip up, say something they didn't intend to.

Dale looked at me, stone-faced, for a good five seconds before he started laughing. "I'll admit," he said, "of all the things I expected you to say, that was not one of them."

I kept a straight face, poised my pen over my notebook, and looked at him expectantly.

"I'm a lobbyist, Riley. Not a butter importer—or a money

launderer, for that matter," he said, amusement lingering in his voice.

"You are the principal investor in Rosalee's Tavern, though, right?"

"Where are you getting your information?"

My source had been Rosalee, of course, but if Dale was really looking for her I didn't want him to have any indication that I might know where she was.

"I can't give you the name of my source. I'm sure you understand."

Dale nodded, keeping his eyes on mine the whole time. It was almost as if I could see the wheels turning in his quick mind, trying to figure out what exactly I knew, how much to tell me, how easily I could be put off the trail. "You're a reporter, Miss Ellison?"

"Riley, and yes."

"Who do you work for?"

"The *Tuttle Times.*"

"Ah," he said. "Tuttle Corner, home of the Johnnycake Festival and the Sterns Copper."

I raised my eyebrows in surprise. The Johnnycake Festival was well known, but not many people besides locals knew about Sterns Copper.

Reading my surprise, he offered, "I'm a bit of a history nerd. I love driving around to all the little towns in this area to learn about how they came to be. In fact, it was something Greer and I used to do all the time when the kids were little. We'd pile them in the car and just take off, stopping in little towns for ice cream or sightseeing..." He got a faraway look in his eyes, but this time I wasn't buying what he was selling. My gut told me he was covering up for letting his knowledge of Tuttle slip out.

"I was born and raised in Tuttle," I said.

His nostalgia was gone as quickly as it had appeared. "You're a friend of Rosalee's?"

"Just a reporter doing my job."

He smiled that false smile again, the one that I was sure had gotten him out of many a tight spot. "I'll tell you what I've told the police. Rosalee and I had a relationship a long time ago when she worked for us as an au pair. My wife, God rest her soul, found out and I ended it. Betraying Greer is one of the biggest regrets of my life, and we worked hard to repair our marriage over the past ten years."

"Did Greer know you moved Rosalee down to Tuttle Corner and bought her a business?"

He stared at me for a fraction of a second too long. "I don't know what you're talking about."

"Rosalee's Tavern. You bought it under the name..." I made a show of checking my notes. "Colonel Mustard Enterprises."

I watched the surprise flare in his eyes. He covered it almost instantly with a breezy chuckle. "Colonel Mustard?"

"I'll admit, it's sort of clever," I said.

"I'm sorry, but I have no—"

"Rosalee is from Dijon, France."

I could have knocked poor Dale Mountbatten over with a feather. His face paled and he was quiet for a long moment. "She was, wasn't she?"

His use of the past tense made me uncomfortable. "Is," I corrected.

"I'm sorry, Riley," he said, standing up abruptly. "I'm suddenly not feeling very well. Must be the stress of the past couple of weeks. I think I need to go lie down."

I was taken aback by his unexpected change in demeanor. "Of course," I said, and stood to leave. "If you can think of anything else, here's my number." I handed him my business card, the one Holman insisted I have printed. It had my name, title, cell number, and work email address.

Dale took the card. "Obituary writer?"

"I work the obit desk as well as the crime desk," I answered, gathering my things. "Small paper. We all pitch in."

Dale led me out the way I'd come in. He shook my hand but said nothing other than "Pleasure to meet you." I found that an odd statement, in light of our conversation. Then again, his whole demeanor had been odd ever since I mentioned Colonel Mustard Enterprises.

I got into my car, confident that I had done what I'd come here to do: let Mountbatten know that if he decided to go after Rosalee, there were people out there who knew her story. I was still new to investigative reporting, but it felt good to be actually doing something, even if it had been a teensy bit dangerous. No one got hurt, I told myself. I didn't break any rules. If I was going to make a good reporter, I'd have to get comfortable following my instincts. And now that I'd done that, I couldn't wait to get the hell out of Dodge.

I got out my phone to call Holman on my drive home, but as I turned the key in the ignition, a funny thing happened: nothing. I turned it over again—two, three, four times, but all it did was rev and wheeze as it tried unsuccessfully to catch. *Damnit Oscar!* What was I supposed to do now? Ring the doorbell and say, "Hi! Me again! I know I just barged into your house and accused you of being a criminal and maybe a murderer, but can I hang out here while I wait for AAA?"

I was about to call my dad, which is what I always did in situations in which I had no clue what else to do, and saw I had missed a text from Holman. It read: R is gone.

I immediately dialed his number. "Hey, what's going

on?" I asked, trying again, unsuccessfully, to start my car.

"Rosalee's gone. I went home to get her to take her over to the sheriff's office like we planned. She wasn't there."

This was not good. "Do you think she's okay? I mean, did she leave on her own? Or do you think..." I didn't finish my sentence, remembering Dale's reference to Rosalee in the past tense.

"There was no sign of forced entry, but there also was no note. I just can't believe she'd leave without telling me."

Holman sounded hurt. I pushed that aside. We were dealing with something way bigger than an unrequited crush. "Do you think she got cold feet about talking to Carl?"

"I don't know. The whole thing was her idea in the first place. If she didn't want to do it, I wasn't going to force her. I don't know why she'd feel like she had to run away," he said. "By the way, where are you?"

I quickly debated whether or not to tell him the truth. He'd be mad at me, for sure, but he probably had a right to know. I braced myself and said, "I'm sitting in Dale Mountbatten's driveway."

"What?" Holman said, his voice as close to panicked as I'd ever heard it. "Why? You need to get out of there right now, Riley!"

"Believe me, I'd like to," I said, and then I told him about my stupid car.

His cold silence told me he was angry, and worse than that, worried. "Holman?" I asked after several seconds had passed.

"I'm thinking." His voice was clipped, serious. I let him think. After a minute, he said, "Stay in your car. If Dale comes out, tell him you've called for help and that it's on the way."

"But I haven't called anyone yet."

"You called me," he said and hung up without another word.

About five minutes later Greer's sister opened the front door and came out to my car. "Can I help you with something?" She asked this not in a can-I-actually-help-you sort of way but in more of a what-are-you-still-doing-here sort of way.

I explained the situation and she sighed loudly. "Come on back inside then."

"Oh no, that's okay—"

"You're not going to sit out here in the driveway like a vagrant," she hissed.

I flinched. "I don't think anyone would think I was a..."

"Don't make me beg, for heaven's sake!" she yelled, and waited for me to get out of my car.

This woman was a study in contradictions. She was insistent on doing the polite thing, but could not have been less polite while doing it. She was clearly annoyed by my presence, but insisted I come inside. Maybe this was a result of her grief? Or maybe she was always this unpleasant. Either way, Carl Haight had been right. There was something very strange about Hadley Lawrence.

I followed her into the massive kitchen. She opened the fridge, poured me a glass of iced tea (which I hadn't asked for), and then pretty much shoved it into my hands. I noticed she moved about the house like it was her own—there was no hesitation about where the glasses were or what might be in the fridge. She seemed very much at home in her sister's house.

"I'm Hadley, by the way. Greer's sister," she said, folding her arms across her chest.

"I'm so sorry for your loss," I said.

She nodded in acknowledgment. "Did you know her?"

"I can't say I had the pleasure."

Between the Botox and the perma-frown, it was hard to tell, but I thought I saw disappointment flicker across her face. "I came in from Charleston to help with things," she said, offering an explanation I hadn't asked for. "There's so much to be done when someone unexpectedly..." she broke off, letting the unspeakable go unspoken.

"That's very kind of you. I'm sure it's a big help."

Hadley shrugged as if being helpful was an unintended side effect. "It makes me feel better to be near them now—the boys, I mean. They're living, breathing pieces of her. All that's left, really. Lewis will be home from Stanford for another week, and Charlie's still a senior in high school. I figure I can be here to do the things their mother used to do for at least a little while."

I thought of the Mountbatten boys and how sad and scary all this must be for them. Not only were they dealing with the pain and shock of losing their mother in such a violent way, but all the media attention as well. I felt a whiff of guilt for being a part of that system, but tried to squash it. I reminded myself it was my job to expose the truth, not manage its consequences.

"How are they doing?" I asked.

She gave me a look that could have cut glass. "How do you think?"

I looked down. I suppose it was a stupid question.

Hadley took a deep breath. "They'll be okay eventually, but it will take time."

I noticed a sense of possessiveness in her voice when she talked about the boys, like they were hers now that her sister was gone. I couldn't decide if it was protective instinct or something less altruistic...perhaps more single-white-femaleish.

I checked the time on my phone. It had been seventeen minutes. I didn't know who was picking me up, but Holman had a lot of connections in the DC area. Hopefully whoever it was would be here soon.

"So you're a reporter?" Her voice went up like this was a question, but the distasteful look on her face told me she already knew the answer.

"I am."

"And you drove all the way up here just to talk to my brother-in-law about butter?"

I stilled. I hadn't told Hadley I'd driven in from anywhere. She'd either been listening in on my conversation with Dale, or she'd done some research on me. She fixed an expectant gaze on me as I tried to think of how to respond.

I was suddenly very aware that I was an unwelcome guest in a house with two people I did not know and did not trust. Thankfully, before the silence stretched out too long, the doorbell rang. I almost passed out from relief. "That'll be my ride!" I set the glass down on the marble island and took off toward the front door. "Thanks for the tea!"

I grabbed the massive door handle, not wanting to spend another second in that house. I didn't know who was picking me up, but I knew whoever it was I'd be better off with them than with Dale Mountbatten and his peculiar sister-in-law.

I swung open the door and almost passed out again—not from relief this time, but from shock. It was Jaidev Burman, DEA special agent and my ex-boyfriend, standing there looking equal parts worried, angry, and jaw-droppingly gorgeous.

CHAPTER 21

The lecture that began with "This is not how I envisioned seeing you again, Riley" lasted almost the entire drive to Jay's apartment. I was quiet for the most part, mostly because I was too stunned to speak. Jay and I hadn't spoken since the day he left Tuttle Corner a few weeks earlier. We'd decided to break up, not because we weren't into each other, but because neither of us wanted to do the long-distance-relationship thing. For starters, we'd been together for only three months, albeit an intense three months, but still. I wasn't likely to move away from Tuttle Corner, and he wasn't likely to move back. But just because we had no future didn't mean we had no chemistry. Seeing Jay again raised all kinds of thoughts and feelings...not all of which were PG-13.

"You had no idea what you were walking into." Jay's voice brought me back to the present. "You could have been killed, or worse."

"Worse?"

"Believe me," Jay said darkly. "There are things that are worse than death."

His work in the DEA had been one of the sticking points during our brief romance. He had seen some really messed-up things, and as a result got pretty freaked out a while back when I'd taken some chances chasing a story.

Granted, he'd been right. I'd angered a killer who ended up attacking me. The spot on my leg where I'd been shot ached with the memory.

"Okay, I get it," I said after a beat. "I just knew that if I waited, I'd lose the element of surprise."

Jay blew out a hard sigh and then in a much softer tone said, "I'm glad you're okay."

"I'm glad you came to get me," I said, a nervous current zipping through my core.

He pulled into a garage connected to a large high-rise building. "Home sweet apartment building."

We got out of the car and I followed him to an elevator, which led to the lobby of his building. It was decorated with low-profile, midcentury modern furniture and large drum lights hanging overhead. The doorman waved hello to Jay as we passed by, and he waved back. We got onto the elevator and Jay pressed twelve. The doors closed and we were alone again.

"By the way, I'm having your car towed to a garage a few blocks from here. I know a guy who works there, and he said he'd take a look at it first thing in the morning."

First thing in the morning? Was I expected to stay the night here? With Jay? "Um," I said, my stomach swooping again.

"It's a studio, but I have a Murphy bed and a pullout couch. You can take the bed and I'll sleep on the couch." If he felt as weird as I did about this arrangement, there was nothing in his voice to indicate it. He sounded as relaxed as ever, like this was a totally normal, non-awkward situation.

The elevator opened and he led me inside his apartment. It was already dark outside, but I could tell that in the daytime this place would have killer natural light. He had a gray flannel sofa, a glass table in the breakfast nook, and along the wall was a large panel behind which I guessed was the pull-down bed. I couldn't help but think that once it was set up and the couch pulled out, the entire apartment would basically be one giant bed. My stomach swooshed again.

"This is a great place," I said, walking over to the large windows at the back of the apartment.

Jay walked up behind me, so close I could smell his cologne. He reached around me to open the sliding door onto the balcony. "It's not a million-dollar view, but at least I have some outdoor space."

We stood on his small balcony overlooking the activity on the street below, the buildings in varying earth tones, and the treetops bare from the impending winter. The streets were filled with cars and people and the sounds of city life. I never pictured myself living in a place like this, but I could see the appeal. As I was looking out at the scene below, I felt Jay's eyes on me. The burning sensation of self-consciousness prickled under my cheeks and I was sure they were candy apple red. I turned to face him. Without warning, Jay pulled me into a hug, a deep, tight, warm, all-consuming hug that felt far better than it should have. He kissed the top of my head just before releasing me. "It's good to see your face again. I've missed you."

If there had been a realtor on that balcony with us, I swear I would have signed a thirty-year lease on the spot. In that moment, there was nowhere else I wanted to be. A flurry of thoughts populated my mind. *Maybe we could make this work? Maybe it had been a mistake to break up? Neither of us had found anyone, perhaps that meant we were supposed to be together. Making the rash decision to come to DC and my car breaking down could all be the universe's complicated way of saying that Jay and I belonged together....*

I lowered my eyes so he couldn't see how much I meant it when I said, "I've missed you too."

And then a sound caught my ear, both of our ears, actually, and we turned toward the front door to the apartment. A key went into the lock, turned, and then a woman walked into the apartment holding two, what looked like heavy, brown grocery sacks. Jay looked at me with an expression I couldn't read for a split second before his face broke into a wide smile as he left me to go help with the bags.

I watched as Jay kissed the woman and took the two bags from her arms. He was briefly out of sight as he set them down in the small kitchen, and in those couple of seconds the woman stared at me. She didn't look surprised—or happy—to see me there.

Jay came back out holding a bottle of wine. "Chloe, this is my friend I was telling you about, Riley Ellison. Riley, meet Chloe Marks."

I stood rooted to the spot on the balcony, a stunned kind of paralysis keeping me from moving. Chloe Marks plastered a smile on her face, clearly for Jay, as she walked confidently toward me, her right hand outstretched. I shook it, still shell-shocked from the turn the moment had taken.

"I've heard so much about you!" Chloe's voice was light, the look in her eyes was anything but. She squeezed my hand. Hard.

Jay had his phone out. "Holman just texted. He's on his way."

"Holman's coming?" I asked, surprised.

"He was worried sick about you."

"Is that your boyfriend?" Chloe asked, taking the bottle from Jay's hand.

"No," I said, "my co-worker."

"You never know," Chloe said in a singsongy tone.

"That could be how it starts...it's been known to happen." She giggled and winked at Jay.

"You'll love Will, C. He is truly one of a kind," Jay said.

"C" opened a drawer to get the corkscrew. Jay took out three glasses from the rolling bar cart and set them on the peninsula, and then Chloe opened the wine. I sat there like an idiot, looking between the two of them, trying to take it all in. The whole thing was like a well-choreographed dance to the tune of domestic bliss. I began to feel a little nauseated.

When we all had glasses in hand, Chloe raised hers toward me and said with a smile that did not reach her eyes, "To old friends...and new."

We were halfway into the second bottle of red when Holman got there. The conversation had been pleasant enough, though I'd had to hear more than I cared to about Chloe Marks. She was from a small town in the Florida Panhandle, came to Washington, DC, on a full ride to Howard University, where she graduated summa cum laude. (Like I cared.) She double majored in finance and marketing and worked as a financial adviser in the 2012 Obama campaign. (Big whoop.) She taught Sunday school at her church, volunteered at the food bank, and twice a month on Wednesday nights drove old people to their doctor's appointments. (Okay, that really was impressive.) I really didn't want to know all of this about her, but I kept asking questions because that was the easiest way not to have to talk about myself, since my biggest accomplishment in the past month had been successfully quitting the gym I'd been trying to leave for nearly two years.

Holman arrived just after nine. Jay had said he'd been "worried sick" about me, but when he got there he barely gave me a glance before attaching himself firmly to Jay's backside. In fact, I suspected that was half the reason he'd decided to make the drive up there. Holman had a bit of a hero-worship thing going with Jay from back when he had saved both our lives. Introductions were made and then true to form, Holman started asking questions about how they met, how long they'd been dating, blah, blah, blah.

Chloe was working as a supervisor in the Human Resources department for the DEA, and the two met when there was a problem processing Jay's paperwork for his new position. He'd gone over on his lunch break to "read someone the riot act," according to Jay, but things had taken a different turn.

"He changed his tune pretty damn quick when he saw *me* sitting behind that supervisor desk," Chloe said, adding that they'd made "an instant connection." (Puke.) They told the story of their meeting and subsequent first date in tandem like an old married couple. I took another long swig of my wine.

"Who's hungry?" Jay said, finally putting an end to the insufferable story. I don't know if it was the wine or wishful thinking—or maybe it was both—but I thought Jay looked uncomfortable. Had he finally realized that telling me the gory details of his new relationship might be a tad inappropriate?

"I am," Chloe said, getting up from the table. "You've got to be starving, Riley. I'll call Mauritizios and have some pizzas delivered."

"It's only two doors down, come with me and we'll pick up. It'll be faster that way," Jay said. "Besides, I think Holman and Riley have some business to talk about, and they could probably use a little privacy."

Chloe, clearly feeling the wine, looked between Holman

and me. "I see. They've got '*business*' to discuss." She gave a stage wink in our direction.

"Wedo," I said, the words running together. It's possible I was feeling the effects of the wine too.

Jay helped Chloe on with her coat and gave me a concerned look before heading out. "You okay?"

"Peachy," I said, which admittedly came out more like, "Peashy."

The door closed and Holman turned to me. "You've had too much alcohol."

"Noshitsherlock."

"We haven't used those code names in ages, Riley. But if you think we need to, I suppose we can start again..."

I flopped down on the sofa, ignoring Holman. I was too depressed and tipsy to care about code names or stories or anything except how cute Jay was and how he'd moved on from me in record time. I let my head fall onto the back edge of the couch. Holman went into Jay's kitchen and returned with a glass of ice water.

"Are you upset that Jay has a new girlfriend?"

I heaved my head up and looked at Holman. I nodded.

"Do you still have romantic feelings for him?"

I shrugged. I didn't think I did, but seeing him this afternoon confused me. Was I mistaking attraction for deeper feelings? Nothing had changed to make a relationship with Jay possible. All the same reasons we broke up still existed. The truth was that I didn't know how I felt.

"Maybe you just didn't want to be replaced so easily?" Holman suggested.

I slumped over onto him and laid the top of my head against Holman's bony shoulder, just south of which was his big, kind heart. He could be so sweet, however he wasn't big on physical displays of affection, a fact made obvious by his ramrod-stiff posture. I could tell I was making him uncomfortable by laying on him, so after a moment I hoisted myself up and wiped at the moist edges of my eyes.

"Sorry." I took a deep breath in. "I'm okay now. It was just kind of a surprise, that's all. I mean, it's only been like a month since we broke up, and they look like they're in pretty deep."

Holman looked at me, his round eyes magnified under his thick glasses, wide and unblinking. He put his hand on top of mine and gave it a gentle squeeze. "I'm sure Jay knows no one could ever replace you."

I was touched. It was exactly what I needed to hear. Sometimes Holman showed so much more compassion than I gave him credit for. "Thank you—"

"—you're like that disgraced Miss America winner who took those raunchy photos."

"Wait—what?"

"You know, the Miss America winner who was dethroned because back in her youth she had taken some nude photos? Apparently, nude photos are against Miss America bylaws. Anyway, after she was stripped of her title, the woman who'd gotten second place was crowned the new Miss America. But even though number two technically had the title, everyone knew she only had it because the first one, number one, had made a poor life choice. Everyone still knew number one was the real winner."

I could feel the crease between my eyes deepening as I stared at him.

Holman blinked, looking confused by my confusion. "Riley, you're like the woman who made the poor life choice. Technically you've been replaced, but everyone still knows you're number one."

I thought about his warped rationale and eventually

decided it was meant to be a compliment. I should take it and run. It was probably the best I was going to get on this train wreck of a day.

I went to the bathroom to splash some cool water on my face. When I got back, I felt better, though I wasn't quite as clearheaded as I would have liked. I looked at the time. We probably had less than ten minutes to talk before Jay and Chloe would be back.

"Have you been able to get ahold of Rosalee?" I asked.

"No. I've been calling and texting her and she hasn't responded. Phone goes straight to voicemail. I'm concerned."

"I'm sure she's okay," I said, not one bit sure, but I felt I had to say something to reassure Holman. "Rosalee is a survivor. I have a feeling she knows how to take care of herself."

"What if Dale found out where she was? Came after her?"

"He was at home all day, at least according to him and his sister-in-law."

"He could have sent his goons after her," Holman offered.

"First of all," I said, "we don't know that Dale has 'goons.' Second of all, Rosalee probably just got nervous about going to talk to Sheriff Haight and bailed. She does have a history of running..."

Holman nodded but didn't look convinced.

"Will," I said as gently as I could, "I think we have to tell Carl."

He raised his bug eyes to meet mine. I could tell he was uncomfortable with my suggestion, but the fact that he hadn't already said no told me he also knew I was right.

I added, "It's for her own good. If she is in trouble, she's going to need help. More help than you or I can give her."

Holman reluctantly agreed that we'd talk to Carl as soon as we got back from DC. Then I filled him in on what Ridley had told me about the shady butter importer and how I'd confronted Dale Mountbatten. Holman was not happy about what I'd done, but he agreed that at least Mountbatten was now on the defensive. If he was guilty—even if only of money laundering—chances are he'd be spooked. Now that we knew what to look out for, we could watch him and possibly catch him trying to cover his tracks.

With that settled, all that was left was where I was going to sleep tonight. I pinched the bridge of my nose to stave off the beginnings of the headache that was starting to take root deep inside my skull.

"You can stay with me," Holman said.

It was a nice offer, but I wasn't sure a night in a hotel with Holman was better than staying here. "Uh, I—"

"Mother won't mind," he added.

Mother? This was the first I was hearing that a.) Holman had a mother, and b.) she lived not even two hours from Tuttle Corner. "Your mom lives in DC?"

He nodded. "For some time. She moved here from Toronto when she and Dad divorced."

In all the time we'd known each other, which I guess upon reflection was only six months, Holman had never talked about his parents. Once he told me his father had been in the Royal Canadian Navy, but that was only in context of a story he was writing.

"Um, okay, sure. I guess," I said.

"I can tell Chloe doesn't like you, so I think you'll be more comfortable at Mom's place."

"Excuse me?" This night just kept getting better and better.

Holman shrugged. "Her body language, the small jabs

she keeps making at you, the way her mouth goes down at the sides each time Jay engages you in conversation. She feels you are a threat, probably because of your past sexual relationship with Jay."

"Are you serio—" I started to say, but then heard voices outside the door. I lowered my voice to a whisper. "To be continued!"

A second later, Jay and Chloe walked in, him holding a pizza and her a brown paper bag. "Who's hungry for pizza and ice cream?" Chloe trilled. "Riley, you look like a girl who appreciates a good bowl of ice cream."

I looked at Holman, my mouth slightly agape, and he just shrugged as if to say *I told you so.*

Chapter 22

Even though I was starving, I ate only one piece of pizza. But because I was still a little tipsy, I somehow managed to get sauce all down the front of my white shirt, which Chloe thought was just hi-frickin-larious. By the time the three of them finished their ice cream (to which I said a very dainty "No thank you"), I was desperate to leave. Holman had been spot-on: Chloe didn't like me, and now that I was tuned into it, the little digs and passive aggressive comments were hard to ignore. Jay appeared to be clueless to the whole thing, which seemed weird. He was a highly trained DEA agent who occasionally went undercover. It was his job to read people. Maybe he was just blinded by love? The thought made me regret my no-ice-cream decision. Had I been home alone, I'd have been knee-deep in that carton of mint chip.

After dinner, Jay fought us on the idea of my going back to Holman's mom's place. "There's plenty of room here," he said. "Like I said, you can have the bed and I'll take the couch."

I felt my cheeks heat up. I must have involuntarily looked over at Chloe because Jay quickly added, "Chloe lives just a few blocks away and I'll be taking her home soon."

Taking her home? Chloe wasn't going to spend the night? I'd just assumed with all the cutesy-cutesy crap, they were serious—or at least serious enough to be sleeping together.

"Um, well—"

Holman jumped in. "My mother has been waiting my entire adult life for me to bring a woman home. Let her have this."

"All right," Jay laughed. "I get it."

"Can't you see they want to be alone," Chloe said, raising her eyebrows up and down. "Besides, Riley looks absolutely exhausted—just look at the bags under her eyes."

"It was so great to meet you!" I said in response and pulled Chloe into a big hug (making sure to squeeze tight enough for the glob of tomato sauce to transfer onto her shirt). And then I turned to Jay. "Thanks for coming to my rescue. Again."

"Anytime," Jay said. "I mean that."

"So..." I wasn't sure where to go with this goodbye. I couldn't really say *See you soon* or *let's do it again.*

"So..." Jay echoed.

"So...*bye*!" Chloe chirped, holding the door open. "Hope you got enough to eat, Riley!"

CHAPTER 23

Five minutes later, Holman and I were in his car en route to his mother's house. I was decidedly more sober than I'd been before, so a flood of thoughts and feelings about the strange afternoon and evening swamped my brain. I forced myself to focus on the moment, however. I was concerned about barging in at nearly 11 p.m. to crash at the home of a woman I'd never met. That was not exactly the best way to make a good impression.

"Does your mom know I'm coming? Will she be asleep?"

"Oh, she won't care a bit."

"Wait—back there you said your mother has been waiting for you to bring a woman home your entire adult life."

"She has."

"Then don't you want to give her a little heads-up?"

"Riley, you're hardly the kind of woman she'd get excited about."

Wow. Well, *that* stung. "Gee, thanks."

He continued, oblivious to my sarcasm. "Mom has been waiting for me to bring home a woman in whom I am romantically interested. Not simply a co-worker."

"Am I simply a co-worker?" I couldn't help but feel a bit hurt. I knew what he meant, but still.

Holman turned down a tree-lined street and slowed down. When he answered me, there was a distinct weariness in his voice. "Are you feeling extra needy because of what happened with Jay tonight?"

"No, I'm not feeling *extra needy,*" I said, clutching my cross-body purse tighter around me. "I just thought that our relationship went beyond 'simply co-workers,' that's all."

"I was afraid this might happen," Holman muttered under his breath. He had pulled in front of an empty spot and was getting ready to parallel park. He placed his hand behind my headrest and turned to face me, which in the confines of a Dodge Neon, was pretty close quarters. He looked directly into my eyes and spoke slowly, deliberately, like you would to a very young child.

"Riley, I think what we have here is a classic case of transference. You're upset about Jay and some of the feelings you have for him are being directed at me. I get it. I'm like the Henry Higgins to your Eliza Doolittle, the Harry Potter to your Hermione Granger, I am the foundation upon w—"

"*Holman!*"

"What? I didn't mean that in a sexual way, if that's what you were thinking..."

I held a hand up to stop him from saying another word. I absolutely could not have this conversation yet again. Holman parked and walked around to the sidewalk, his backpack slung over one shoulder.

"Sometimes you exhaust me," I said as I climbed out of the Neon. "And I don't mean *that* in a sexual way, in case that's what you were thinking!"

"Now, now, kids," a woman's velvety voice wafted down from the steps of the massive row house I just noticed we were standing in front of. "Save the pillow talk for later, okay?"

Will Holman's mother was not what I expected. With all of his eccentricities, I guess I assumed Holman's mom would also be a few degrees south of normal. I assumed wrong. Camilla Holman was elegance personified. Everything from her chic gray stacked bob to her monogrammed cashmere robe to her short, perfectly manicured buff-colored nails dripped with posh sophistication.

"You look good, honey," she said to Will as he kissed her on the cheek. "Thin. You are eating, aren't you?"

"Obviously, Mother. The human body needs food for survival."

"You'd be surprised," Camilla said drily. "I know a senator's wife who exists solely on cigarettes and animosity."

Holman gave his mother a quizzical look.

"Hyperbole, dear."

He nodded. "Mother, this is Riley Ellison, my co-worker at the *Times*. She is also my friend." He then looked at me and added, "Is that a more acceptable definition of our relationship?"

I felt my face turn red. I ignored Holman and stuck out my hand to shake hers. "Hi, Mrs. Holman. Pleasure to meet you. Sorry about the late arrival."

"Camilla. And I don't sleep," she said by way of absolution. "I'm glad you're here." Her steely blue eyes were sharp and alert, and when she looked at me it felt like an appraisal. I found myself instantly wanting her approval.

Camilla led me to the back bedroom on the main floor, which I gathered was one of several in the house that went unused most of the time. Will's room was upstairs. Despite her earlier joke about pillow talk, there was no question that we would be staying in separate rooms. I wasn't sure if this was out of a sense of propriety or because she knew we were not romantically involved, but either way I was relieved not to have to explain it. I was also exhausted. After changing into the freshly pressed pajamas set out on the bed for me and using the brand-new toothbrush left in the bathroom, I climbed under the cloud-like covers feeling like I'd just checked into a fancy hotel. I was asleep in ten seconds flat.

Self-Care Assignment #3:
A Better You Through Prudent Risk-Taking

Nine Strategies to Become a Responsible Risk-Taker:

1. Begin before you're ready
2. Be ridiculously irrational
3. Make your own mistakes rather than let mistakes make you
4. Develop a growth mind-set
5. Eschew consensus
6. Become a Failure Genius
7. Gamble on Yourself
8. Don't Boil the Ocean
9. Adopt and Adapt

Identify an area of your life, personal or professional, where you can employ one or more of the above strategies. Do not be alarmed if you feel afraid, hesitant, or unprepared. That is just your trapped negative energy trying to work its way out.

Spend at least fifteen minutes journaling about how employing that particular strategy made you feel, noting the sensation of emotional bravery on a macro and micromolecular level. (Personal molecular change detector, $289.99).

Yours in Loving Alignment,

Regina H,
Personal Romance Concierge™ and F.L.Y.
Guy™-in-training
Click.com

*

Dear Miss Ellison,

Thank you for your email. I am sorry you are having trouble understanding the list of Nine Strategies to Become a Responsible Risk-Taker. I understand you feel frustrated by the "incoherent jargon" and "meaningless platitudes" you feel the list offers. I can assure you that was not our intention! #youconfuseyoulose #corporatemotto

I have forwarded your concerns to our F.L.Y.™ Content Development Concierge™, Frederick L. He should get back in touch with you as soon as he returns from his *Secrets of the Swiss: Happiness Mountain Retreat* (he's beta-testing this for inclusion in the F.L.Y.™ program for early next year!). #yesplease #icouldbehappyinswitzerland #swissmiss

In the meantime, please do your best to embrace your inner prudent risk-taker. You never know where it could lead. #norisknoreward

Yours in Loving Alignment,

Regina H,
Personal Romance Concierge™ and F.L.Y.
Guy™-in-training
Click.com

*

Dear Miss Ellison,

I'm glad you have been "working ahead without even knowing it," but I feel I must point out there is a difference between self-care through prudent risk-taking and straight-up risky behavior. The idea of the exercise is that you might take a new route to work or perhaps choose a new menu item at a favorite restaurant, not confront a potential homicidal maniac! Putting yourself in mortal danger is the opposite of self-care. #youcantimproveifyouredead

Our legal department has asked me to remind you that the contract you signed includes a hold-harmless clause explicitly stating that Click.com is not responsible for any liabilities, costs, expenses, damages, and/or losses you incur as a part of the **Sugar, How'd You Get So F.L.Y.™** program, including but not limited to loss of property, loss of limb, or death. #readthefineprint

Yours in Loving Alignment,

Regina H,
Personal Romance Concierge™ and F.L.Y. Guy™-in-training
Click.com

Chapter 24

THURSDAY

I woke up several blissful hours later with the sun in my eyes and the smell of coffee in my nose. It was 6:52 a.m. The Holmans were early risers. I put on the soft, luscious robe hanging on the back of the door and wandered down the hall toward the kitchen. Framed pictures of Will from his childhood lined the soft slate-colored walls. From the looks of it, Holman came out of the womb wearing the same thick, round glasses he wore today. As a toddler, he looked like a cartoon character, those big, round eyes of his looking even bigger and rounder on his small face. I stopped to admire one particularly nice black and white of a very young Holman sitting in the grass. Camilla knelt beside him holding a dandelion puff, the camera catching the exact moment Holman blew on the flower like a birthday candle, sending the tiny translucent seeds scattering into the air.

"Nicholas took that," Camilla said, appearing beside me like a well-heeled ninja. "Will's father."

"Oh," I said. I did a quick scan and noticed there were no pictures of a family of three on the wall, no pictures of Holman and his dad at all.

"Will doesn't talk about him very much, does he?" She turned her attention from the photo to me.

"Um," I said, trying to think of a nice way to say that until last night Holman hadn't mentioned either of his parents. "Not really."

"I'm not surprised," she said, looking back to the pictures on the wall. "It was very painful when he left—for both of us. Nicholas wasn't a bad man exactly, he just couldn't accept that Will was never going to be the son he imagined."

"He left because of Will?" I was shocked at the cruelty of that.

Camilla cocked her head to the side, a subtle question in the gesture. "He hasn't told you?"

I shook my head, feeling embarrassed for what I didn't know about my friend.

"Well, it's probably just as well. We ended up doing just fine on our own," Camilla said, straightening up. "He's happy in Tuttle Corner?"

I wasn't sure I had the authority to answer that question. "He seems like he is."

"Good," she said with a firm nod of her head. "He can be tough, but he really does have an extraordinarily big heart."

"Yes, he does," I said. That I knew for sure. "Speaking of, is he awake?"

"In the kitchen." Camilla motioned down the hall and then excused herself to get ready for the day.

I walked into the kitchen and found Holman reading the newspaper and eating a doughnut. He was fully dressed in new clothes (he must keep some here), and I suddenly felt silly in the borrowed robe and pj's. "Morning," I said when he didn't look up.

He glanced over the top of the page he was reading. "Good morning." He went back to reading. Okay, then. Not chatty in the morning. I added it to the growing list of things I hadn't known before about Will Holman.

The white marble-top tulip table contained three placemats, each set with a small plate, silverware, a coffee cup, and a juice glass. One of the plates had a folded section of newspaper on it, so I took the other remaining seat, the empty one.

Holman handed the folded newspaper section over to me. "For you." It was the obituary section of *The New York Times*. "Coffee." He pointed to a white ceramic carafe sitting on the table, then slid his long, pointed finger over to the glass container. "Juice. Mother doesn't keep croissants in the house, but there are some berries in the fridge." He went back to reading the paper.

The whole scene was laughably civilized and not a bad way to start the day. I quietly poured myself a cup of coffee, added copious amounts of sugar and cream, and then read through the obits. It was a treat to have a tangible paper, as I usually read online. I savored the way the black ink set against the thin white-gray paper made the words seem weightier, more legitimate somehow. That day's tributes were for a famous drummer of a 1970s rock band I'd never heard of but felt sure my parents had; the first female head of a political party in Tunisia who'd fought for democracy during the Arab Spring; the original head chef at one of New York's most famous restaurants; and a woman who invented a small but essential component of a C-47 transport plane engine used during World War II.

After I finished reading, I checked the time. It was already past seven-thirty. "I should check on my car."

Holman agreed. We decided if they could fix it in a couple of hours, we could wait. If it would take longer, we'd head back to Tuttle and I'd come back to get it another time. I dialed the garage and asked for Ivan, like Jay had told me to.

"You need a new timing chain. I can do, but it will take three, maybe four, five days."

"Five days?"

"Is not difficult," he said with a heavy Eastern European accent. "But I just get orders for work on government fleet. Ivan is only one Ivan."

"All right." I sighed and then asked the question I was dreading getting the answer to. "How much?"

"Not too bad." He paused, and I let my shoulders relax, relieved to finally get some good news where this car was concerned.

Then he continued. "Five, maybe six, seven hundred bucks."

"Are you kidding me?" Old Ivan must be doing pretty well if he thought seven hundred dollars was "not too bad." That would make a sizable dent in my already paltry savings account. A feeling akin to grief took root. Having already been through the denial and anger stages, I moved onto bargaining. "Is it drivable? I mean, could I drive it back to Tuttle and maybe get it fixed closer to home?"

Ivan laughed like I'd said something hilarious. "Car doesn't go without timing chain. You want I have it towed to Tattle Corner?"

The cost to tow my car 150 miles back home was sure to exceed any savings I'd get by having it fixed there. "No, that's okay," I said, firmly in the depression stage but moving toward acceptance. Retirement is overrated anyway. "I'll leave it with you."

"Ivan is good. Ivan fix you up."

"Thanks, Ivan," I said.

"You're welcome, friend of Jay."

I hated to leave my car behind, but I didn't really have a choice. As pleasant as it was, I couldn't stay at Hotel

Camilla forever, and I sure as hell couldn't call Jay again. I needed to get back to Tuttle. For one thing, I had a dog to take care of. Thankfully, my mom had agreed to take Coltrane last night during my unexpected stay. For another thing, I had a story to follow.

When I got back to my room, there was a handwritten note on delicate stationery embossed with a CH at the top. "I took the liberty of throwing your clothes in the wash. There's a fresh outfit for you in the closet. xx, C."

Camilla came in here to get my laundry? That felt both intrusive and comforting at the same time. I said a silent *phew* that I'd made the bed before I went to eat breakfast. I opened the closet, which was empty except for two hangers. One held a tailored tweed dress in a soft pink with thin metallic gold threads woven throughout, and on the other was its matching jacket. I stood and stared at the garments for a good solid minute trying to figure out what I should do. Could I really wear Camilla's suit? Not only did it feel weird to borrow clothes from a woman I just met, but I could tell by looking at them that they were majorly high-end garments. Definitely not my usual thrift store style. I'd look like I was playing dress-up. But what choice did I have? I couldn't very well stay in pajamas all day. So I did the only thing I could do: I took a shower and put on an outfit that far exceeded the current value of my car. And probably of my bank account as well.

CHAPTER 25

"I had a feeling it would look nice on you," Camilla said when I walked into the front entryway wearing her magical suit.

"It's incredible." I snuck another glance in the large mirror in the foyer. I felt like a princess—no, an heiress—no, a girl boss! Whatever it was, I felt powerful. I never realized that clothes could have such a significant effect on how one felt on the inside. Then again, I'd never worn anything like this before. The material was thick and luxurious, and the cut somehow highlighted every curve and glossed over every flaw. It was as close to a supersuit as I was ever going to get. "Are you sure you don't mind me wearing it?"

"Looks better on you than it ever did on me," Camilla said with a warm smile.

"I'll bring it back when I come to pick up my car," I said, reassuring her.

Camilla waved a hand as if she wasn't concerned. Holman stood silently holding his backpack.

I turned toward him and did a little twirl. "So, what do you think?"

"About what?"

"About the clothes, dear," Camilla said. "I gave Riley something to wear because her clothes were dirty."

Holman looked at me as if he was noticing for the first

time that I was wearing a suit, or anything at all. “It looks like something you’d wear, Mother.”

She took a step closer and put a hand on his elbow. “Yes, well, that’s because it is. But doesn’t Riley look pretty in it?” I noticed she spoke in the gentle, leading way mothers have when talking to small children. *You remember cousin Richard, don’t you? Tell Grandma how much you love the scarf she knit you. Isn’t Aunt Janice’s fruitcake delicious?*

Holman looked at me again, moving his big eyes over the length of me, then gave a disinterested shrug. “Riley always looks pretty.”

It was both a compliment and an insult, the variety of comment Holman so often doled out. After he said it, I caught Camilla’s face in the mirror. She was trying to suppress it, but I could see a faint smile tugging up the corner of her lip.

We were not even out of Georgetown when my phone rang. The phone number came up as *Blocked* and I thought it might be Ivan calling me with an update on the car. I assumed wrong.

“Riley Ellison?” a woman’s voice came across the line.

“Yes,” I answered, a little hesitant.

“I have some information about a story you’re reporting on.”

“Okay,” I said, reaching into my bag for my notebook. I put the phone on speaker so Holman could hear the call too. “To whom am I speaking?” I couldn’t be sure, but it sounded a little like Hadley Lawrence if she’d thrown a tea towel over the speaker of her phone.

“That’s not important,” the woman said. “What’s important is Dale Mountbatten’s crooked financial dealings.”

“Okay...” I said again, now pretty sure it was Hadley. I’d

listen to what she had to say and maybe I could persuade her to eventually go on the record.

"Colonel Mustard Enterprises," the woman said. "It's a shell company."

Of course I already knew about that, but I wanted to know what she knew—and how she knew it. "A shell company?" I asked.

"A company that exists only on paper." She sounded annoyed.

"Yes, I know what a shell company is," I said, slightly annoyed myself. "I was wondering what sort of shell company it is, and what connection it has to Dale Mountbatten?"

"Then you should have said that."

I saw Holman smirk out of the corner of my eye. He had chastised me for being "imprecise" with my language on a number of occasions.

"I apologize," I said, mounting a herculean effort to keep the sarcasm out of my voice. "Please go on."

"Colonel Mustard Enterprises is, on paper anyway, a distributor of French butter. But in reality, Dale and his business partner," she said these last words with heavy sarcasm, "have been using it to launder money."

This could be independent corroboration for Rosalee's story, I thought. Although this woman—most likely Greer's sister—was clearly indicating Rosalee was a willing participant in the financial crimes, which was not exactly the story Rosalee told.

Holman pulled the car into the nearest parking lot in order to give this conversation his full attention. I looked over and put a finger to my lips. I didn't think it was a good idea for him to start asking her questions. She might get spooked and hang up.

"Tell me more," I said.

"You've heard of Paul Manafort, right?"

"Of course." Paul Manafort was the infamous lobbyist who worked for President Trump's 2016 campaign. He was indicted for allegedly taking millions in fees from foreign Ukrainian/pro-Russian oligarchs without declaring himself as a foreign agent.

"Dale Mountbatten is a small-time Paul Manafort—only he had the good sense to stay out of any presidential campaigns."

"Wait—are you telling me that Dale works for the Ukrainian government?"

"No, you silly twit!"

"Hey, hey," I cut her off. "Slow down on the insults, okay? You called *me,* remember?"

I heard her take in a breath. "I'm sorry. I get upset sometimes."

"It's okay, Hadley," I said, fishing. When she didn't respond, I asked, "This is Hadley, isn't it?"

There was a pause. "No."

"Are you sure?"

Another pause. "Who's Hadley?"

"I can tell it's you, Ms. Lawrence. We just met yesterday and I remember your voice."

"I don't know what you're talking about."

"You forced me to have a glass of tea in your sister's kitchen..."

"Do you want the information or not?" she snapped, dropping the towel and the last pretense of her anonymity.

"Yes, of course. Go ahead," I said, and then unable to stop myself, I added in a much softer voice, "Hadley."

She cleared her throat before continuing. "Dale quietly took on a client about nine years ago from Qatar, a high-ranking political adviser to the royal family. They wanted Dale to help improve the image of the Qatari government within certain US political circles."

I wrote this down as quickly as I could. "Okay," I said, "but that's not illegal, right? He's a lobbyist. That's kind of what he does."

"Well, it wouldn't be a problem if he had gone through the proper channels and registered under FARA."

I'd watched enough news coverage over the past couple of years to know that FARA stood for the Foreign Agents Registration Act, a statute requiring lobbyists to disclose their associations with foreign governments. It had been on the books for years and years and was almost never enforced, that is, until Paul Manafort came along.

"Dale's not registered under FARA?"

"Not for his work with Qatar."

This was easy enough to fact-check and I would certainly do so, but I wanted to keep her talking, so I played devil's advocate. "If Dale had been illegally taking money from a foreign government for years, how come he hasn't been caught?"

Hadley laughed. "Honey, only the dumb criminals get caught. And Dale is many things, but dumb ain't one of them."

"I can check this pretty easily, you know?"

"I'd expect nothing less."

Holman got out his phone and immediately started Googling.

"So tell me about the connection to Colonel Mustard."

She sighed as if burdened by my ignorance. "The Qataris paid Dale well for his services, and since he wasn't officially registered with them, he had to do something with the money."

"Nine years..." I said out loud as the connection hit me.

"That's right," she said, finally sounding satisfied with something I said. "Right about the time he moved that little whore down to the sticks and opened a restaurant."

I saw Holman's jaw tighten at the insult. I put a hand on his arm to calm him. We couldn't risk making Hadley mad, not yet.

"So you're saying Dale and Rosalee funneled the money from the Qatari official through Colonel Mustard Enterprises under the cover of butter?"

"Spread over the course of nine years, I'll bet they've run close to ten million dollars through there."

"Ten million dollars?" I said, surprised. "That's an awful lot of butter."

"You'd be surprised. One hundred thousand dollars in butter per year doesn't raise any flags in the restaurant business."

"How do you know so much about this?" I asked. "And why are you calling me and not the authorities?"

She was ready for my question, or at least she answered quickly enough that it appeared she'd been waiting for me to ask. "Everyone knows the press is way faster than the FBI. Do you have any idea how long an investigation would take? It could be months before they even got the paperwork to begin looking into all of this. Especially with someone as well-connected as Dale."

There was distinct bitterness in her voice when she said his name, like she resented his notoriety. This struck me as odd because when I was with her the day before, I'd gotten the impression she was very much at home with Dale and the boys, like she'd stepped into her dead sister's shoes almost a little too easily.

"So you're hoping that I'll look into these allegations and print them to force some sort of federal investigation?"

"I'd also like to see him go to prison for murdering my sister."

That got my attention. "You think Dale killed Greer?"

"I think she found out exactly what her beloved was up to and probably threatened to turn him in—"

"Probably?" I said. "Wait, is this something you know or something you're guessing?"

"I have reason to believe that is what happened." She clearly didn't like me drilling down for details.

"As I understand it, Dale has a solid alibi for the time Greer was killed."

"There are ways of being responsible for someone's death even when you're not there. Surely, you understand that."

Her haughty tone was really starting to chap my hide. "Okay, so suppose you're right and Dale did have your sister killed. Why? If he'd been laundering money for years like this, why would Greer all of a sudden threaten to expose him? Why now?" I asked.

"You really aren't very bright, are you?" she said in a barely controlled voice. The word *unhinged* came to mind.

Out of my peripheral vision I saw Holman open his mouth, probably to launch some sort of lukewarm testament to my mental competency, but I held up a hand to stop him. I was trying to bait her. The more frustrated she became, the more likely she'd be to let something slip out in anger.

"*Why now?*" she said, mocking my voice. "Because *now* is when he planned on leaving his wife for that trashy little baguette. Greer wasn't about to let that tramp reap the benefits of all of her years of support and silence. She was the one who made everything he did possible, she took care of everything else in his perfect life so he could concentrate on his work," she said, her voice rising. "She could put up with the cheating and the lying and the moral ambiguity, but she could not abide being tossed away like yesterday's trash—" she broke off and I heard her take a deep breath. When she spoke, again her voice was lower, calmer. "You've upset me, Riley. I have to go."

"Wait!" I said before she hung up.

"What?" she snapped.

"Um," I said, trying to think of something to get her to stay on the phone. "Um, I just wanted to say I think it's really nice how you're there for your nephews. I mean, it must be so nice for them to have you around." It was the only quasi-compliment I could come up with, and I figured I had a better chance of catching this cuckoo bird with honey than vinegar.

The comment seemed to mollify her. "This is a very difficult time for them."

"Is it hard for you to be away from your own family?" I asked, fishing again.

"I'm not married," she said tersely, then added, "anymore."

"No kids?"

"I wasn't able," she said, answering almost automatically. Before I could respond she snapped, "Why are we talking about me? We should be talking about Dale!"

"I'm sorry, you're righ—"

"You know what? Forget it!" she yelled into the phone. "I thought you seemed like you had it on-the-ball and might be able to take this information and do something productive with it. Obviously, I was mistaken—"

"Hadley, wait—"

"I guess I'll just have to take care of this myself like I have to take care of everything else. Goodbye, Riley!"

CHAPTER 26

Holman and I sat shocked in the silence of the car for a moment, trying to make sense of what had just happened. Eventually he pulled back onto the highway and we continued our drive toward Tuttle Corner, hashing through all that we'd just heard. Holman was ready to write her off as a loon, but I wasn't so sure.

"She's an unreliable witness," Holman said as confidently as if he were saying *the Earth is round.*

"What do you mean?"

"She clearly has a bias against Rosalee because of the affair. She could be saying all this just to get back at her, to get back at them for hurting her sister."

I wasn't anxious to come to Hadley's defense, but I also wasn't ready to reject everything she said out of hand. She'd given us some pretty incriminating information about Dale that'd be easy enough to check out. "I don't know..."

"Did you catch how sensitive she was when you asked if she had kids of her own?" Holman said, trying another tact. "With her sister dead and her nephews' father in prison, Hadley would most likely become their guardian. That would not only give her the family she never had, but also possibly control of their trust until they reached maturity."

"You think Hadley could have killed her own sister and is trying to frame Dale for it in order to get custody of their near-adult children?" It was a sick thought. Then again, Hadley Lawrence was not a well woman. Still, I had a hard time buying that. "What about Balzichek?"

"Did you hear her comment about how 'she had to take care of everything herself'? Maybe she took care of Balzichek? Let's also not forget that Balzichek led a high-risk life and fraternized with some very dangerous criminals. Maybe he was killed by someone else and the deaths are unrelated?"

I couldn't help think of what Carl had told me, about how he was looking at the same possibility.

"Okay," I said, pumping the brakes on this conversation. Holman was obviously trying to come up with any theory that would exonerate Rosalee from wrongdoing. But facts were facts and we needed to sort through what we knew. "Let's back up and think this through. Let's just say what Hadley told us is true and Greer found out about Dale and the money laundering and Rosalee and everything. It makes sense she might have confided in her sister."

I tapped my pen against my bottom lip. "But why would Hadley call a reporter and not the police? If she thinks Dale killed her sister, why not go straight to the cops? I'm not buying her answer that the press is faster."

"I agree," Holman said.

"And why me? I mean, there are tons of other reporters covering this story for far bigger news outlets. Why do you think she decided to give me this information?"

"Another good question. I'm telling you: unreliable witness."

I ignored him. "You know, another thing that has been bothering me is, remember when someone vandalized Rosalee's Tavern? Balzichek was arrested for that crime, and he said Greer had hired him to do it."

"Yes," Holman agreed. "Rosalee said that was Greer's way of trying to get the authorities to look into the Tavern more closely so they'd get in trouble for money laundering."

"Again—why not just call the authorities and tell them?"

Holman shrugged. "Maybe she wanted to threaten Dale but not actually turn him in. She had a pretty lavish lifestyle. If he got caught, I'm sure the first thing they'd do is freeze his assets."

"I guess," I said, not feeling completely satisfied with that explanation. "But she had money of her own. And besides, it just seems like the long way around. Just like Hadley calling me, a reporter, instead of the police. What if—and I'm just thinking out loud here—what if Rosalee hired Balzichek to vandalize the Tavern herself? And maybe even to kill Greer?"

I could feel Holman's resistance to my suggestion in a kind of molecular shift around him. "Why would she do that?" His voice was tighter than usual when he spoke.

"Well, if she and Dale had been laundering money together all this time...what if she got tired of waiting around and decided she wanted it all for herself? She'd have to get Dale out of the way somehow. And what better way than to have him go to prison for murder."

Holman was shaking his head before I even finished my sentence. "No, that doesn't make sense. If Rosalee was really after the money and she's the cold-blooded killer you think she is, then why wouldn't she just kill Dale? Then she could escape with the money before anybody even figured out she did it."

I had to admit he had a point. I thought some more. "What if none of this has to do with the money at all, and Rosalee killed Greer out of good old-fashioned homicidal jealousy?"

"After nine years? I would think the fire would have gone out of her jealousy in that length of time."

Again, he had a point. I couldn't explain it, but I just *felt* like Rosalee was involved in these killings somehow. The more I thought about her story, the more I found parts of it unbelievable. Like why did she suddenly break things off with Dale after all this time? And if she felt so scared for her life, why not go to the sheriff? At best, her story was filled with half-truths. At worst, it was an elaborate lie. Holman obviously disagreed with me, and it was time to address the reason why.

I turned my shoulders so I could face him. He was driving, so his eyes were straight ahead, but I knew he could feel me looking directly at him. I took a deep breath. "Will, I know you like Rosalee. And I know you think she's pretty, and smart, and sophisticated...and she *is* all of those things...but I think she may also be dangerous."

"I disagree," he said immediately, his eyes fixed on the road ahead.

Since Holman was someone who relied on facts, I presented him with the facts as we understood them. "Okay, let's think about what we know: Rosalee told Ryan and Ridley she was going to be leaving town—"

"—lots of people take vacations, Riley," Holman said, a defensive edge in his voice.

"She has no alibi for the time of either murder—"

"She lives alone. Is that a crime? Because if it is, you and I are guilty as well."

"She bought a sledgehammer just days before Greer—her lover's wife—was bludgeoned to death *with a sledgehammer.*"

"Rosalee was planning to do renovations in the Tavern's cellar. She even told Ryan that! What else do you use to break up brick and plaster?"

"Holman..."

"What?"

"I think you're letting your feelings for Rosalee get in the way of your judgment. I'm not saying she's guilty, I'm just saying we shouldn't rule her out because you like her."

Holman said nothing, my accusation hanging in the air between us like thick smog. After several seconds of silence, he said, "You don't know her like I do, Riley. She isn't capable of killing anyone." He said this with such finality I knew there was no point in trying to convince him...until I had proof.

Chapter 27

"Oh look, it's the Queen of England and her merry man," stupid Spencer jeered as we walked into the *Times* office.

It took me a second to figure out what he was talking about until I realized it must be Camilla's suit. I had nearly forgotten I was wearing it until his comment. I could have quipped something back at him, but I decided to let Holman take this one. This was a perfect opportunity for his particular skill set.

"Riley is from Virginia, not England, Gerlach," Holman explained. "And if you were meaning to describe me as her 'merry man,' " he went on, "I should tell you that despite my genial countenance, I'm not feeling very merry today. I'm also not her man. To put a finer point on it," he continued, raising a long finger into the air, "because we live in a time when people no longer belong to other people—thankfully—no one really is anyone else's anything, man or woman. But I recognize the idiom you were using, that people who are dating are said to belong to each other. For instance, Kanye West regularly refers to Kim Kardashian as 'his woman' and I don't think she minds because they are married and she knows he doesn't mean it literally, i.e., she does not legally belong to him. However, idioms aside, since Riley and I are not romantically involved, it would not be appropriate to refer to me as her anything, except her co-worker." He stopped, then quickly added with a furtive glance at me, "Or friend."

Spencer, who got more than he bargained for (but less than he deserved) stared back at Holman, slack-jawed. As we walked past him on the way to Holman's office, I gave him a royal wave and whispered, "Cheerio, old chap!"

I got the final version of the Klondike obit turned in just before the deadline. Flick did an excellent job, as always, and my contributions were minimal, but I was proud of how it turned out. I thought our readers would enjoy it. Of particular note was an interview Klondike had given a few years earlier in which he said, "I believe you should live generously. Use butter generously, pour gas on your fire generously, pour your drinks even more generously, laugh generously, give generously, and love generously." Good advice to live by, I thought. One of the reasons people in Tuttle liked our longer-form obits so much was because they were full of small details that make up a life well-lived. We didn't focus on the big contributions that changed the world, we left that to *The New York Times*. Our column focused on the small things the average Joe or Jane—friends, neighbors, community members—did that people remember after a person has passed on. I hoped people would learn from Jonathan Klondike. If there was one thing working the crime beat had taught me, it was that the world could use a little more generosity.

As soon as I finished with the obit, I walked into Holman's office. He sat behind his computer, the movement from his fast typing causing him to bob up and down on his ergonomic ball chair. He didn't look up when I came through the door. I knew he was still upset with me for what I said in the car ride back from DC. What I didn't know was if he was upset because he knew it was true or if he actually believed he was being objective about Rosalee.

"You ready to head over to the sheriff's office?" I asked. We'd decided we would go tell Carl everything we knew as soon as we'd both caught up on a few things.

He kept his eyes on the computer screen. "Give me five minutes." His voice was flat, terse.

"Will, I—"

Kay Jackson's voice crackled over the intercom on Holman's phone, interrupting me. "Can you and Ellison come to my office, please? Now."

That couldn't be good. Holman finally looked up. I shrugged; I had no idea what we did wrong. We walked to the far end of the hallway in silence, neither of us sure what awaited us. Kay sat behind her desk. From the threshold of the doorway, I could see the back of a man's head and a grim expression on Kay's face.

"There's someone here to see you," she said.

Right on cue, Dale Mountbatten swiveled around to face me.

Confusion and dread hit me like a wrecking ball. *What on earth was he doing here?* Whatever it was, it couldn't be good.

"Hi, Riley," he said, looking me up and down. "Nice dress." His expression then morphed into a poor facsimile of contrition. "You said to call if I thought of anything else. I decided to just come on by. Hope that's all right?"

Once we were settled in the conference room, Kay made sure Dale understood that nothing he told us would be kept confidential; this conversation was not privileged.

"We're reporters, Mr. Mountbatten," she said, looking him directly in the eye. "Our job is to find out the truth and reveal it."

"I understand," Dale said.

After getting preliminary disclosures out of the way, Kay left the three of us to do the interview. We set up Holman's phone to record and he asked the first question. "Why are you here today, Mr. Mountbatten?"

"Because I believe that Rosalee Belanger killed my wife and is now trying to kill me."

I saw Holman's hand clench under the table, but when he spoke I was glad to hear his voice was even, controlled. "Tell us why you think that," he said, maintaining strong eye contact the whole time.

Dale's story started out much the same way Rosalee's had. The two had a passionate affair. Greer found out and forced Rosalee to leave the house. She agreed not to have her sent back to France if Dale would agree to stay in the marriage. That was the deal they made.

"I loved them both," Dale said. "Greer, for giving me the family I'd always wanted, and Rosalee for...everything else."

He said he was familiar with Tuttle Corner and thought it would be a perfect place for Rosalee to live while he figured out what to do next. "It was selfish. I can see that now," he said, stating the obvious. "But I wasn't thinking clearly. Rosalee was like an addiction. I was consumed with her—being with her, trying to find a way for us to have a future. I just thought if enough time passed, eventually the path forward would become clear."

"You wanted to have your cake and eat it too," I said, unable to help myself.

"Yes, I suppose that's right," he said without meeting my eyes. "I bought the restaurant and set Rosalee up in the little house on Ninth Street. We were in love, and even though it wasn't ideal, there was a sense of optimism about the whole arrangement. Rosalee told me she loved small towns and had always wanted to own her own café, so I felt like she was getting something out of the deal too, you know?"

I didn't, but I kept quiet.

"We saw each other every chance we got under the cover of business travel or whatever. After a while, it seemed like Greer either accepted my relationship with Rosalee or convinced herself it was over. Greer could do that—convince herself of whatever it was she needed to believe. Either way, we never talked about it. Life went on at home as usual. And if Rosalee minded sharing me with my family, she never said."

Although Dale insisted they were happy, that both Greer and Rosalee were content with things, I very much doubted his rose-colored assertion that his wife and mistress were perfectly happy about this barbaric, male-first sort of relationship, but whatever. He obviously had convinced himself the arrangement worked.

"Everything was going fine in that regard," Dale said, looking down at his fingers. "But Greer has—I mean, had—" he corrected himself, "very expensive tastes, and frankly, money was becoming an issue. I was making a good living, but between the private schools, camps, lessons, cars, donations, college prep, and just generally keeping up with the Joneses, money was getting tight."

"And you were paying all of Rosalee's expenses too?" I added.

"It was the least I could do for her," he said, an emotion I couldn't readily identify rolling across his face.

"It was stupid, so stupid, looking back—but when I started consulting with a diplomat from Qatar, I just 'forgot' to disclose it on the year-end FARA forms. It was reckless, but you have to understand that back then everyone was doing that kind of thing. I could name ten lobbyists right now who work for foreign governments and haven't disclosed it. That requirement was a joke, seen as more a suggestion than a law."

If he was trying to convince Will Holman that his lawbreaking wasn't that big of a deal, he was barking up the wrong tree. "It was a way around paying taxes, which is illegal," Holman clarified.

Mountbatten looked out the window, then back at Holman. "Well, yeah, I guess...there are a lot of loopholes in the system where this kind of thing is concerned, but yes, not disclosing my relationship with Qatar meant that I didn't have to declare the money."

"But you needed to do something with it," I said.

He nodded. "You asked me yesterday about Colonel Mustard Enterprises. That was Rosalee's idea." Dale took a sip of his coffee before continuing. "I did it for her—for us. The deal was that I'd take the consultancy with Qatar in order to make enough so that when I left Greer, I could take care of her and the kids. And Rosalee and I could be comfortable too." He stared out the window again for a good five full seconds, and when he turned back to us his eyes were moist with emotion. "No one was supposed to get hurt."

We sat silently as the gravity of what he'd just said sank in.

"What happened next, Dale?" Holman asked when the silent seconds stretched on.

Dale wiped his nose, which had started running as his emotions spun closer to the surface. He was truly upset by this point, and whatever else he may have been lying about, I could tell his sadness was genuine.

"Greer must have found out about the money somehow...I honestly don't know how she did. I obviously didn't tell her and kept no records of any transactions, but maybe she had my phone bugged or followed me or something. I still have no idea, but she came to me about a month ago and said she was going to go to the FBI. The hell of it was she didn't even care about the corruption; she was mad because I was planning to leave. She said she'd keep quiet if I stayed."

Dale wiped away a tear that fell out of his right eye. "I told Rosalee later the same day Greer made the ultimatum. In fact, it was the only time in all these years that I ever came to Tuttle Corner and parked right in front of her house. I told her we had no choice. If Greer went to the authorities, we'd go to prison."

Holman interrupted him. "*You'd* go to prison. Rosalee didn't technically do anything wrong."

Dale looked at Holman like he was speaking Swahili. "Rosalee laundered all the money. Colonel Mustard Enterprises? The butter company? That was all Rosalee. You can't just deposit millions of dollars into the bank without saying where it came from, you know."

I saw Holman's jaw clench. He didn't believe Dale, or didn't want to. I wasn't so sure. I thought back to my conversation with Rosalee the other night. She hadn't explicitly said she'd been involved in the money laundering, but she also hadn't said she wasn't. Now that I looked back, all she'd said was that Dale laundered money through the Tavern and she knew about it. I forced myself to come back to the moment as Dale continued talking. The details of what happened to the money were the least of our concerns.

"Rosalee went ballistic. She absolutely lost her mind." He widened his eyes as if the shock of her reaction was still surprising to him. "She said we couldn't let that happen and Greer had to be stopped." He paused. "She told me she knew someone who could 'take care of her.' "

"What did she mean by that?" I asked. We would need Dale to say the words if we were going to be able to report it.

He ignored my question, lost in telling his story. "I told her no—*emphatically* no. In fact, I was so shocked, so horrified that she would even suggest something like that...I couldn't believe it. That was not the woman I'd known and loved all these years. I'm afraid I didn't handle it well. I was just so outraged she'd even suggest something like that...I stormed out. That was the last time I saw her."

"When was that?" I asked.

Dale dropped his head into his hands, and when he raised it his eyes were red-rimmed and glassy. "November fourth. The day before Greer went missing."

Dale said he'd left Tuttle Corner and had gone straight to Manhattan, where he had meetings and that scheduled interview on NPR's *All Things Considered*. The next evening he talked to his son Charlie, who was worried because he hadn't seen his mom all day. When he wasn't able to get ahold of Greer, he called the police, who later found her car covered in blood.

"I just couldn't believe it—any of it. Greer gone, Rosalee responsible...it was like a living nightmare."

"What makes you think Rosalee was responsible?" Holman asked. "Did you talk to her afterward? Did she admit to killing your wife?" Holman sounded more like a defense attorney than a reporter in that moment. I put a hand on his arm in a warning gesture. We were reporters and should at least try to convey impartiality.

Dale knitted his brow together. "My wife is killed right

after Rosalee said she knew a guy who could make her disappear? What would you think, Mr. Holman? I didn't want to believe it—I still don't—but there's no other conclusion to come to. Rosalee said she was tired of waiting around and wanted us to have a life together. When she found out Greer was a threat, she must have just snapped."

"So, you haven't seen or spoken to Rosalee since that night you went to her house and she suggested she knew someone who could," I check my notes, " 'take care of' Greer?" I asked, trying to clarify what he'd told us.

"That's right. I knew the police were going to be all over me—they always look at the husband—so I knew if I tried to call or get in touch with Rosalee, it would just make me look like I was involved."

That seemed a pretty calculated move for someone shocked and grief-stricken. It seemed to me if your wife was murdered and you thought your lover did it, you'd tell the police. Or at the very least, call them up and accuse them of it.

"Why not tell the sheriff everything right after you found out about Greer? If you really thought Rosalee had her killed, why not turn her in?" I asked.

Dale looked down at his hands again and twisted the gold band still in place on his left ring finger. "I love her—loved—love, hell, I don't know," he said. "I didn't want any of this to be true. I didn't want Greer to be gone, Rosalee to have—have—"

"And you didn't want to get caught," Holman said.

I kicked him under the table. He needed to keep himself in check. Acting like Rosalee's lawyer right now wasn't doing anybody any good.

"Yes, you're right. There was an element of self-preservation at play too, but honest-to-God that was mostly for my kids. With their mother gone, I'm all they have. If I got sent to prison, they'd have nothing left. I've failed them in a million different ways, but I didn't want to take their future as well."

"So what changed?" I asked.

"Honestly? It was you," Dale said, looking at me directly. "I knew deep down that it was only a matter of time until someone figured out about the money laundering. When you showed up yesterday asking questions about Colonel Mustard Enterprises, I knew it wouldn't be long till the whole sordid story came out. I was up all last night debating what to do."

"And?" I asked when he paused.

He took a deep breath in and blew it out slowly. In a stronger, fuller voice he said, "After I leave here, I'm going to Sheriff Haight and am going to tell him everything—all about the affair and the Qataris and the money laundering. I wanted to do this interview first because I figure at least this way, I can get my side of the story out there. I may be guilty of a lot of things," he said with a steely edge, "but I did not kill my wife."

Chapter 28

The rest of the afternoon was a blur. Word had gotten out that Dale Mountbatten was in Tuttle Corner, and when we walked him out of the newsroom to accompany him to see Sheriff Haight, there was a small herd of reporters already waiting there.

"What are you doing at the *Tuttle Times*?

"Did you come to confess to killing your wife?"

"Were you and Rosalee Belanger in it together?"

"What was the motivation for killing Justin Balzichek?"

"Did the reporters from the *Times* persuade you to turn yourself in?"

"Why are you so dressed up, Miss Ellison?"

The questions were coming almost as rapidly as the click-click-click of the cameras. Holman stood on one side of Dale, and I on the other. We moved slowly through Memorial Park, our path blocked by the growing crowd of reporters and bystanders. Kay Jackson called the sheriff's office to warn them what was coming their way, so when we got about halfway across the park, Butter and Deputy Wilmore came out to help.

"Step aside, step aside," Butter said to the crowd of reporters. "Let the man walk. You'll all get your chance to ask your questions eventually." He put his arms out to keep a safe distance between the crowd and us.

The press was not allowed inside the sheriff's office, so once we got inside, we all took a deep breath. For the first time, I felt sympathy for people like Harry Styles and Reese Witherspoon, who were hounded by reporters everywhere they went. No one understood the impulse to get the story more than me, but that frenetic kind of question-shouting and crowding just wasn't my style. I could see how a person might lose it and smash a camera here and there after a while.

Carl was waiting just inside the station to take Dale back to an interrogation room. "Thanks, guys," he said to Holman and me as he led Dale, flanked by Butter and Wilmore, toward the back. "I'll be in touch."

"Hey," I said, before he turned to go, "can we have a quick second?"

He told Butter to take Mountbatten back. "What's up?" he said, looking between Holman and me.

I felt like it was important for Holman to start this particular conversation, so I waited for him to speak up. Thankfully, he did.

"Rosalee came to see me," Holman said.

"What? When?" Carl kept his voice low, but I could tell he was freaking out.

"A few days ago—"

"A few days ago?" His surprise turned to anger. "Why am I just now hearing about this?"

"She was scared. Says she's innocent and Dale is trying to frame her for the murders."

"And just so you know," I said, lowering my voice and leaning in, "Dale says the same thing about her."

"Great," Carl said. "Just great." He blew out a gale-force sigh and put his hands on his hips. "I need to go talk to Dale, and then I really need to talk to Rosalee. Where is she?" He looked at Holman.

"I don't know." Holman looked down.

"Don't toy with me, Holman. I'll have the DA slap you with an obstruction charge if I have to..."

"He doesn't. Honestly," I cut in. "He'd persuaded her to turn herself in yesterday, but then she took off. No one has heard from her since."

"Well, if this isn't the biggest shitshow I've ever seen—" Carl stopped himself. He rarely cussed, and I could tell he was angry for letting his temper flare. He paused as he looked across the room toward where Dale Mountbatten was waiting in the conference room. "I've gotta go. But one of you two better call me the nanosecond she gets in touch, you hear?"

We agreed and asked if we could be let out the back entrance to avoid the press, which Gail thought was just the height of (hilarious) irony.

We went back to the office and got straight to work writing up the story on Dale Mountbatten. Holman was taking the lead, and Kay and I were helping by fact-checking certain details like dates that Rosalee worked for the couple, his previous FARA disclosures, and any records we could find pertaining to the establishment of Colonel Mustard Enterprises. We were trying to establish a paper trail between Colonel Mustard Enterprises and Dale Mountbatten personally. Being that it was nearly six o'clock on a Thursday evening, most of the offices that we needed to get in touch with were already closed for the day.

"We'll run what we have," Kay said, looking over our notes from the interview. "By tomorrow morning, every paper who sent a reporter down here is going to have a similar story. Let's get out ahead with something, even if we can't run everything."

Holman and I agreed, and we sketched out a rough plan of what we thought we could print without crossing any ethical lines.

I was on my way to the break room to make another pot of coffee when I got a text from a number I didn't recognize. **R u free?**

Who is this?

Ash. Can u come to funeral home?

How did Ash get my number, and why did he want me to come to the funeral home right now?

I texted back. **At offIce. Big story. All okay?**

Not really. Could use ur help.

It can be hard to decipher tone over text, but I was picking up on a kind of frightened tenor unusual for Ash. Or at least what I knew of him. He didn't strike me as a guy who scared—or asked for help—easily.

I walked back into Holman's office and told him I had to run out for a short while. Both he and Kay looked at me like I had ferrets coming out of my ears.

"I wouldn't leave if it wasn't important."

"Is it Rosalee?" Holman's voice was so childlike and hopeful in that exact moment, I thought my heart might break in two.

"No," I said. "I'd tell you if it was."

He blinked at me twice and then turned back to his laptop. Kay gave me a confused look, and I just shrugged in response. The last thing I would do was tell Kay about Holman's complicated feelings for Rosalee. I would never sell out my partner like that. If Holman's Rosalee-bias became a problem, it would be a problem I'd have to deal with on my own.

CHAPTER 29

Since the funeral home was technically closed, it was dark inside except for the light coming from Franklin's office down the hall. Ash's face was half in shadow, the light hitting just one of his eyes giving him an ethereal—if a little spooky—look. "Thanks for coming," he said as I walked inside. "I didn't know who else to call. Wow, you look nice." He nodded to my dress.

"Thanks," I said, my face reddening. I really needed to go home and change. Or start dressing better on a regular basis.

I followed him back to the office, and despite the fact that we were alone in the building, he closed the door behind me. I took one of the chairs across from Franklin's desk, but instead of sitting in his grandfather's chair, Ash sat on the corner of the desk, right in front of me. He wore jeans and an off-white Henley that was just fitted enough to reveal that he must spend time in the gym. Not that I was looking at his pecs or anything. I was there to help. As a professional. Or something.

"You look stressed," I said, leaving out that he also looked kind of hot. "What's going on?"

"I screwed up, Riley. Like, really screwed up."

"Okay..."

He let out a mirthless laugh. "For the past week, all I've

been thinking about is a way to get out of taking over the family business, and now ironically—there isn't going to be any business left when this gets out."

"Ash, slow down," I said. "Tell me what happened."

He took a deep breath before speaking. "Remember how I told you I talked to that woman, Sofia Scheiner?"

"Justin Balzichek's next of kin, yes. I spoke to her on the phone too."

"Right. Well, she came by this afternoon."

"I thought she was coming Saturday?"

"She said she decided to come up earlier 'to get it over with.' "

"Hmm, okay. So, what happened?"

"Well, technically the fourteen-day waiting period isn't up until tomorrow, so the body has yet to be cremated. Javier has it scheduled for the morning."

"Right." I was having trouble seeing where this story was going, but Ash was clearly terribly so upset about something to do with Sofia Scheiner and her unscheduled visit that he was telling the story in halted clips.

"She seemed so disappointed and said she'd taken off work just to drive in all the way from Arkansas and...well, I just felt so badly for her..."

"For God's sake, Ash, just spit it out!"

"I gave her his stuff. I gave 'Sofia Scheiner' Justin Balzichek's personal effects."

"Why did you put air quotes around Sofia Scheiner?" I asked, leaning in against my growing sense of dread.

"It wasn't her."

"*What?*"

He shook his head like he still couldn't believe it. "She seemed convincing—she knew a lot of details about Justin and how he died and even referenced our conversation on the phone...when she asked if she could have his things so she could 'start the healing process' I just...I just gave it all to her."

I felt a sudden stab of guilt. The article I posted contained all that information. Anyone could have read that piece and used the information to pretend to be Sofia Scheiner. I wasn't sure if Ash realized that yet, and I wasn't about to enlighten him, but when he did, he would not be happy with me. This would not bode well for his already deep dislike for the press.

"Wait," I said, trying to think if this was all what it appeared to be. "How do you know it wasn't the real Sofia Scheiner?"

Ash took out his phone and handed it to me. It was an article from the *Northwest Arkansas Democrat-Gazette* with the headline "Local Lady Awarded Best Buns," and there was a photo of a woman with stringy gray hair, a wide nose, and brown eyes holding a tray of what looked like sticky buns. I took the phone for a closer look and saw that the photo caption read "Sofia Scheiner, 58, of Morrilton, wins 'Best Buns' contest for Grandma Balzichek's caramel sticky buns recipe."

Ash waited as I read before saying, "That was not the woman who came here tonight."

"Are you sure?"

"Positive. The woman who showed up here about an hour ago had dark hair and was younger looking than this person." He held up the phone in his hand. "And besides, I know it wasn't the real Sofia Scheiner because when I realized I forgot to have her sign the form she was supposed to sign, I called her to ask her if she could come back by..."

I closed my eyes against what I knew he was going to say next.

"She had no idea what I was talking about," he said grimly.

"Oh gosh..."

"I covered, of course. Told her I had the wrong number. And then she asked if we were still on for Saturday, and I said yes. What else could I do?"

I had no answer for that. "So when the fake Sofia came in, I take it you didn't ask for ID?"

He shook his head. "Nope. She seemed upset, I felt badly for her...hell, I've never done this before and I didn't think anyone would actually try to steal a dead guy's worthless stuff."

This was not good. "What did she take?"

"That's the thing," he said and grabbed a piece of paper off his desk and handed it to me. "Nothing really—at least nothing of value. This is the personal property inventory. It has two dimes, a nickel, three pennies, and a set of rosary beads. The sheriff kept everything valuable or that might be needed for the investigation—wallet, keys to his apartment, stuff like that."

I tried to think of a reason why someone would want that stuff, but I couldn't come up with anything.

"It doesn't matter, though," Ash said, despondent. "It's my fault and once word gets out—and it *will* get out with as high-profile as this particular corpse is—no one will ever trust Campbell & Sons again, certainly not with me running things."

He had a point. People in Tuttle Corner weren't particularly forgiving of newcomers. And, ultimately, he had screwed up. Not asking for identification before releasing Balzichek's things was a Grade A mistake. I couldn't help but feel a tiny bit responsible for the situation, however, because if Ash hadn't done me a favor by sharing the information about Aunt Scheiner, it never would have appeared in the newspaper and the imposter wouldn't have been able to so convincingly pretend to be her. I felt a responsibility to help make things right.

Ash was still sitting on the edge of the desk, despondent, his eyes fuzzed out and staring at the floor. Lord knows what kind of dark thoughts were rolling around inside that pretty little head of his. I stood up and took hold of his forearm. "Listen," I said firmly. "We can fix this—" And when he started to argue, I amended my statement, "—or at least make it better. We need to figure out who came here tonight and more importantly, why."

"But how?"

"I'm a reporter, remember? We never quit till we get what we're after."

CHAPTER 30

I called Holman and told him I'd be another thirty minutes to an hour. He said that was fine and didn't even ask where I was. I took that to mean that he was in the zone writing the article. Or he trusted me. Or possibly both.

If I was going to help Ash figure out who came in pretending to be Justin Balzichek's next of kin, I was going to have to go into full-on list-making mode. It was a trait I got from my mother, who made lists for everything, from what groceries to buy to what books she wanted to read to which clothes she was going to bring on vacation. I got out my notebook and turned to a new page and wrote "Things We Know about Justin Balzichek" at the top.

Ash took another approach. He pulled a bottle of bourbon from the bottom drawer of Franklin's desk. "Drink?"

I arched an eyebrow. "Is that yours or PopPop's?"

"PopPop knew there are some times when 'I'm sorry for your loss' doesn't cut it," Ash said and looked down. "I remember being here once after a service—this man had just buried his wife of fifty-seven years and he just couldn't bring himself to go home. All the mourners were gone, the service was long over, and this man just sort of wandered around the place looking for last-minute things he could do. He read through the guest book, collected the leftover leaflets, brought the flowers into the entryway. PopPop knew he was lost, that he didn't want to go home, and so he brought the man in here and the two of them finished an entire bottle of Bowman's while the man told stories about his wife. It was such a compassionate thing to do." His eyes glistened at the memory.

"Franklin sure has a way about him, doesn't he?" I lifted the glass he'd poured for me. "To PopPop."

Ash tilted his glass toward mine, then drained it in one long swallow.

"It's going to be okay," I said. I knew this wasn't a particularly helpful or insightful comment, but sometimes it helped just to hear someone say it. I thought now might be one of those times for Ash.

"You think?" he asked, his light brown eyes glassy from emotion or the bourbon, or both. Either way, it triggered my empathy response. I found myself wanting to comfort him, but we didn't have the luxury of time for comfort. And I figured the best way to help him was to focus on solving his current problem.

I went into work mode. "Okay. Let's talk theories. Why would someone want to take Balzichek's seemingly worthless personal effects?"

"Hell if I know," Ash said, running a finger along the rim of his glass. "He's been dead for almost two weeks and we haven't been able to get anyone to even acknowledge they knew him, let alone claim him. I can't figure it out."

"Let's start with what we know. His parents are both deceased, correct?"

Ash nodded. I jotted this down. "And his only sister is currently serving a lifetime prison term in Fluvanna for drug charges, right?"

He nodded again. I made another note, and as I wrote, I noticed Ash's eyes were starting to fuzz out a little as he absently lifted a second shot of bourbon and knocked it back. Then he said, "The sheriff's office kept all of his personal effects as evidence. Javier said Justin came in naked as a jaybird. He put him in some of the extra clothes we keep for these kinds of situations."

"All right," I said, making more notes. Out of my peripheral vision I saw Ash lift the bottle and pour himself a third shot.

"Listen," I said, trying to keep any prickliness from my tone. "I don't mean to judge, but you might want to keep a clear head if we're going to solve this."

He raised his lion eyes to mine and without breaking eye contact, Ash drained his glass.

"Okay, I guess not," I murmured. I wasn't his mother. If he wanted to get drunk, I supposed that was his business, but there was something unsettling about the way he flip-flopped between a sensitive soul asking for my help to an arrogant jerk who doesn't care. I pushed my irritation aside; I had my own reasons for wanting to break this story. Not only would it make me feel less guilty for printing the details that helped whoever did it, but the person who came here tonight must have had a damn good reason for it—and that reason was almost certainly tied to why Balzichek and Greer Mountbatten were killed.

"Let's think of who it could have possibly been," I said, mentally ticking through everyone who had a stake in this case. Rosalee was the obvious answer as far as females were concerned. And she had been missing for the past twenty-four hours. It occurred to me that Ash had probably never seen her. She could have easily walked into Campbell & Sons and pretended to be Sofia.

I took out my phone and scrolled through until I found an old picture of Ryan and me with Rosalee from the summer before our senior year in college. It was the day Rosalee taught me to make a croissant, and the picture was of the three of us proudly showing off my slightly lumpy creation. I held the phone out to him. "Does she look familiar?"

Ash leaned forward to get a better look. "Nope. Never seen her before."

Damn. That would have been the perfect kind of proof to show Holman that Rosalee wasn't the angel he thought she was.

Ash sighed and leaned forward in his chair. The bourbon had clearly begun to take effect and he was noticeably more relaxed. "The timing is suspicious too..."

"How so?"

Ash stood up and walked over to the file cabinet at the back of the room and pulled out a manila folder. He moved like molasses, slow and unhurried. He walked back over and threw the file onto the desk in front of me. "Take a look. See anything odd?"

I opened the folder and saw the Proclamation of Death signed by the Richmond medical examiner, the death registration form, signed by the Tuttle County recorder. The cause of death was respiratory failure due to cyanide poisoning, like Carl had said. I continued to flip through the paperwork in the folder but didn't see anything out of the ordinary. "What am I supposed to be looking for?"

He walked up behind me and leaned over my shoulder. I could smell the bourbon on his breath and feel the heat coming off his skin. The sensation wasn't altogether unpleasant. He flipped through the folder to a blank form that was bracketed inside the back cover of the file. "Here."

I read it out loud. "Cremation Authorization Form." I scanned the document. "Signed by Sheriff Haight."

"Like I said, the cremation was scheduled in the morning," he said, straightening up. "Standard procedure in cases like this is to bury or burn religious items along with the body. It's why the sheriff's department gave us the rosary instead of keeping it like they did with the other things."

"So," I said, turning to face Ash, "the person who came here was after the rosary?"

"I guess it's possible."

It was a bizarre theory, but it made as much sense as anything else. Somebody was clearly after something of Balzichek's; I supposed it could be his rosary. But then a thought hit me like a smack to the face.

"What?" Ash said, reading my expression.

"I just remembered something..." I said slowly. "I interviewed Balzichek's childhood pastor for the profile I'm writing about him."

"So?"

"*Pastor,*" I said, emphasizing the word. "Not priest. Balzichek wasn't Catholic."

Ash's face went slack. We looked at each other silently until he finally spoke the question we were both thinking, "Then what was he doing with a rosary?"

CHAPTER 31

Ash and I decided we needed to go straight to Sheriff Haight with this new information. For one thing, it was definitely connected to the murder investigation. For another thing, his people would have inspected the rosary beads when they came in and might be able to venture a guess why someone would want them badly enough to commit a crime to get them.

We gathered our things and were heading out of Franklin's office when we heard a loud thud come from the front of the building. We both stopped moving. There was another thud and the sound of glass breaking. My heart leaped into my throat. Ash put a finger over his lips and moved silently to the desk. He opened the third drawer and pulled out a handgun. Seeing my eyes widen, he signaled again for me to be quiet, calm.

He snuck out the door, creeping silently down the corridor. My heart was beating so hard against my chest, I thought it might pop right out. I didn't know what to do, so I followed Ash, careful to stay several steps behind him.

He turned the corner into the chapel and I heard him shout, "Don't move!" There was the sound of crunching glass under foot, another thud, and then a shot rang out. The sound was deafening.

I ran toward the sound without thinking. "Ash?" I

scanned the room for him, but it was dark. I first saw the outline of a person standing in the back corner of the room near the lectern where people stood to read tributes and eulogies. It was impossible to tell in that split second who the person was, or even if it was a man or a woman. They had a black hood over the top of their head, a black ski mask on their face, and wore baggy clothes. Ash, who was standing in the opposite corner of the room and had his gun drawn, trained on the stranger, turned at the sound of my voice. "Riley, stay back."

That second was all the person needed to turn and run out the emergency door, instantaneously setting off a blaring alarm. Ash followed out the door, as quick as lightning.

"Ash! Wait!" I went to the door, trying to raise my voice over the screeching of the alarm bell.

A few seconds later, he came back through panting heavily. His shoulders slumped as his chest heaved with breathlessness. "Damnit! He's gone..." He pounded a fist, the one not holding the gun, against the open steel door frame.

"Did you see who it was?"

He shook his head as he limped over to a keypad on the wall near the door. He punched in a code and mercifully the alarm quieted.

"Did they take anything?" I asked, looking around the room. There wasn't much in there except pews, hymnals, and some fake floral arrangements.

"I don't think so." Ash sounded thoroughly defeated. "What in the hell is going on here, Riley?"

I had absolutely no idea. But I knew instead of going to see Sheriff Haight, he'd be coming to see us. Campbell & Sons was now officially a crime scene.

As we waited for someone from Carl's office to come out and take our statements, Ash gave me the grand tour of the funeral home in the hopes that we could figure out what the intruder was after. I knew it would be a while, as Carl was still probably taking Dale Mountbatten's statement—or arresting him—and since it wasn't a true emergency, we would be bumped to the end of the list.

"Here's where we keep the bodies." Ash led me through a discreet door at the back of the chapel, beyond which was a concrete staircase leading to the morgue.

I wasn't particularly squeamish, but descending into a windowless basement full of dead people set me more on edge than I would have liked. I took a deep breath in and blew it out slowly.

"It's okay," Ash said. "It used to freak me out too, but you get used to it."

"I'm fine," I said, but as I looked around the room, I didn't think I could ever get used to this. The morgue was basically a large concrete room. It was cold down there, like probably sixty-five degrees or less, and there was a distinctly chemical scent in the air, which to me smelled like a combination of rubbing alcohol and bleach. Along the back wall there was a large piece of metal furniture that would best be described as an oversized filing cabinet. It had six drawers, each with a chunky metal handle similar to the kind you'd find on a meat locker. Those must be the refrigeration units.

In the center of the room there were two stainless steel tables that had shelves underneath with various equipment in powder blue plastic tubs. There was a tall steel cabinet on rollers with a lock on the outside, still in place.

"Is there an entrance on this floor?" I asked.

"Through here," Ash said, and walked over to a door

that I hadn't noticed. It was along the side wall of the basement, directly opposite the stairs. He dug a key from his pocket and opened the door.

"Is this door always locked?" I asked.

"Far as I know," he said, pushing it open. The doorway led directly into a set of concrete steps that sloped up sharply to ground level. I walked out, taking a deep inhalation of fresh cool air while I had the chance. I went up a few steps until I could see out behind the building into the covered portico where the hearse was parked. It was dark outside, and without any lights in the parking lot I could barely make out the white headstones that dotted the cemetery just behind the building.

Ash was right behind me on the steps and when I turned around to come back down, I almost ran straight into his chest. "Oh sorry."

He stepped up so we were on the same stair and pointed east into the darkness. "That's Sterns right there." He pointed toward the headstones. "To the right of the parking lot is First Baptist, and three doors down this way," he said, his voice low, almost a whisper, "is St. Paul's."

I nodded. My eyes were beginning to adjust to the darkness, and with his directions I realized where I was. "Got it. Obviously the thief couldn't have gotten in this way because the door was locked, right?" I said, and then added a last-minute thought, "unless they had a key."

Ash's mouth flattened into a thin line. Clearly, he didn't like the idea of one of the funeral home employees being involved.

I walked back down the steps and into the basement, the antiseptic smell hitting me with force as soon as I got inside. I could feel a stinging sensation behind my eyes. "How many people have a key to this door?"

"Three. Me, Javier, and my grandparents."

"No one else? No one with the cleaning crew or graveyard staff?"

Ash shook his head. "I don't think so."

"Hello?" We heard a voice calling from upstairs. "Tuttle County Sheriff's Department. Anyone here?" It sounded like Butter.

Ash and I went upstairs and found Butter and Sheriff Haight standing in the chapel. Carl rolled his eyes when he saw me. "I should have known you'd be mixed up in this."

I tried not to be offended.

"We got a call someone broke in here tonight?" Butter asked, looking around at the glass on the floor near the back door and the fallen podium.

I looked at Ash. This was his story to tell.

"That's right," he said and took a deep breath. "But before I tell you about the break-in, there's something else you ought to know."

Self-Care Assignment #4:
A Better You Through Daily Detox Diet™

Today we will explore the connection between our physical and emotional states of being. It should come as no surprise that the food with which we nourish our bodies nourishes our spiritual selves as well. If we choose to fuel up on empty, chemical-laden processed foods, our conscious and unconscious minds can become egocentrically obese or, worse, emotionally malnourished.

Spending just one day per week on our Daily Detox Diet™ will cleanse and purify your body while reinvigorating the light that lives within your spirit. #weightwatchersforthesoul

Daily Detox Diet™

7 a.m.: Rise and drink 60 oz. of F.L.Y. Juice™, a proprietary blend of herbs, microgreens, and the finest cupuaçu extract, found only in the most secluded rain forests of Papua New Guinea (Six 12oz. bottles, $39.99).

10 a.m.: Prepare a large bowl of ethically sourced bone broth flavored with cilantro, turmeric, ginger, and collagen hydrolysate. Be sure to say a blessing for the creatures who gave their bones in service of your detox. (F.L.Y. Bones™ soup starter, $17.99.)

12 p.m.: Lunch is a high-quality probiotic such as No Guts No Glory™ (30-day supply, $44.99), followed by a guided meditation podcast on the metaphysical benefits of denying

yourself (available for iOS or Android in the App Store, $5.99).

2 p.m.: Count out twelve pomegranate seeds, and chew each seed eleven times to honor the number eleven, the most intuitive of all numbers (companion workbook, *Add It Up: A Beginner's Guide to Numerology* by Dr. Diana Yarsborough, $24.99).

6 p.m.: Prepare another large bowl of ethically sourced bone broth, this time flavoring it with cumin, turmeric, ginger, and collagen hydrolysate for a completely different taste profile! Eat in silence, alone if possible, taking care to open your mouth just the minimum amount possible. This helps avoid the pesky bloating that can come from swallowing air while you eat.

10 p.m.: Bedtime snack is a high-quality probiotic. #yum

Do not be alarmed if you experience dizziness, tiredness, jitters, sluggishness, hyperactive bowel movements, brain fog, extreme irritability, or intense headaches. This is just trapped negative energy trying to work its way out.

Spend at least fifteen minutes journaling about how you feel after your Daily Detox Diet™, paying specific attention to the sounds emanating from your intestinal track, as these can provide great insight into the effectiveness of your detox. (Companion workbook, *Decoding Your Duodenal Sounds with Dr. Erik M. Grossmann*, $32.99.)

*

Dear Miss Ellison,

Thank you for your email. I am sorry to hear you feel the Daily Detox Diet™ represents a "reckless reduction in calories" and that you would sooner "throw yourself into the James River with weights around your ankles" than to eat something called fly bone broth. #notreallyfromflies #fliesdonthavebones I assure you it is the latest IT-superfood, according to Sustenance Concierge™ Faith T in our Nutritional Sciences department.

In any event, I certainly understand your reluctance to make such a drastic change to your eating habits. Sometimes it's best to take these things slowly, particularly if, as you say, your current diet consists of eighty-five percent cheese, fifteen percent potato chips, and fifteen percent croissants. #doesntaddup #eatsomefruit.

Yours in Loving Alignment,

Regina H,
Personal Romance Concierge™ and F.L.Y.
Guy™-in-training
Click.com

CHAPTER 32

Despite being at the newsroom late to help Holman with the Mountbatten piece and write mine about the break-in at Campbell & Sons, I woke up early the next day. I wanted to give Coltrane a little TLC before I went into work. I'd been neglecting him all week and I felt badly about it. I knew the old boy would forgive me for the price of one hard-boiled egg and one long walk before sunrise. Coltrane was easy that way. The truth of it was that the walk would do me some good too. I'd need to sleep eventually, but for now I was running on adrenaline. Today was going to be a big news day around Tuttle Corner, with Holman and me at the center of it. There was nothing wrong with enjoying a few moments of relative calm before the impending storm.

The sun was still below the horizon, its warm glow bleeding into the night sky. The peaceful exchange of power between light and darkness was a daily phenomenon made no less spectacular by its regularity. I could still make out the faint glow of Venus against the inky backdrop—a beautiful reminder of how small a place we occupy in the universe. Stargazing was in the blood of the Ellison family, a hobby my dad and granddad were both extremely passionate about. As a child, my enthusiasm for amateur astronomy was mandatory, and I'm pretty sure I was taught to spot the Big Dipper before I could walk. But my love for it was my own now. There was nothing like looking up at thousands of pinpricks of light—all of which are millions of times brighter than our sun and millions and millions of years old—to give your life a little perspective.

It wasn't cold, but chilly enough that my breath created little gray puffs as we took our usual route down Salem Street, then left onto Beach. I could see lights turning on in kitchens and bedrooms as we walked past, the gradual awakening of our town.

The grass was brown at this time of year, and with Thanksgiving just around the corner, most of the leaves had already fallen. The tidy Hamiltons had their leaves bagged in yard-waste-approved plastic bags stacked neatly at the end of their driveway. The Daltons next door clearly favored a more "natural" approach. And Oliver Washington, who lived across the street, had decided six years ago to rip out all his grass and rock his entire yard with pea gravel. He said that not only did it make his life easier, it cut down on his water bill too. This was one of the things I loved about living in Tuttle—how you kept your property was your business. There were no rules specifying length of grass or height or type of fence. If you wanted an aboveground pool, have at it. If you wanted to throw your old '64 Mustang up on blocks in your front yard, no one was going to stop you. (However, if you lived within spitting distance of Charlotte Van Stone, you'd be in for some nasty looks.) Tuttle Corner was like a person of a certain age who has been around long enough not to care about looks. We didn't have to put on airs; we knew who we were.

I turned left again onto Forest Avenue, and up on the right I could see the house Ryan and Ridley were set to move into in a few weeks. It was directly behind mine. Ryan said he bought the place because it has a full apartment in the basement where he could live, while Lizzie and Ridley took the upstairs. He said it was a way for them to live together as a family even though he and Ridley weren't together. That was six weeks ago. Now I supposed he was hoping for a different kind of arrangement.

A feeling I couldn't quite name, something north of nostalgia but south of angst, bloomed in the pit of my stomach as I thought about Ryan and Ridley and what the future would look like for them. I truly had no idea how Ridley would react when she found out about his feelings for her. If I had to guess, I'd bet she would be willing to give a relationship a try. They were a family, after all. And whether Ryan and Ridley were together or not, they were forever bonded by their deep love for and commitment to their little girl. I didn't begrudge them their happily ever after, but was it wrong that I didn't want to be a part of it? As I walked past the house that they'd soon share, I decided it wasn't. I wouldn't stand in their way, but I also didn't have to be the conduit for them to get together. If Ryan wanted a future with Ridley, he was going to have to figure it out on his own.

Feeling settled having come to that very pro-self-care conclusion, I decided to give Coltrane an extra-long walk and turned down Maple Street toward St. Paul's church. We didn't always go this route. Usually we just did the square block around my house, but given how much we were both enjoying being out, I thought, *What the hell.*

Coltrane and I were rounding the far corner back onto Forest when I saw Tom Bell of Bell Construction pulling out of his driveway. He stopped when he saw us. "Morning, Riley," he said, "I see you guys are up with the sun today."

"Hey, Tom," I said, letting Coltrane put his paws up

on Tom's truck door to say hello. "Yeah, nice out here this morning. You heading to work?"

He nodded as he scratched behind Coltrane's ears. "We're doing some work over at the Bluth property. Mary likes us to be out of there before Hank takes his 2 p.m. nap."

Mary and Hank Bluth lived in one of the oldest homes in Tuttle, just off the town square. Bell Construction did a lot of work on the older, more historic homes in the area, and they'd even been involved in a few restorations over in Williamsburg. It occurred to me that the Bluth house was probably built the same time as Rosalee's Tavern. I was still bothered by her story about the sledgehammer and the supposed basement remodel. I knew those old buildings were tricky to remodel. Plus, she'd been in that space for nine years, why renovate now? I remembered Melvin said she'd ask him to move the equipment so she could go down into the basement a couple of times a month to make plans. How long did it take to plan a basement storage room?

"Hey, have you ever done any work on the basement under Rosalee's Tavern, by any chance?"

Tom thought for a minute. "Not since Rosalee's been in there, but I did do some work on the building back when Jack Harper owned it. Why do you ask?"

"No reason," I said. "It's just I was talking to Ridley Nilsson, who's working over there now, and she mentioned something about Rosalee planning to remodel the basement to use as storage. I just wondered if Rosalee ever had you come take a look since you do so much of that kind of work?"

"No, she never got in touch. But as I recall, it was your typical colonial cellar—a big empty space, with low ceilings, cold and damp. Probably make a pretty good root cellar."

"You say it was a wide-open space?" My hackles went

up. I distinctly remember Rosalee saying the basement was full of half walls and other odd angles, and that that was the reason she needed the sledgehammer.

"Oh yeah," Tom said. "Back in the day, people used to use them as kitchens. I probably worked on a dozen or more houses like that around here. They're all about the same. Big empty rooms with stone walls, dirt floors, and wooden beams. Depending on how well they've been preserved, some of 'em are pretty neat. The Tavern's basement is pretty representative of the era. You should check it out if you can."

What a good suggestion, Tom, I thought to myself. *I think I'll just do that.*

CHAPTER 33

I walked into the newsroom and immediately knew we'd hit a home run. Normally we were a pretty laid-back office, but not today. Everyone was dressed better, walking faster, standing taller. Even stupid Spencer had trimmed his mustache and tucked in his shirt. For one shining moment, the *Tuttle Times* was the news leader. We broke a story that was certain to get national attention, despite the fact that there were several bigger news organizations following it. Not too shabby for a little weekly paper in the middle of nowhere. I felt a swell of pride for the part I'd played in getting this scoop. I just wished Flick was here to enjoy the moment with us. I hadn't heard from him since his last call and really wished he'd get in touch.

Kay was already in her office meeting with Pedro, the *Times* webmaster and tech guru, to make sure the site would be able to handle the increased traffic. AP picked up the story and asked if they could link it, so Pedro was trying to make the necessary adjustments.

I walked into Holman's office and found him with a large mug of coffee and a half-eaten bear claw on a napkin in front of him. He didn't look like he'd slept or changed clothes since I left him here late last night.

"Hey," I said. "You get any rest?"

He looked up at me, then blinked like he didn't understand

my question. I guess that answered that.

"Have you heard if Carl is still holding Dale?" I asked, taking one of the doughnuts out of the box on his credenza.

Holman's eyes followed the doughnut from the box to my mouth, and he watched with a slight frown as I took the first bite. I could tell he wanted to protest, but he looked like he was having trouble finding the words. He just stared, wide-eyed, at my cruller.

"*Holman!*" I snapped my fingers at him.

"What?"

"Is Dale Mountbatten still at the sheriff's office?" I repeated the question, despite my mouth full of food.

"No," he said. He picked up a piece of scrap paper on his desk and read off his notes. "It's all really complicated, but Carl said since the crimes Mountbatten confessed to—failing to register as a foreign agent, conspiracy to launder money, etcetera, etcetera—were federal crimes, they were out of his jurisdiction. He had nothing to charge him with in terms of the homicides. He's being called another 'person of interest' in the case, and Carl asked if they could meet again today. Mountbatten agreed."

"But Carl called the FBI, right?"

"Yes. He called it in last night. Not sure what the next step on that will be, but I imagine Dale Mountbatten is in quite a lot of trouble."

"Did he ask for a lawyer?"

"Yes. She came down from DC this morning."

"Wow," I said, swallowing down the last bit of my doughnut. "So he's still here? In Tuttle?"

Holman nodded. "He's staying over at the Ottoman Inn."

The Ottoman Inn was a six-suite bed-and-breakfast overlooking the James River, an old Georgian Colonial on the historic register of buildings. For years it had been a private home, but about ten years ago, Heather and Mike Flanagan bought it and turned it into a B&B. When they were asked about the name, as they always were, Mike said they fought for weeks about what to call the place, and then during one particularly acrimonious discussion while Mike was trying to watch the Masters Tournament on TV, he pointed toward his feet and yelled, "We can call it the goddamn *ottoman* hotel for all I care!" Heather loved the idea, and that was that.

"Any word from Rosalee?" I asked gingerly.

"Nothing."

I waited to see if Holman had any more to say on the subject, but he did not. "Okay," I said, walking toward the door. "Well, I'm going to do a little more digging on 'Aunt Scheiner' and see if I can find someone who might have seen her going in or coming out of the funeral home. I'm also going to follow up on Colonel Mustard Enterprises and see what I can find out there."

I didn't mention to Holman that I also planned to check out the basement of Rosalee's Tavern. I wasn't sure why I decided to keep that from him; I guess maybe I just didn't feel like arguing about Rosalee again. "Why don't you go home for a little bit? You look exhausted."

"Mother called this morning to congratulate us on the story," he said, ignoring my suggestion. "And she told me how much she liked you. She says she thinks you are nice."

I felt an inner flush of happiness. "Wow, tell her thank yo—"

"I told her that calling a person nice is about as illustrative as calling them human. I gave her a selection of other words she could use to describe you, such as inquisitive, polite, intelligent, high-strung, slightly disorganized, quick to anger—"

"Okay thanks," I said, cutting him off. "Tell Camilla I said hi back!"

Holman gave me his trademark blink, twice. "Well, technically she didn't say *hi* to you, as I said, she called you—"

I walked out and closed the door behind me before he could finish that sentence. Or that list.

CHAPTER 34

Carl had scheduled another press conference for 4 p.m. That gave me enough time to follow up on the stolen-property story and maybe even get Ridley to let me sneak down and check out the basement of the Tavern. I was bicycling around town today because Ivan still had Oscar, and I was on my way over to Campbell & Sons when I saw Ash walking through the park toward me. Perfect, I thought, this would save me a trip.

He had sunglasses on, so I couldn't tell if he was looking at me as I waved. He didn't wave back, so I called out his name. No response. As we got closer, I waved my arm comically like I was signaling a plane. "Ahoy there!" I said (I inexplicably tend to make Dad jokes around cute guys—it's a problem). But he didn't even crack a smile.

Ash stopped walking when he got about two feet from me. I slowed down and stopped my bike.

"I can't believe you," he said in a tone of voice that could only be described as disgusted.

"What?" I was genuinely taken aback.

"You totally screwed me last night!"

Old Mrs. Deaver, who was walking her two Chihuahuas past us at that very moment, let out a little yelp and clutched Mr. Deaver's arm. The four of them hurried away from us as fast as they could.

"What're you talking about?" I lowered my voice, hoping he would follow suit.

"That article you posted?"

"Yeah?"

"Do you have any idea how much that is going to hurt my family's business? Or my grandparents?" he scoffed. "What am I saying...you don't care about that. You just had to get your precious scoop, hell-be-damned who it hurts."

I felt blood rush to my face. "Are you serious? Did you honestly think I wasn't going to report what happened last night? I was an eyewitness to a crime. I'd have been fired for gross incompetence if I didn't write that up!"

"If the Converse fits..."

"Hey," I took a step closer and pointed a finger at his chest. "You don't get to talk to me like that. I was just doing my job."

"You know what?" Ash said, switching from irate to ice cold in two seconds flat. "That's fine. You're the kind of person who puts her own career ahead of people's feelings. Now I know. I'll just file that little piece of information away for the future: Riley Ellison cannot be trusted. Good to know."

I was so angry, I almost couldn't speak. *Almost.* "I will have you know that is not at all what I—"

"Save it." Ash cut me off. "I really don't care. Now if you'll excuse me, I have to go see my grandmother and reassure her that her only living grandson hasn't tanked the family business while she's been caring for her dying husband." He brushed past me and continued on his way.

I followed him, calling after him several times, but he just kept going. Finally, riding alongside him, I grabbed the elbow of his shirt. "Hey, just stop a second—please."

When he finally stopped, I was caught up short by the

pained expression on his face. Gone was the arrogance and ire of a few minutes ago; now Ash just looked sad. "What?" he asked, his voice weary.

"I'll go with you." I'm not sure why I said it—it just popped out of my mouth.

Ash looked about as surprised as I was at the offer.

"I can help explain to her what happened, or at least provide backup for your explanation. Your grandmother knows me and knows that I work for the paper. I think in Tuttle there's a certain amount of trust that comes with that."

He looked across the park at two men who were heading toward us. One was holding a camera. "More reporters," Ash mumbled. "C'mon, let's go before they get here. I've had just about enough of the free press for one day."

The ride over to the long-term care facility was an awkward one. I tried to make small talk—I asked Ash where he was staying while he was in town, did he have any friends here, had he decided how long he was going to stay—but each question was met with stony silence. Clearly, Ash Campbell knew how to hold a grudge. During the entire ten-minute ride, the only thing he said to me was, "You sure ask a lot of questions."

Patricia Campbell, who, as it turned out, had not read my story online, reacted with a subdued sort of surprise when we explained all that had happened over the past twenty-four hours at the funeral home. Her eyes widened and narrowed at different points in the story, but when we finished talking, she took her grandson's hand in hers and said, "It's such a blessing to have you here to take care of all of this, Ashley." Then her gaze returned to her husband of fifty-four years who lay, barely conscious, in the bed beside her. Patricia's priorities had shifted, and it was clear she didn't want to think about the family business. We stayed for a few minutes longer, and when the nurse came in to check Franklin's vitals, we said goodbye.

Back in Ash's truck, both of us sat silent with the sad reality of what was now clearer than ever. His grandpa was not going to recover, and his grandmother was not going to be able to run Campbell & Sons, at least not for a while. It would be up to Ash whether or not to carry on the family business. He'd have to choose between the future he wanted for himself and the past his family had created. I didn't envy that choice.

"I'm sorry," I said, turning to face him.

His head was lying against the back of the headrest and he rolled it toward me. "No," he said, his voice soft, "I'm sorry." He reached a hand out in my direction, rolled his palm upward. "Can we be friends again?"

I looked at his outstretched hand for a couple of seconds. Could we be friends again? Were we ever? Ash was cruel one moment, sweet the next. He switched between cold and flirty and vulnerable like he was changing lanes on a highway. Every time I thought I had him figured out, he did or said something that put me on shaky ground. But despite all that, there was something about him I liked. Before I could think too much about what it meant, I reached over and put my hand in his.

He closed his fingers around mine and gave them a gentle squeeze. "Good," Ash said, giving me the full glory of those honey-colored eyes. "Because if I'm going to be living here now, I'm going to need all the friends I can get."

Chapter 35

When I got back to the office, it was pretty much mayhem. Calls and emails had been coming in from all over the country about the Mountbatten story—requests for comments, verification of facts, link requests, etc. Kay was on the phone with her door closed. Stupid Spencer, who had been assigned to cover the updates coming out of the sheriff's office (it was now all hands on deck with this story), said Dale was meeting with Carl at the sheriff's office again this morning. District Attorney Lindsey Davis was with them, as well as four other individuals thought to be federal investigators and possibly Mountbatten's attorney. *Carl must be having a day*, I thought.

No one over at the sheriff's office would comment officially, but speculation was that assuming Mountbatten made the same admissions as he had when he spoke to us, the federal agents would file paperwork with the courts to file charges and probably take away his passport. Being that it was Friday afternoon, I doubted anything would get processed before the weekend.

Back at my desk, I checked my messages and was glad to hear there was one from a Nicole Breedlove with the prothonotary's office (a fancy name for the chief clerk in some jurisdictions) in New Castle County, Delaware, the municipality where Colonel Mustard Enterprises had been incorporated. I had left her a message the night before asking for some information I had a right to under the Sunshine law, which required that certain information from government agencies be available to the public. Nicole said she'd be happy to help. When I called her back, she confirmed, as I had suspected, that Dale Mountbatten had filed a DBA (doing business as) certificate under the name Colonel Mustard Enterprises nine years ago just before he moved Rosalee down to Tuttle Corner. She agreed to fax me a copy of the certificate.

This was a big deal. Even though Dale Mountbatten had basically told us this much, up until now all we had was his word. And I didn't trust Dale Mountbatten's sudden desire to come clean. It wasn't that I didn't believe him about the foreign money and scheme to launder it, I suspected he had an ulterior motive for his sudden confessional. It didn't make sense to me that a guy who spent the better part of a decade breaking the law for monetary gain would give it all up so easily. He said it was because Rosalee killed his wife and was trying to set him up to take the blame for that, but I wasn't so sure. There was too much finger-pointing going on between Rosalee and Dale. Neither was acting innocent. And neither seemed to care one bit about Justin Balzichek. Which is what made it all the more odd that someone out there, presumably a third person involved in this whole mess, wanted Balzichek's things badly enough to commit fraud to get them. A rosary and twenty-eight cents in coins wasn't exactly a treasure. I couldn't understand why someone would want to steal them badly enough to risk being found out. If Ash had been any more knowledgeable or experienced, he would have asked the person for their ID. What would they have done then?

On a hunch, I decided to swing by St. Paul's church, the

one that was just down from Campbell & Sons. I thought Father Dunn might have some insight for me on why someone might want to steal a rosary.

"The rosary is basically a meditation on the life of Christ," Father Dunn said as I followed him from pew to pew helping him put the hymnals into their correct spot after that morning's Mass.

"Is there any other use for them? Something less...pious, perhaps?" I asked carefully.

Father Dunn looked concerned. "I'm not sure what you mean, Riley."

"Oh no, it's not for me," I said. "It's a story I'm working on for the paper."

His face lit up like a Christmas tree. "A story on the tradition of the rosary!" He clapped his hands together. "How joyous!"

"Oh well..." I said, sheepishly. "It's not exactly that kind of story."

"No?"

"I mean, well, it is about a rosary...but more about a crime that someone committed using one..."

He sucked in a sharp breath and then crossed himself. Father Dunn was known for being a little dramatic. People in town still told the story of the Palm Sunday picnic when a king snake slithered into the He is Risen! Balloon Filling Station and Father Dunn was convinced it was Satan himself. When Millie Hedron grabbed it behind the head and took it down by the river, he insisted on taking her straight back to the church and dosing her in Holy water.

"It's nothing to worry about," I said, trying to calm him (although I'm pretty sure if I told him the rest of the details, he might conclude that Satan was once again among us). "I was just wondering if there's any reason you can think of why a person would want to take someone else's rosary beads? Are they valuable?"

Father Dunn sat down as he thought about my question. "Value, of course, is in the eye of the beholder. My own rosary was given to me on my first communion by my beloved grandmother, who has since passed, so to me it's priceless."

"But there's no intrinsic value, like they're not made of precious metals or anything like that?"

"No," he said, shaking his head. "Not usually. There are artifacts, of course, rosaries from throughout history that would have some value. And I suppose there are probably some out there adorned with valuable stones or gold and silver and whatnot, but the real value of the rosary comes from within. The key is what it means to each individual person."

I stilled, a thought slowing starting to take shape in my mind. "Say that again, Father."

He looked confused. "I said, there are rosaries from throughout history—"

"No," I said, startling poor Father Dunn. "Sorry. Not that part—what you said at the end."

He knitted his brow together. "I said the key to a rosary is what it means to the individual."

"That's it!" I said, running for the door. "Thank you, Father! You've been such a huge help!"

"A key?" Ash said, looking at me like I was crazy.

"Yes, I think the rosary was either holding a key or possibly the key itself." I held up the results of my Google search to show him. "Look at all of these. Every single one has a mechanism by which you can slide the top of the crucifix over or unscrew a tiny little invisible screw on the bottom to reveal a hidden compartment."

He took the phone from me and studied the images. I moved around to his side of the desk so I could look with him. "And these," I said, taking the phone and calling up the search I'd done for crucifix keys, "you slide over this shield, and the sides of the crosses have been carved into the shape of a key. It's very subtle, not something you'd necessarily notice if you didn't know what you were looking for."

Ash studied the pictures silently. Every now and then he'd enlarge a photo and bring the phone closer to his face.

"Did Balzichek's rosary look anything like these? Could it have had a hidden chamber?" I asked.

"I suppose it's possible," he said as he handed back my phone. "It was bigger than most of the other rosaries I've seen, but I'm not Catholic. I'm no expert."

"See, that's the thing. Most people here aren't. Carl isn't. And even if you were, it's not like you'd be suspicious of someone hiding something inside a rosary. It's kind of brilliant, actually."

"If it is a key, what do you think it opens?" Ash swiveled his chair around to face me.

I'd thought about that on my bike over here from St. Paul's. "The obvious answer is some sort of a safe or safe deposit box."

"Maybe it contains proof of who murdered him—like in the movies where the person leaves a letter saying, 'If you're reading this, then I'm probably already dead.' "

I laughed. "I know this all sounds a little far-fetched, but if there's one thing I've learned over the past few months, it's that you just never know."

"You going to tell the sheriff your theory?"

"Definitely."

"They probably have pictures of it in the evidence locker. Maybe someone over there could blow up the images."

"Good idea," I said, putting my phone back into my purse. "I'll let you know what he says."

Ash stood up to walk me out. "Thanks for...well, for everything you're doing," he said as we got to the front door of Campbell & Sons. "I know it's not all for me or anything, but..." he let his sentence trail off.

I felt a blush beginning. "Just doing my job." I smiled. "But I hope it'll help."

I was halfway down the steps toward my bicycle when he called out, "Listen, after this is all over, maybe I could take you out for a drink to say thanks or something?"

"Fraternize with a reporter? You sure about that?"

He laughed. "Maybe I'm reconsidering my position on reporters?"

I slung my purse across my chest and climbed onto my bike. "If you're not careful there, Ash, I just may start to think you're actually a nice guy."

CHAPTER 36

I was pedaling my way back to the newsroom when I saw Ryan in the Sanford Farm & Home delivery truck turning down my street. He was probably dropping off my monthly dog food order. I had a couple of minutes to spare, so I turned to follow him. I figured if I caught him in time maybe he could lug the bags inside instead of me.

"How's that for timing?" he said as I rode into the driveway behind him. He smiled, his dimples appearing like two adorable parentheses around his mouth. Even in the dorky white golf shirt with the store emblem embroidered on the sleeve, Ryan looked cute enough to be the lead singer of a boy band.

"Hey," I said, leaning my bike up against the house. "Want to do me a favor?"

"Always."

"Mind bringing the bags into the garage for me?"

"Of course not," he said. "By the way, where's your car?"

I flared my nostrils. "Long story."

"Sounds juicy." He gave me an easy smile as I opened my garage and let Coltrane out so he could come jump on his favorite person in the world other than me (and maybe Ridley). After a few rounds of "Who's a good doggie?" Ryan slung a large bag of dog food over his shoulder and carried it over to the back of the garage.

After he dropped the second bag in the designated spot, he handed me the invoice to sign. “Hey, did you have a chance to think about what I should do with Ridley yet?”

Damn. I had hoped he would drop the whole thing.

“Ryan,” I said, unable to look him in the eye. “I just don't think I can play cupid for you two. It's too weird.”

“What do you mean ‘too weird’?”

“What do you mean ‘What do you mean’?” I didn't want to have to spell it out. Surely he could understand why I would feel weird helping him get closer with Ridley.

He let out a nervous laugh. “I'm confused, Riles.”

I sighed. He was going to make me say it. “Listen,” I said, intensely studying a crack in my garage floor. “I want you to be happy. I want Ridley to be happy. And I definitely want Lizzie to be happy.” I paused to figure out how to say the next part. “But it's kind of hard for me to see you... falling in love with someone else, okay? There. I said it. Are you happy?” It all came out in a rush. I wanted to get this conversation over with as quickly as possible.

Ryan didn't say anything for so long that I actually looked up to make sure he was okay. When I did, I found him looking at me with a strange expression. Gone was the laid-back smile from before. Replacing it was a look somewhere between frustration and anger. “What are you doing to me here, Riles?”

“What? Nothing—”

“I beg you for months to take me back and you refuse and now just when I'm finally ready to move on, you tell me you can't stand to see me with Ridley...”

“No,” I said, my defensive reflex kicking in. “That's not what I'm saying.”

“Then what are you saying?” He crossed his arms in front of his chest.

"It's just...I mean, it's just that I know you're moving on, but you can't come to me for advice on this stuff."

"Why not?"

"Because...it's..." I was frustrated because I knew what I wanted to say but was having trouble finding a way to say it that didn't sound hypocritical. It had all seemed so clear and reasonable to me on my walk this morning. "I just can't be there for you in that way—"

"Are we friends or not, Riley?" He sounded straight-up angry now. He rarely called me Riley. It was always Riles or Ri or Sweets or Sugar...

"Of course we're friends—"

"Then what's the problem? Friends are supposed to help friends, right?"

"Yeah, but—" I was getting confused now. It felt like he was twisting my words. Just because we were friends, did that mean I had to give him relationship advice?

"Ah," he said, sounding like he'd just solved the case. "Maybe this doesn't have anything to do with *friendship*?"

"What?" I snapped.

He raised his eyebrows.

"Oh, you think it's because I'm sitting at home pining for you or something like that?" I rolled my eyes.

"Maybe." He shrugged. "I mean, you don't have anyone right now. Maybe you see what Ridley and I have and it makes you wonder about what could have been. The baby, buying a house...I mean, you're not getting any younger and I've heard girls' clocks start ticking..."

I opened my mouth, but no sound came out. Was he kidding me? *Clock-ticking?* I was barely twenty-five! Besides, I was the one who'd been walking around town quoting T. Swift for months now, saying that we were never, ever, ever getting back together.

"I can assure you that's not the case," I said through gritted teeth.

"You know," he said, a patronizing sort of diplomacy dripping from each word. "I never really thought about it before, but it's got to be hard for you to see me and Ridley moving on while you're all alone."

"I am not all alone—"

"No, of course not. You have Coltrane, your job, your parents." He stopped as if he'd exhausted the entirety of my life by listing three things, one of which was a dog. Before I could open my mouth to defend myself, he cocked his head to the side and put a hand on my shoulder. "You're a great girl, Riles. Don't worry, you'll find somebody eventually."

If I was a cartoon character, this is where my head would have spun around and blown off. A flurry of comebacks swam through it, but the smugness in Ryan's voice told me getting angry would only strengthen his unbelievably arrogant belief that I was somehow still in love with him. "I'm so relieved you think so."

"And now I can see why you don't want to give me advice about Ridley," he said, oblivious to my sarcasm. "Sorry I asked."

I would not be responsible for my actions if he stayed here much longer. "Okay, well, I should get back to work!"

He gave me a sad little smile that seemed to say *Be brave, little Princess,* and I swallowed my outrage so I didn't punch him in the face. Fortunately, before he could say anything else, my phone rang.

Ryan waved goodbye as I checked the display. It was Holman.

"Hey."

"What's wrong? You sound upset."

That was one word for it, but the last thing I wanted to

do was talk about it with Holman. “I’m fine,” I said. “What’s up?”

“Carl called and wants to see us before the press conference. Can you meet me over there in ten minutes?”

“Yeah, fine.”

“You sure you’re okay?”

I sighed. “I don’t know what I am, Holman.”

“Well, I do. You’re a reporter,” he said in that matter-of-fact way of his. “And you’re going to be late if you don’t get moving.”

There were times when you just couldn’t argue with Will Holman’s particular brand of logic.

CHAPTER 37

"First off," Carl said, "have either of you heard from Rosalee?"

Both Holman and I shook our heads no.

"Okay." He seemed relieved and disappointed at the same time. "What I'm about to tell you is pretty much what I'm going to announce at the press conference, but I wanted you to have it first. I want to make sure the reporting out there is accurate, and I trust you to get it right."

"Thanks, Carl," I said.

"Don't thank me," he said. "This isn't a gift. That leak from a few days ago? I don't want that repeated, so this time I am controlling the information much more tightly."

I shut my mouth and took out my notebook.

"I'm going to ask you not to report certain things I tell you, at least not yet. But as soon as we're ready to release this publicly, you can run it."

It was a tricky thing agreeing to not report information in exchange for a scoop. On the one hand, we didn't want to obstruct Carl's investigation by printing something that could make it difficult to catch the killer or killers. On the other hand, we had a responsibility to our readers. It was a complicated ethical dilemma, and I was glad Holman was there to answer for me.

"Okay," Holman said. "Deal."

Carl gave us both a long look and then nodded for me to close the door to his office since I was standing closest.

"A lot of what I'm sharing at the press conference today is stuff you guys already know. Dale Mountbatten has come forward with new information pertaining to the death of his wife and Justin Balzichek, etcetera, etcetera. You already know all that because he stupidly decided to go to the press before coming in and talking to me." Carl rolled his eyes.

Dale Mountbatten's bid to control the narrative around his wife's death had been both transparent and effective. Getting out there with his side of the story—that just happened to point the finger directly at Rosalee—was sure to garner some points in the court of public opinion. He turned himself in for financial crimes, which made him appear repentant, apologetic. When in reality, he knew that day I showed up at his house and mentioned Colonel Mustard Enterprises that he was going to be exposed. Coming out ahead of the story in the press was smart, and it also gave him the perfect opportunity to blame everything on Rosalee. I can see why it annoyed Carl.

"I'm sure there will be a lot of questions about what's gonna happen next with Mountbatten's federal case, none of which I'm going to answer. I couldn't even if I wanted to, and that's the honest truth."

"Has the FBI shared anything with you?" I asked.

He shook his head. " 'Course not. They don't share with the local yokels. My guess is once they confirm some of the things he's told them about his foreign contacts, they'll charge him pretty quick. Wouldn't be surprised if something happened early next week. The money laundering stuff is another issue. Either way, it's not my problem." He paused as I finished writing. "I'm going to go public with the fact that we are looking at the possibility that Greer Mountbatten and Justin Balzichek were killed by two different people, like we talked about, Riley. And I'm going to announce that Balzichek was poisoned."

He paused again, letting us catch up.

"Now," Carl said, scooting forward in his chair, "Riley, I told you the other day that it was cyanide."

"Right," I said. I hadn't told Holman yet, so this was the first time he was hearing this information.

"What I didn't tell you was that the medical examiner knew it was cyanide even before the results of the tox screen came back because he noticed a strong smell of burnt almonds when he was doing the autopsy."

"Is that what cyanide smells like?"

"Apparently."

"Interesting," I said, making a note.

"But there was also something else," Carl said.

He was clearly building up to some kind of dramatic reveal. It was annoying, but I forced myself to wait patiently like a good reporter and not someone who used to dare him to eat rubber cement in preschool.

"Balzichek's stomach contents revealed undigested almonds and pastry dough."

I broke out in goose bumps from the top of my head down both arms. "Almond croissants."

Carl nodded, his face grim.

I didn't even turn my head toward Holman. I knew he had to know how bad this looked for Rosalee. He'd wanted her to be innocent so badly, and with each new piece of evidence it was getting harder and harder to believe that she was. My heart hurt for him. I knew how infrequently he allowed himself to care about people, how few friends he had, and how he hated to be wrong about anything, least of all something like this.

After a moment, Holman cleared his throat. When he spoke, I could tell that his voice was stiffer than usual, more stilted. “Was the medical examiner able to tell whether or not the poison had been administered via the pastry?”

“That’s what we’ve been waiting on,” Carl said. “We’ve known for some time about the stomach contents and the cyanide, but it took some additional testing of the remnants of the undigested food to know for sure, but yes. Results came in today. Dr. Mendez feels he can say with a high degree of certainty that’s how the cyanide got into his system.”

I wrote down what Carl said exactly, my forearm beginning to cramp from writing so fast.

“There’s more, and this is a big one,” Carl said. “There’s evidence to support the idea that Balzichek killed Greer Mountbatten.”

Both Holman and I stopped writing and looked at Carl in astonishment. “What evidence?” I finally asked.

Carl opened a file on his desk. “The blood found in the vehicle is his blood type, AB Negative, relatively rare. We’re waiting on the DNA results, which should be back in about two weeks. Also, we were able to match a print left in the mud at Riverside Park to Balzichek’s shoes. We also got her cell records that show a call in the hours before she went missing from a burner phone with an 804 area code, presumably Balzichek’s. We don’t have a complete picture, but it’s sure starting to look like he might be guilty.”

“Then who killed him?” I asked.

“We’re still working on that,” Carl said.

“You’re going to announce all of this today?”

“Nothing about stomach contents, nothing about cyanide. I’m going to keep it general during the press conference and use the word *poison*. If and when we get a suspect in for questioning, I want to be able to see just how much they know. Someone comes in knowing about the cyanide or what Balzichek ate just before he died, that'll tell us a lot. If every little detail is splashed all over the news, it won't be so easy."

I had a feeling he was going to say that, so I wasn't surprised as much as I was disappointed. Kay Jackson would give up her firstborn for a scoop like this.

"I'm releasing the details about the shoe print and the blood type and that we're working off the theory that Justin Balzichek may be responsible," Carl finished.

"But Balzichek was obviously just a hired gun—or sledgehammer, I guess," I said. "The real question is who hired him?"

Carl turned to Holman, who looked like he wasn't even listening to us anymore. "Maybe, maybe not. Coulda been that Balzichek and Greer had a dispute of their own, and he got mad and killed her. At this point, we just don't know anything about motive one way or another."

I looked at Holman to see if he was planning to contribute anything else to this conversation. "Will? Do you have any questions for Carl?"

"She's not the only person in the world who makes almond croissants," Holman said, his voice one notch below pleading.

Carl looked at me, closed his eyes, and gave a gentle shake of the head. When he spoke his voice was soft and compassionate. "As hard as it may be for us to believe, Will, it's looking more and more like Rosalee could be behind Balzichek's murder."

I could tell by his tone that Carl must have figured out that Holman had feelings for Rosalee. Then again, Holman was the kind of man who didn't just wear his emotions on his sleeve; he wore them as a full body suit.

"I'm just saying it's important not to jump to conclusions," Holman said. "If someone were trying to set her up, wouldn't that be the perfect way to do it?"

"Fair point. But let me assure you we will not be doing any conclusion jumping. We are going to follow the evidence wherever it may lead, and when the time comes to charge someone, you'd better believe it'll be because we feel confident we've got the right person."

Holman nodded, having done his level best to stand up for Rosalee.

Carl looked at the clock on his phone. "I gotta get going." He stood up. "Remember, hold everything about the cyanide and croissants. As soon as I'm okay with releasing it, I'll let you know."

I wanted to tell Carl my theory about the rosary, but Mayor Lancett and Toby were already outside his office door. Mayor Lancett gave me and Holman a pleasant hello, while Toby, who wore track pants, a T-shirt that read "Real Deal Flex Appeal," and a houndstooth blazer, said, "My, my, aren't you just everywhere these days, Riley Ellison." His sneering tone told me he didn't mean it as a compliment.

"I see you're all dressed up today." I smiled sweetly.

Toby preened at the compliment. "I do try to look my best, especially when we've got so many out-of-town visitors. I like to think of myself in some ways as the face of Tuttle Cor—"

"Toby!" Mayor Lancett snapped her fingers at him like he was a Yorkipoo. And like a Yorkipoo, he scrambled after her on his stubby little legs.

CHAPTER 38

Holman said he wanted to be alone for a few minutes, so we agreed to meet back for the press conference, which was scheduled to start in fifteen minutes. I found a spot on a bench in Memorial Park and was about to start writing the lede for the press conference story when my phone rang. The call was from a 202 area code. Washington, DC.

"Friend of Jay? This is Ivan from garage."

"Hey, Ivan," I said, relieved. Maybe this call meant my car was finished and I could go pick it up. "What's up?"

"Your bill."

I laughed; he didn't.

"What we have here is worst-case scenario. When your timing chain break, the valves and pistons collide like in... what was that show? You know with the nerds?"

"Um," I said, a little thrown off. "*The Big Bang Theory*?"

"Yes. I loved that show—*bazinga!*"

He laughed; I didn't.

"Oh, well, maybe you have to be there. Anyhow, the valves and pistons collide in big bang and start poking holes in engine block."

I had no idea what he was talking about, but it sounded expensive. "So what do we do?"

"Well," he said, "this is up to you. Ivan can fix and it'll

run you about three, maybe three and a half, four thousand dollars."

Four thousand dollars? I did not have four thousand dollars. I cradled my head in my free hand. "Please tell me there's another option."

"Yes. Always other option," Ivan said merrily.

"Okay. What is it?"

"Option two is sell car."

"Sell the car? Are you serious?"

"I'm sorry, friend of Jay. I wish I had better news for you. Maybe you think it over, yes?"

"Yes," I said sulkily. "I will. Thanks, Ivan."

"You have beautiful weekend." Just before he hung up, he said, "By the way, Jay call this morning to check on car. Jay is good man. You have good friend in him."

I laughed, in spite of myself. It had been quite a day in the love life of Riley Ellison. I'd been sort of asked out by a mercurial funeral home director, pitied by my ex-boyfriend who thought I was still in love with him, and now my mechanic was telling me what a good man my other ex-boyfriend was.

"Why you laugh?"

"No, you're right," I said. "Jay is a good man."

"Ahhhh." There was a twinkle in Ivan's voice. "I see. You have the hots for him." His otherwise charming Eastern European accent meant that every time he used a word that began with the letter h, it sounded like he was hocking a loogie. *You chhhhave the chhhhots for chhhhhim.*

"No! That is not—"

"Yes. Yes," he said, confidently. "Ivan is almost as good at diagnosing relationships as he is diagnosing car. Back in Bulgaria I was like Oprah."

I started to argue but then realized the absurdity of this

conversation. "I think we're going to have to agree to disagree on this one."

"It's okay. I think he might have hots for you too. He was very concerned about your car, if you know what I mean."

I didn't, but thankfully at that exact moment, I saw Holman walking toward me. I told Ivan I'd call him later with my decision about the car. Holman sat next to me on the bench, his perfect posture somehow even straighter and stiffer in light of his current state of mind.

"You okay?" I asked.

"I just don't understand how I could have been so wrong about her."

I hoped by just being there with him I could lift some of his disappointment or at least share in it. After a few moments, I said, "When we like somebody, sometimes we make excuses for them. I did it for years—am still probably doing it—with Ryan. And Rosalee is tough...she's manipulative and—" I broke off. I knew I had to be careful not to insult her too much. Holman was still very much holding onto the belief that she was a decent person. I tried to think of what Regina H would say. "Well, she's like a psychic vampire."

"A what?" Holman looked alarmed.

"A psychic vampire. Someone who drains your energy by manipulating or charming you into...oh, forget it." I lost steam halfway through the explanation. Psychic vampires were really outside my emotional IQ. "She played you, Will. It sucks and that's all there is to it."

Holman blinked hard, twice, and when he spoke it seemed like he'd put his Rosalee-feelings away for the moment. "Okay. So what was it you were going to tell Carl about the rosary?"

I explained to him my theory about there being a key

hidden inside the rosary or possibly the crucifix being the key itself. "I've been thinking about it and—this is wild speculation, by the way," I admitted, "but I'm bothered by Mountbatten's sudden decision to unburden himself to Sheriff Haight. It's true, I was onto the whole Colonel Mustard Enterprises thing and would have probably eventually written about it, but it would have taken me a while to prove it. By then he could have covered his tracks or fled to another country, for that matter."

"And he lives in Washington, DC. He could have walked into the FBI office—it's under their purview anyway," Holman added.

"Right. It's like he wanted to come to Tuttle Corner. We know he's been laundering money through the Tavern for years...what if there's something else here that he wants?"

Holman's mouth flattened into a thin line. "Rosalee."

"What? No, I don't think so," I said. "I was thinking more along the lines of something tangible."

"Like what?"

"I don't know, like what if Dale bought some gold or silver? Maybe he had more money than he could run through the butter distributor without risking raising a red flag." I was again in wild-speculation territory. "Or I guess he could also just have stashed some actual cash. Remember that case of the mobster who hid millions inside the drywall of his crappy little house in Miami?"

"And you think the rosary found on Balzichek when he died held the key to a safe in Rosalee's Tavern?"

"I think it's possible. Dale clearly has another reason for coming all the way down here. Maybe it's Rosalee, but given that he's just ratted her out to the sheriff, I'd guess not. If I had a bunch of cash or gold that I was trying to hide from the government and my wife, I certainly wouldn't keep it in a bank safe deposit box, let alone in my home."

"Then who was the person who stole the rosary from Campbell & Sons?"

"I don't know. Maybe someone Dale is working with? I showed Ash a picture of Rosalee, and he said it definitely wasn't her."

Holman was quiet as he thought. "If what you're supposing is true, then maybe Dale was the one who killed Balzichek for the key!" Holman came to life. "Yes. This makes sense. What if he knew Balzichek had the key and killed him for it using a tainted croissant because he knew that would implicate Rosalee?" Holman started pacing back in forth in front of me. "Dale kills Justin and then can't find the key because it was hidden in the rosary. So he invents a reason to come down to Tuttle Corner so he can steal the key before it gets cremated along with Balzichek's body." He was talking faster and faster. "If the key is to a safe that contains cash or something just as good as cash, like gold, he could get it and be on a plane to Singapore before he's even charged with anything!"

"Well, yeah," I said, a little uncomfortable with all the leaps Holman was making. He wasn't usually a leap-to-conclusion kind of guy. He was usually a stickler for data collection, followed by analysis. In fact, he'd treated me to several lectures on the subject during my training. "But there are lots of 'ifs' there, one of them being, if it was Dale's key, why would Balzichek have it?"

It was like Holman couldn't hear me. I could practically see the little gears inside his head churning. "Yes, this makes sense. I'll bet it was Dale who killed Justin Balzichek!"

"Holman," I said, standing up to get his attention. "I think we need to slow down a little. I was just thinking out loud, trying out some theories...we don't even know for sure that the rosary contains a key."

But I'd already lost Holman to his fantasy world in which he saved Rosalee from certain doom. "It must have some value if someone went to the trouble of stealing it."

As soon as the words were out of his mouth, Holman and I looked at each other, both of us remembering the same thing at the exact same moment. I said it first. "Rosalee had a key made at Sanford Farm & Home on the day she bought the sledgehammer."

"Maybe that's just a coincidence?" Holman said, his voice shrinking back from the excitement of a second ago.

"I don't believe in coincidences." I crossed my arms in front of my chest. "And neither do you."

CHAPTER 39

As it turned out, our argument would have to wait because it was time for the press conference to begin. Holman and I made our way through the growing crowd toward the front/side of the courthouse steps where I'd stood for the first press conference. There were even more reporters than had been here then, and there were even a few TV crews. News of a prominent lobbyist coming forward to help with the investigation into his wife's murder even though it meant admitting to financial wrongdoing and exposing himself to federal prosecution was apparently more newsworthy than the murder itself. I guess everyone loves a martyr.

Toby stood front and center, guarding the steps like a bouncer. Unlike a bouncer, he was barely taller than your average sixth grader and tragically out of shape. But he was trying to look the part, so he had on dark sunglasses (even though it was cloudy), and I could have sworn that I saw the shadow of a wire coming out from behind one of his ears. Lord only knows what it was connected to.

Carl came out flanked by Butter and Wilmore, just like the last time, and thanked his department again. He sounded nervous, but maybe it was just because I knew he was. He gave a recap of the two open investigations and then delivered the new information. The crowd of reporters was silent as he spoke. He detailed the facts about Balzichek's poisoning, the theft of his personal belongings, the shoe print, etc. It wasn't until he got to the information about Dale Mountbatten that reporters began murmuring and stirring. Holman and I already had all the information, so when Carl finished his prepared remarks and began taking questions, Holman left to go back to the office to start writing. I stayed to make sure we didn't miss anything.

We didn't. After fifteen solid minutes of far more questions than answers (Carl was on-point with "I'm not at liberty to discuss/elaborate on/divulge that, as the investigation is still very much ongoing"), Carl ended the press conference and the crowd began to dissipate. I was on the far side of the park, closest to the Tavern. Since Ridley was serving only breakfast and lunch, they were long since closed, but I wondered if I might be able to catch her there cleaning up and ask her if I could take a peek into the cellar. Melvin said Butter had been down there, but I still wanted to have a look myself. No offense to Butter or anything, but unless there was a snack bar down there, I didn't necessarily trust him to be all that thorough.

I walked over to the Tavern, but all the lights were off, doors locked. I remembered that Rosalee/Ridley's office was in the back of the restaurant, so I walked around to the back. No luck. And the back door was locked too.

It was just starting to get dark outside. I should probably have gone back to the newsroom to help Holman write up the article about the press conference, but the truth was he didn't really need my help with it. Besides, knowing him, it was probably already done and logged.

I sat down on a bench facing the parking lot behind the town square. It was a cloudy night and the air was heavy with the sort of humidity that signaled an impending storm.

Nights like these always made me think of my granddaddy and how whenever he was babysitting me and it would storm, I'd cry and insist I couldn't possibly sleep. He always had the same response. "Let's just go see about that storm," he'd say and bring me out on the front porch of the house. He'd wrap me in a blanket and we'd sit on the porch swing and he'd point out what was happening in the sky. He talked to me about how lightning was really just a giant spark of electricity, like the shock I got when I wore fuzzy slippers on the carpet and then touched the doorknob. He explained how thunder is the sound of the lightning and then how speed and light traveled at different rates. He'd tell me all about nimbus clouds and cirrus clouds and cumulus clouds, and on and on and on until eventually I got tired and begged to go back to bed. I don't know if it was his intention to bore me to sleep, but whatever it was, it worked.

When I got older and was no longer afraid, I asked him about why he did that instead of just telling me a storm was God bowling like all my friends' parents did. I remember he turned to me with that special look he reserved only for me, a perfect balance of adoration and amusement, and said, "I didn't ever want you to be afraid of something because you didn't understand it. You were scared of storms, so I explained them to you. The more you understand something, the less afraid of it you're going to be. That goes for thunderstorms, flying in airplanes, traveling to new places, hearing new ideas, and especially meeting new people." Granddad was full of that kind of wisdom. I would give anything to have him back, to get to share one more storm with him.

Thinking about Granddaddy of course made me think about Flick, and I decided I was finished waiting for him to get in touch with me. I was worried about him, and the longer he went without calling, the more worried I got. I took out my phone and dialed his number. Straight to voicemail. "Flick here. Leave a message." I told his voicemail that I was worried and begged him to call me back. Then I texted him, and for good measure, sent an email as well.

It was almost 6 p.m. and I was about to head back to the newsroom when I saw Ridley's car pull into the spot reserved for Rosalee's. "Hey there," I called out as she got out of her car. She was alone, no Lizzie this time.

"Riley!" She sounded happy to see me, as she always did. "I just came up here to finish up some paperwork. What're you doing here?"

I got up from the bench and walked over to meet her. "I was looking for you, actually."

"Well, you found me." She smiled, showing off her line of perfectly straight, perfectly white teeth.

"I was wondering if you'd mind if I poked around in the basement for a minute?"

"Sure." She put the key into the lock and turned it. "What're you looking for?"

"I have no idea, actually," I said, following her inside. "But I think I'll know it when I see it."

CHAPTER 40

Ridley helped me move the long narrow stainless steel prep table over to the side of the tiny kitchen. It took both of us to move it the few feet we needed to in order to reveal the trapdoor in the wood floor. The door was a rectangle, about three feet by five feet and had a small round handle set flush.

I looked at Ridley, still breathing heavy from the effort of moving the table. "You ready?"

She nodded. I lifted the handle, turned, and pulled. It was heavy, but not as heavy as the table had been, and I was surprised that I was able to lift the door all the way up to a ninety-degree angle. I was also surprised to see someone had installed one of those hydraulic thingies that kept it open.

I went down first. The staircase was basically a glorified ladder, and I had to climb down into the basement backward like I was climbing into a swimming pool. When I reached the bottom, I looked around, my eyes adjusting slowly to the dark. Tom Bell had been right. It was a wide-open space, dirt floor, large fireplace, low ceiling. In the corner I saw something that I thought could be a shedded snakeskin. At least that's what I hoped it was.

At six feet tall, Ridley could just barely stand up straight down here. It was one time I was glad for my height, or lack thereof. “What are we looking for?” she whispered.

“You don’t have to whisper,” I said in my full voice. “We’re not doing anything wrong.”

“Right,” she said, still in a whisper.

I shot her a look.

“Sorry.”

“Okay.” I looked around. The truth is I wasn’t exactly sure what we were doing here. Trying to find evidence that Rosalee had been planning a remodel that would involve a sledgehammer? Maybe the sledgehammer itself, although I had a sneaking suspicion the sledgehammer in question was the same one sitting inside the evidence locker at the Tuttle County Sheriff’s Department, despite Rosalee’s denials. “I guess, let’s just look around for anything that looks strange or out of place.”

“Like an electrical panel?”

I laughed. It was the kind of literal thing Holman might say. “Yes, Ridley, exactly like that.”

“No, I’m serious,” she said. “Look.”

I followed her outstretched finger, and sure enough there was an electrical panel built right into the stone wall. Why on earth would a cellar with no lights, no outlets, and no electricity need an electrical panel?

Ridley walked over to it and was about to open it when I yelled, “Don’t!”

“What?”

“That could be evidence,” I said. “I’m guessing that’s not a real electrical panel.”

“Well, you’re not as stupid as I thought you were,” a voice that did not belong to Ridley curled out into the dark basement.

My throat went dry. I saw the dark outline of a woman a second before Hadley Lawrence stepped out from behind the edge of the fireplace wielding a large kitchen knife and what I was sure was meant to be a menacing look had the botulinum toxins not deadened her facial nerves.

"Who are you?" Ridley demanded. Then bless her sweet perfect heart, she took a step forward, putting herself between me and that long, sharp blade.

"Do you want to tell her or should I?" Hadley asked, looking around Ridley.

I moved out from behind her. "This is Hadley Lawrence, Greer Mountbatten's sister. Hadley, I'd like you to meet my friend Ridley Nilsson."

"Pleasure," Hadley said, proving you couldn't take the Southern out of a psycho.

"Ridley has nothing to do with any of this. She doesn't know anything. Why don't we just let her go on and get out of here. She won't tell anyone anything, will you?"

"Nice try," Hadley said, raising the knife slightly and nudging it at us. "You—Wonder Woman, get over there against the wall with your little friend."

Your little friend? I didn't love that, but given that Hadley was definitely a few sandwiches short of a picnic, I did what I was told and walked over toward the far wall.

"Sit," Hadley ordered.

We sat.

"You killed your own sister? What kind of a monster does that?" Ridley said, her voice full of the kind of courageous defiance that was as admirable as it was likely to get us chopped into tiny bits.

"She didn't kill anyone," I said quietly.

"Of course I didn't kill my sister!"

Ridley flinched at her shrill tone.

"My brother-in-law and his little whore did that. And I am going to make sure they go to prison for the rest of their lives!"

"Oh," Ridley said. "Wait—then why are you threatening us? We're trying to do the same thing."

Hadley looked at me to see if I knew the answer. I hadn't been sure until I saw her down here, but now I knew I'd been right about the safe. "She's here for the money."

"And why shouldn't I be?" she barked. "They murdered my sister—my own flesh and blood—they *owe* me. And besides, it isn't like they're going to be able to spend it when they're rotting in their jail cells."

"What money?" Ridley asked, confused.

Hadley looked at me and raised her eyebrows. "She really doesn't know?"

"Not a thing," I said. "Just let her go...she can't tell the sheriff something she doesn't even know."

Hadley actually looked like she was considering it until Ridley lifted her chin and said, "I would never leave you here with this *sinnessjuk*!"

Dear, sweet, naive Ridley. She was so brave, so stupid.

"That settles that I guess," Hadley said sharply. You didn't have to speak Swedish to know *sinnessjuk* was no compliment.

"You don't want to do this, Hadley," I said.

Hadley again hoisted the knife in our direction, but her eyes began darting around the cellar. She looked shaken, unsure.

"You're not a killer. You're not like them," I continued.

Her hand began to shake. Hadley Lawrence was not a stable woman. While it was true I didn't think she was a cold-blooded killer either, I wasn't sure what she might do under duress.

"The money will help me take care of the kids when Dale goes to prison," she said loudly, as if the louder she said it, the more legitimate it became. "I need it, I deserve it!" I could see the light from the open trapdoor bouncing off the blade of the knife as her hand trembled.

"I thought you had family money..." I said, thinking back to what Holman had told me.

She made a guttural sound, a rough eruption of sarcasm. "That's what everyone thinks. Our father has made millions, but he's spent 'em too. Plus, he's been married and divorced four times. I'll get what's left, if anything, when he dies, but who knows how long that'll be. And I'll need money to care for Lewis and Charlie. They...they expect a certain lifestyle..."

"You know, I might go insane too if someone killed my sister," Ridley said out of nowhere. We all turned to her in surprise.

"I don't think we want to call her insane, Ridley," I whispered.

"No, she's right," Hadley said after a beat. "I mean, look at me." She raised her arms. "I'm in a basement holding two women at knifepoint. If that isn't insane, I don't know what is!"

"See?" Ridley smiled. "Exactly."

I was not at all sure what was going on, but it seemed like Ridley and Hadley had come to some sort of understanding.

"I just want them to pay for what they did," Hadley said.

"Of course you do. We all do."

Hadley looked over at me, then at Ridley. She let out a humorless laugh. "The craziest part is I can't even open the safe," she said. "The damn thing takes two keys, like a nuclear bomb or something."

I looked over at the electrical panel.

Hadley followed my gaze. "Pretty obvious, isn't it? Why would there be an electrical panel in an eighteenth-century cellar?" She walked over to it, unclipped the hidden latches on the side, and the whole front panel swung open, revealing a wall safe with two silver locks and an electronic keypad. "But the damn thing is like Fort Knox."

I studied the safe for a minute. Two keys. It all made sense now. "And you only have the one from Justin Balzichek—the one he was hiding in his rosary. You pretended to be his aunt and got it from the funeral home."

She looked at me with what appeared to be newfound respect. "Right. Except it was Greer's key—he took it from her when he killed her."

"I thought you said Dale and Rosalee killed her?" Ridley asked, confused again. It wasn't her fault. I'd kept her in the dark on a lot of these details to keep her out of danger. It hadn't exactly worked out as I'd planned.

"They hired Balzichek to do it for them," Hadley said, the bitter edge back in her voice now. "Greer knew what was going on and was going to expose them."

"So why didn't she?"

"Love," Hadley said simply. "She loved that stupid man and thought they could get past this like they'd done before. She thought she could make him stay. She always was a fool when it came to Dale."

"Love can make a fool out of the best of us," Ridley said quietly. I immediately thought of Ryan and had to squash the impulse to yell out, "Preach!" This was definitely not the time.

"When Greer found out that Dale had been hoarding money with Rosalee, she was angry. So she came down here and found that disgusting Balzichek and hired him to attack their restaurant. She thought that would scare Dale, make him believe his money wasn't safe here. I told her not to do it, that it wasn't going to work, but she wouldn't listen to me."

I could see Hadley getting agitated again as she told the story. "Dale or Rosalee—I'm not sure who—must have found out Greer was behind the incident. My guess is they tracked down Balzichek and hired him to kill her, thinking it would look like their shady deal with the vandalism had gone wrong. Greer told me Balzichek called her after the incident and wanted to meet. Said he was going to tell the police that she hired him unless she paid up. The problem was, she didn't have any money, not really. She knew Dale had a safe somewhere down here, and she'd found the key he kept hidden in his rosary."

"Wait—it was Dale's rosary?"

"You didn't know that?" Hadley looked genuinely surprised.

"No, I thought it was Justin's."

"I met Justin Balzichek once and let me tell you, I'd sooner believe that man was the devil himself than a practicing Catholic." Hadley rolled her eyes. "Not that Dale is a whole lot better. He was only a Catholic when it was convenient. Didn't start carrying that thing around until about the same time he moved Rosalee down here. I always told Greer that I thought that was suspicious. It was like he replaced his Rosalee with a rosary. Creepy as all get out, if you ask me. 'Course now we know why."

"Who has the other key?" Ridley asked.

"Rosalee probably." Hadley shrugged. "I'm guessing that's why she hasn't left town yet. She wants the money."

"Interesting. Clearly, they didn't trust each other."

"So you think Balzichek was paid to kill Greer and then took the key for himself?" Ridley asked.

"I'm thinking that Greer tried to bargain with him," Hadley said, closing her eyes as if the thought was painful.

"Tried to tell him she'd give him money if he let her..." she broke off and took a deep breath before continuing. "And Balzichek decided to kill her anyway and just take the key for himself."

If Justin Balzichek was the kind of man he appeared to be, it would make sense that he'd take the key and either try to find the safe or possibly blackmail Dale and Rosalee with it. That was the most likely option, seeing that Balzichek ended up dead just a couple of days later.

The more I thought about it, the clearer things were becoming. We still didn't know who killed Balzichek for sure, but given the stomach contents showed undigested pastry dough, my money was on Rosalee. We had to tell Carl about the safe. It was the last puzzle piece, the thing everybody was after, the reason Dale and Rosalee were both hanging around Tuttle Corner, the reason Rosalee had a key made at Sanford's, and the reason Balzichek was dead.

"Hadley, if Dale and Rosalee did what it looks like they did," I said, softly, "they need to be held accountable."

Hadley looked up, her face wracked with grief. She wasn't going to hurt us; I could see that now. She was upset and desperate and probably struggling with some mental health issues, but she was no killer. I stood up slowly.

She looked at me, then down at the knife in her hand. I continued to meet her gaze until she finally lowered her hand and dropped it. The knife made a dull thudding sound as it fell onto the dirt floor.

"We'll go with you to the sheriff," I said.

She nodded, turned around, and that's when the tears began to fall.

The three of us climbed up the ladder and out of the cellar, exhausted from the tension of the past thirty minutes.

Hadley seemed calmer now that she had made the decision to do the right thing. I felt certain that going to the sheriff with her story would provide her with a kind of resolution and peace that no amount of money ever could.

It had started to storm while we'd been in the cellar, and I could hear the rain pounding on the roof along with intermittent bouts of thunder. It would be a soggy walk to the sheriff's station. I pulled out my phone and saw that I'd missed several calls from Holman, but he hadn't left a message. He texted once, about a minute ago, but it was just the letter "r." Sure it was just a butt-dial text, I slipped my phone back into my pocket and was about to help Ridley close up the door to the cellar when she said, "Shit. I think my phone must have fallen out of my pocket down there."

Hadley was leaning against the cooktop, lost in her own thoughts. She didn't seem likely to take off on me, especially not in this rain, so I told Ridley to just go down there real fast and get it. We'd wait.

As Ridley climbed back down, I was about to ask Hadley how she was doing when I heard the back door open. I stilled. Hadley must have heard it too because she looked at me, her eyes wide. We heard footsteps coming down the short hallway seconds before Holman and Rosalee appeared in the tiny kitchen. They were soaking wet.

"Riley!" Rosalee said, rushing over to me and throwing her arms around my neck. "Thank God you're safe!"

Stunned silent, I stood there as she hugged me, paralyzed with shock.

"What is she doing here?" Hadley sniped, her voice heading into batshit-crazy territory again. "Is this some sort of a setup?"

Unsure of what else to do, I tried to communicate to Holman with a single look that Dale and Rosalee had hired

Justin Balzichek to kill Greer and were now both trying to figure out a way to get to the millions they'd been hiding in the creepy old cellar beneath her restaurant and that Hadley had figured it all out and was planning to take the money for herself but instead decided to go to Sheriff Haight and tell him everything. It was a tall order for a look, but I tried anyway.

Holman's eyes never left mine until he blinked, then blinked again, then blinked again. *Like a toad in a hailstorm.* He was nervous, which could only mean one thing: That magnificent bastard already had figured it out. He knew Rosalee was a killer, and he was here to stop her.

CHAPTER 41

Rosalee," I said, trying to make my voice sound casual and not at all scared to death. "Where have you been?"

"You bitch!" Hadley screamed and launched herself at Rosalee, who whipped around with surprising agility, turning me around like a human shield. It wasn't until I saw the fear in Hadley's and Holman's eyes that I felt the pressure of cold steel at my neck. Rosalee had a gun at my throat.

"Get back," she said, calm and cool as ever. "Both of you."

"Rosalee," Holman said. "What're you doing? Let her go—"

"Don't." She cut him off, her voice as sharp as an ice pick. "I know you figured it out on the way over here. You're a terrible liar."

Holman pressed his lips together and looked down. He spoke softly. "You knew Balzichek was poisoned with cyanide. The sheriff never released that." The look of complete and utter betrayal on his face was heartbreaking. "How could you do it?"

"Justin Balzichek deserved everything he got," Rosalee said. "He was a bottom-feeder. Vermin."

"Takes one to know one," Hadley hissed.

"Oh, please shut up," Rosalee said. "I would hate to get

upset and let my trigger finger slip."

An involuntary whimper escaped me, but I was careful not to move. The barrel of the gun was pressing into my flesh.

"Where's the key?" Rosalee said to Hadley. "I know you have it."

Hadley gave her a triumphant look. "I'm guessing that was you who tried to break into the funeral home to get it off poor dead whatshisname? Too bad I got there first."

So it had been Rosalee who tried to break in that night at Campbell & Sons.

"I'm serious." Rosalee tightened her elbow around my neck. "Give it to me."

"Think for a second, Rosalee," Holman tried again. "How will you escape? Even if you do manage to kill all of us and get the money, you won't be able to get away. Someone will hear the shots, the police will track you down in a matter of minutes."

He had a point and Rosalee knew it. What Rosalee didn't know was that Ridley was down in the basement at this very moment with the knife Hadley had dropped. She had to have heard the commotion up here, and if there was a God in heaven—or maybe more aptly, a signal in the cellar, she would have already called 911. We just had to stall long enough for them to get here.

"He's right," I said, my voice quavering. "If you stop now, it'll be better for you."

"I just want to get my money and leave. That's all I've ever wanted. That night in the cemetery when you saw me," she said to Holman, "I was looking for the key. I thought it might have fallen out of Balzichek's pocket when I dragged him out there. I needed it—that stupid safe Dale installed requires two keys plus a pass code. Three failed attempts and it goes into permanent lock-out mode. I'd already tried once."

"With the key you had Ryan make," I said, putting things together.

"Right. But the keys aren't the same. So when you offered to help me," she again addressed Holman, "I had no choice. And then I realized I could use you to bait Dale."

Holman's ears turned bright red, his shoulders rounding as if he was trying to disappear.

"It was all his idea," Rosalee said. "Dale said if we got rid of Greer, we could take the money and be long gone before the police even knew what happened. Then that stupid Balzichek demanded we pay him. Said he had Greer's key and that he was going to tell the cops everything if we didn't pay up."

So Hadley had been right. Justin Balzichek took the key from Greer when he killed her. She must have brought it to their meeting as a bargaining chip. Sadly for her, Balzichek wasn't interested in a trade.

"Dale took everything from me—my youth, my innocence, my ability to live a normal life. I was practically his prisoner all these years. But I loved him, or thought I did, and I believed his lies. He promised that once we had enough money, we would go live out the rest of our lives on a beach somewhere away from here, away from *her*."

For the first time in all the years I knew Rosalee, she didn't sound bored or uninterested. There was real emotion in her voice. Unfortunately, that emotion was homicidal rage.

"So what happened?" Hadley said, a sneer pulling at the corner of her lip. "He betrayed you just like he did his wife? What a shocker!" It was clear there was a part of Hadley that was enjoying this.

I felt the muscles in Rosalee's arm tense up. "We agreed that I would take care of Balzichek. We figured the police would think he killed Greer and they'd close the case. I arranged to meet Balzichek at my house, flirted with him a little to disarm him."

I saw Holman's nostrils flare in anger, the humiliation settling in.

"I offered to fix him a nice plate of almond croissants—your favorite." She tugged at my neck. "The almond paste perfectly masks the scent of cyanide, did you know that?"

"No," I said, even though I did thanks to Carl. I had a strict policy against being a know-it-all around anyone holding me at gunpoint.

"Dale was supposed to come down to Tuttle and help me get rid of the body. Then we were going to get the money out and I was to fly to Belize. He said he would join me after the funeral, after the investigation had settled down. That was the plan. But he never showed up that night, and he wouldn't answer any of my calls." Her voice got louder, faster as she talked. "I tried for hours until finally I realized he was not coming. He was going to let me take the fall for all of it. No one other than Greer and me knew about his illegal dealings with the Qataris. With both of us out of the way, he would be free to do whatever he wanted. With *whomever* he wanted. So I dragged Balzichek out my back door and dumped him at Sterns and decided I would clean out the safe and disappear."

Just then, a dull thunk sound floated up from the basement. Rosalee jerked toward the trapdoor, still standing open. "Who's down there?" She addressed this question to Hadley. When Hadley didn't say anything, she tightened her grip on my neck. "Who?"

"No one—" I stammered, my heart thumping in my

throat so hard, I was surprised I could speak at all. "Probably just a snake or a rat or something."

Holman knitted his brows and titled his chin toward me, asking the same question without words. I couldn't very well answer him, so I just widened my eyes and hoped he understood that meant we need to keep Rosalee from going down there.

"You're a terrible liar too. Someone better tell me who is down there or else I am just going to start shooting," she said, her voice rising. "One...two..."

"Rosalee?" A male voice called everyone's attention toward the back door. Dale Mountbatten stood in the entrance to the kitchen. In all the commotion about the noise from the basement, none of us had heard the back door open or Dale walking in.

"You," Rosalee growled. Her breath was hot in my ear and I could feel the sinewy muscles in her arm tense.

"Christ on a cracker!" Hadley blurted out. "What's next?"

"Honey, what's going on here?" Dale said, taking a step toward Rosalee.

"Don't. Move." Rosalee backed up toward the sink, my feet sliding as she tugged me along. "And don't 'honey' me either."

Dale stopped. He looked around the kitchen at Holman, Hadley—whom he seemed surprised to see—and lastly, the wide-open trapdoor. "I'm gonna need a little help understanding just what in the world is going on here, Rosie. Is this all part of your plan to set me up?"

"Set *you* up?" she seethed at him. "You set *me* up. You never came that night to help me with Balzichek. I called and called and you didn't pick up. I waited for hours!"

With her ire directed at Dale, it seemed like she'd forgotten about the noise in the basement. I looked at Holman, who, I noticed, took the opportunity to move a step closer to the swinging door that led to the front of the café.

"No—you never called—" Dale said, sounding almost as hurt and betrayed as Rosalee did. "I had our phone with me all night. I was waiting. You never called. I was worried sick."

"Liar!" Rosalee shouted.

Another involuntary whine bubbled up from my chest.

"Why would I set you up?" Dale said. "I wanted us to follow the plan so we could be together, and the next thing I know you stopped contacting me, you wouldn't answer my calls. And then I found out you told her—" he pointed at me like I was a side of beef "—about Colonel Mustard Enterprises and I thought you were setting it up for me to go down for the whole thing."

At that moment, Hadley started laughing, cackling really, a sharp incongruous sound. "You guys are so stupid," she said, barely able to catch her breath. "I mean, it was as easy as catchin' fireflies in a jar." She broke off into more uncontrolled bouts of laughter.

Holman took another half step closer to the door. He was only about two feet from it now.

"What are you talking about, Hadley?" Dale's voice was sharp and abrasive. "And what are you even doing here?"

"Yes, what *are* you talking about?" Rosalee said and swiveled the gun from my neck to Hadley's chest.

Hadley didn't even react except to wipe a tear from the corner of her eye as she sighed with satisfaction. She looked straight at Dale, ignoring Rosalee and the gun completely. "Greer knew all about your little Colonel Mustard business," she said, using air quotes around the words. "She knew everything. And she told me everything, too. She thought she could get you to break things off with little miss frog over here, but then..." she skipped over the unpleasant business of murder-for-hire. "Do you know how easy it is to have calls forwarded from a cell number? I mean, it's so simple, a monkey could do it."

Dale looked confused for a moment, and then understanding started to set in. "When you came to stay with us..." he said, almost to himself.

"Now you're getting it," Hadley said with a mock congratulatory tone.

"You never got my calls?" Rosalee's voice sounded as vulnerable as a child's.

Dale shook his head, almost in disbelief.

Hadley seemed to revel in the silence as she watched them absorb what she had done. "I found your stupid burner phone—you really shouldn't have left it lying around your office, you know." She made a tsk-tsk sound. "My initial plan was just to record you admitting to Greer's murder. 'Course I couldn't have known y'all were going to kill Justin Balzichek too."

"So you weren't planning to leave without me?" Dale looked at Rosalee, a pained expression on his face.

"No," she said. "Not until I thought you—"

Dale ran a hand through his thick hair before bringing it to rest behind his neck. He asked, "Did you bring your key?"

"Yes. In my back pocket," Rosalee said, then quickly added, pointing toward Hadley, "she has yours."

In the look Dale gave Hadley, you could practically see years of resentment and anger, not to mention the frustration of the past few weeks. "It'll be my pleasure to take it back," he snarled. He started to walk toward Hadley when another sound came from the basement. It sounded like rocks skittering across dirt and hitting stone. Everyone froze.

"What was that?" Dale asked.

"I think there's someone down there," Rosalee said. Then, keeping the gun pointed toward Holman and Hadley, she released the hold she had around my neck and pushed me forward. "Go. Over there."

Shaken, I scrambled over next to Holman. He grabbed my hand, a rare but comforting gesture of affection.

"Go down and see who it is," Rosalee said. "I'll stay here." It was clear Dale and Rosalee were a team once again. That did not bode well for us. Or for Ridley.

"Wait—" I said, trying to stall for time. I kept thinking that surely Carl and Butter would come blazing in at any moment. Everyone looked at me expectantly, but my mind went blank. "I don't think you should go down there!"

Dale looked at me and scoffed. Then he turned to Rosalee and nodded toward her gun, "You have another one handy?"

"This is the one you gave me for protection all those years ago." She sounded like she was talking about a ring or a bouquet of flowers, not a handgun. It was surreal.

"Take one of those." She gestured with her chin toward the magnetic knife rack on the wall.

Dale grabbed a large knife and headed over to the open door in the floor. He brushed past Rosalee, kissed her cheek, and whispered something that made her blush. Yup. They were back on again, a real-life Bonnie and Clyde. Lucky us.

In a panicked attempt to warn Ridley, I started to make the sound of a European siren. It was all I could think to do. *"Eeee-oooo-eeee-ooo-eeee-oooo!"*

Dale stopped mid-climb. Rosalee looked one part surprised, three parts enraged. "Shut up!" they said in unison.

I shut up. I hoped Ridley heard me and got my warning,

no matter how ridiculous it might have sounded.

Dale continued his climb down, and after a few silent seconds, in which Rosalee didn't take her eyes off of us, he called up, "All clear down here. Probably just a rat."

Rosalee visibly relaxed. I snuck a look at Hadley, who was the only other person in the kitchen who knew Ridley was down there. She gave a little shrug. I hoped that meant Ridley found the hiding place behind the far edge of the fireplace where Hadley had been hiding when we went down there.

A couple more silent moments passed until we heard Dale say, "What the—" and a loud thwacking sound. *Ridley.* I squeezed Holman's hand and closed my eyes. I couldn't bear the thought of what he might have done to her.

"Dale?" Rosalee called to him, her eyes—and gun—still on us. "Everything all right down there?"

There was no response for maybe three or four seconds. I could see Rosalee was getting nervous, and I wasn't sure what she would do. We all waited, our eyes on the trapdoor.

"Actually," the voice that carried up from the cellar was not Dale's. It was Ridley's, sounding as strong and clear and brave as ever. "There's been a change of plans."

Rosalee turned in surprise at the sound of Ridley's voice, and in that split second Holman yanked hard on my hand and pulled me out through the swinging door that led to the front of the café. I heard a shot go off in the kitchen and what I thought was Hadley screaming. Part of me wanted to go back in there to make sure she was okay—and more importantly that Ridley was—but Holman had a tight grip on my hand as he pulled me through the restaurant and out the front door. We ran in the pouring rain down the sidewalk, and the second we rounded the corner, I pulled out my phone and called 911.

CHAPTER 42

She was like Crocodile Dundee down there!" Butter was telling the story for what seemed like the tenth time over at the sheriff's station. He laughed and shook his head like he still couldn't believe it. "Once we got Rosalee in cuffs, I looked down into the floor and there was Ridley in the cellar, standing with one foot on top of Dale Mountbatten, who was hog-tied within an incha his life. Ridley was pointing a kitchen knife this long—" he held his fingers comically far apart (I'd seen the knife and it wasn't two feet long) "—at that poor man's carotid and he was bawling like a stuck pig. Ridley looked like she was just out for a stroll in the park."

Apparently, Ridley, who was taller than Dale by at least two inches, had conked him over the head with a loose stone from the fireplace. She used her belt to hog-tie him while he was semiconscious, then positioned him in front of her so that Rosalee couldn't get a clean shot off without going through Dale. Ridley said that she and Rosalee had a "nice chat" about how quickly Dale would bleed out if anything happened to make her hand slip. Carl and Butter got there within four minutes of our 911 call. Rosalee didn't even resist.

Dale and Rosalee would both likely face a laundry list of criminal charges from the prosecutor, including armed criminal action, conspiracy to commit murder, and murder in the first degree, among the other charges for the financial crimes that would come from the federal courts. Carl assured us that first thing in the morning, he'd be meeting with DA Lindsey Davis to go over the evidence and get the criminal charges filed ASAP.

"They're already starting to rat each other out," Carl said. "Dale says hiring Balzichek to kill Greer was all Rosalee's idea. Claims he knew nothing about her plot to poison him either." Carl rolled his eyes. "Funny, she's saying the whole scheme was his idea."

"I wonder if we'll ever really know what happened?" I said.

"I think now that we know what we're looking for, the evidence and testimony will paint a fairly clear picture. Fact is, they got greedy. No one probably would have ever known about the money laundering if they hadn't killed Greer. The amount they ran through that fake butter distributor wasn't enough to raise any flags. They'd been getting away with it for years."

"Have you been able to get into the safe yet?" Holman asked. We had been speculating about what might be inside, given the intense security measures.

Carl shook his head. "Not yet. We're gonna have to get a team down here Monday to open it. They've both indicated there's cash in there. Rosalee said something about gold coins as well. We'll see. It's probably whatever Dale got from the Qataris that he couldn't launder."

Holman had been quiet the whole time we were at the station, and it was obvious he was taking it hard, finding out about Rosalee. Every so often, he'd look down the hall toward the room where Rosalee was being held for questioning. Carl picked up on it. "Don't feel bad, buddy," he said, clapping Holman on the shoulder. "It wasn't just you. She fooled us all for a long time."

I was always surprised at how long it took to process and book people, and by the time those of us not being charged with a crime were allowed to leave the sheriff's station, it was close to midnight. We were all exhausted. As we walked out into the cold night air, Holman thanked Ridley again.

"You showed incredible bravery tonight. Not to mention an admirable sense of ingenuity. How did you know how to tie someone up like that?"

Ridley smiled, her perfect white teeth reflecting light from a street lamp overhead. "Let's just say this was not my first rodeo." She threw her head back and laughed, somehow appearing humble, sexy, and brilliant all at the same time.

"Where's Hadley?" I asked, looking around. Fortunately, Rosalee's shot missed Hadley by a foot, so I knew she was physically okay. Her emotional state was another story.

"The sheriff had some more questions for her," Holman said.

Hadley Lawrence wasn't someone I'd want to be best pals with, but I did feel sorry for her. She loved her sister, and in her grief and desperation after Greer was murdered, she made a few really bad decisions. I hoped this whole experience would lead her to get the help she needed. I also hoped she had a good lawyer.

On the subject of lawyers, Ash had been called down to the station to identify Hadley as the person who took Balzichek's stuff. He now stood with us outside the station as we downloaded the craziness of what had happened.

Ryan stood next to Ridley, as he had since the moment he'd burst into the sheriff's office wild with panic. I could tell he was truly terrified at the thought of her being in danger. Ridley seemed surprised by his level of alarm, but also flattered. At one point, I saw her take his face into her hands and look into his eyes. "I'm okay," she said softly. I watched as he closed his eyes, visible relief washing over him.

After a few more minutes spent speculating about what would happen to Dale and Rosalee, Ridley and Ryan left to go back to his parents' house, because as Ridley said, "The Tavern will open tomorrow at 6 a.m. as usual. Almost being killed is no excuse to let down our customers." She really was Wonder Woman. I hated—and loved—that about her.

"I'm gonna get going too," Ash said, then turned to me and with a casual shrug added, "You want to get that drink sometime this weekend?"

I had almost forgotten it was Friday. "Uh, sure."

"Great." He shoved his hands into his pockets as his eyes moved over toward Holman and then back to me. "I'll call you, okay?"

"As long as you don't call me 'honey.'" I couldn't resist.

Ash laughed and walked off in the direction of the parking lot.

Although I was exhausted, I didn't feel like going home just yet. Holman and I walked in companionable silence in the direction of the back parking lot. The clouds had moved out after the earlier storms, leaving the air refreshed and crisp. It was a moonless night that allowed the stars to stand out in all their glory against the inky sky. That was another perk of living in Tuttle Corner—no ambient light to compete with the heavens.

"He doesn't seem like your type," Holman said after a few seconds.

"Who, Ash?" I asked. "What does that mean?"

Holman tilted his head to the side, seeming surprised

that I required an explanation. "Ryan is warm, friendly, open...he's basically the human version of a golden retriever. Jay is polished and charming and very brave. And Ash... well, I don't really know him, but he seems to have a darker sensibility than your typical boyfriends."

"Slow down," I said. "He's not my anything right now."

"Mmmm." That was the sound Holman made when he disagreed with me but didn't want to say why.

"Besides, I think there's more there beneath the surface. He's been through some really tough stuff lately. I think he's a good guy deep down. But don't worry," I said, "I'm not jumping into anything. I think it's time to concentrate on me."

The feeling had been sneaking up on me for a while now that it was time to take a break from love and romance. (Even Regina H had been able to see I wasn't in a good place to start a new relationship.) I wasn't going to swear off men forever, but it was time to learn who I was outside of a relationship. Everywhere I looked I saw examples of love's power to transform, for better or worse. It was like a pendulum that swung from the highest highs to the lowest lows. And it wasn't just seeing the Dale Mountbattens of the world hiring hit men to kill their wives—those kinds of things are born of pure greed. More disturbing to me was seeing how easily Hadley was able to manipulate two people who were supposedly so much in love. She engineered a tiny deviation in their relationship—an unreturned phone call, a missed date—and suddenly they were ready to believe the worst of each other. It reminded me that love was a powerful thing and not to be trifled with. Of course, I'd been reminded of that when I saw how quickly Jay had moved on. It hurt more than I cared to admit. Obviously, I had some unresolved feelings there I probably needed to deal with.

Perhaps Holman got it worst of all, though. I worried for him. When we got to where I'd chained up my bicycle, I turned to him. "I'm sorry Rosalee let you down."

He looked down at his shoes. "She said she liked me." Holman sounded one part confused and ten parts hurt. It killed me to see him in so much pain. I didn't know what to say, but I knew the usual "There are other fish in the sea" kind of pep talk wasn't going to cut it.

Holman was a unique person, and I don't mean that in the way Southerners used the word. ("*Unique*," like "bless her heart" and "God love 'em," took on new meaning south of the Mason-Dixon line—and not a good one.) Holman was unique in the sense that he was truly singular, exceptional. Finding someone who would love him for all his exceptional singularity would not be easy. I suspect it had already been hard, particularly in light of what Camilla had said about his father leaving.

I lifted my arm and pointed into the sky. "Do you see Orion's Belt there?"

Holman's eyes followed to where I was pointing. "Yes."

"Okay, so you see those three stars that sort of look like they're hanging from Orion's Belt?"

He squinted and scrunched up his nose. Eventually he said, "Yes."

"So that's Orion's Sword. Now, I want you to look about midway down the sword. Do you see that hazy area that sort of looks like a reddish glowing apostrophe?"

It took him a minute, but he found it. "Yes."

"That's Orion's Nebula. It doesn't look like much from here, but if we were looking at it through a telescope, you'd see four bright blue stars surrounded by hundreds of other stars in every celestial color imaginable. They look like jewels in a felt-lined box—red rubies, yellow diamonds, blue sapphires—surrounded by wispy tendrils of orange, purple, and pink. It's magnificent, one of the most awe-inspiring structures in our galaxy." I paused. "From here, the view is sort of ordinary, but if you look closer, it takes your breath away."

Holman continued to stare at the spot, straining with the effort of trying to see it as anything other than a chalky smudge in the sky.

"That's you." I turned to him and smiled. "You're just like Orion's Nebula. On the surface you may appear kind of ordinary, but when you take a closer look, what you see is truly remarkable."

He was quiet for a long few moments, his gaze held steady at the sky. "Thank you, Riley," he said eventually. He paused again and then added, "You are more than merely a co-worker."

I laughed. "Thanks, Will. You are more than merely a co-worker too."

Dear Miss Ellison,

Thank you for the thorough email with your thoughts on the **Sugar, How'd You Get So F.L.Y.™** program. We at Click.com are always interested in hearing from our customers, even when that feedback is less than complimentary! #ouch #youcantwinthemall

I am sorry to hear you feel the program is a "thinly veiled marketing scheme to get people who are interested in self-improvement to spend crazy amounts of money on even crazier products." You'll be glad to know that I have shared your email with the Director of our F.L.Y.™ division, Dr. Haven-Shapiro-Foster-Klein. Please note it may take some time to get a response, as Dr. Haven-Shapiro-Foster-Klein is currently on a spiritual pilgrimage/ product research trip to Mount Kailash in Tibet. #nocellservice #youcanthearmenow

Please don't feel badly about opting out of the seven-day free trial. To be honest, it comes as something of a relief. You were my first client, and while I believe deeply in the ideals of the program, I don't think I am cut out to be a F.L.Y. Guy.™ I've decided being Personal Romance Concierge™ is a better match for my talents! #byebyebigcommissions #hellointegrity #andramennoodles

Furthermore, I understand your decision to take some time off of dating to focus on yourself. At the risk of internal sanction, I applaud your decision! Please know that when you are ready to get back in the game, we at Click.com will be here ready, willing, and able to assist. Until that day comes, I wish you the very best on your journey of self-discovery. #youdoyou #alonenot-lonely #beyourownhero

Sincerely,

Regina H,
Personal Romance Concierge™
Click.com

CHAPTER 43

SATURDAY

I woke up before dawn to the sound of my house phone ringing. My landline had never rung before. In fact, the only reason I even had a landline was because my parents insisted I have a security system installed a few weeks ago, after my house was broken into. I had no idea who could be calling me this early. I hadn't given anyone that number, mostly because I didn't even know it myself.

I reached for the cordless phone sitting in the cradle on the floor by my bed. "Hello?" I said, sounding unsettlingly like one of Marge Simpson's sisters.

"Ellison?" It was Kay Jackson.

I sat up, struggling to rouse myself from sleep. "Kay?"

"I've been calling your cell and couldn't get you."

I picked up my cell from the nightstand and sure enough there were four missed calls from her. I must have really been asleep.

"Sorry to wake you," Kay said, sounding overly kind. Something was wrong.

"What is it?" I swung my feet onto the floor and gathered the blanket over my lap, a chill seizing me that had nothing to do with the temperature of the room.

"It's Flick."

The words knocked the wind out of me, and for a moment

I couldn't speak. "What happened?"

"He's been in an accident." She paused. "It's bad."

My pulse began to pound in places you shouldn't be able to feel your pulse, like the edges of my eyeballs, inside my eardrum, and at the base of my throat. "Where?"

"Carilion Memorial Hospital in Roanoke."

"What happened?"

"His car went off the road on Route 58."

"Fifty-eight?" I asked, rising to my feet. "No. No, Flick was in Chincoteague just the other day. He—he..."

"The police called me because they found his business card tucked into the breast pocket of his shirt." Kay paused. "I think you should get up there, Riley."

Flick didn't have any children of his own. He had a niece who I think lived overseas and a couple of nephews on the West Coast. His ex-wife was living in Washington, DC, and had remarried years ago.

I grabbed my jeans from the chair where I'd thrown them last night, holding the phone between my shoulder and ear. "I'll drop Coltrane at my parents and then I'll—shit," I said, realizing I didn't have a car.

"What's wrong?"

"Nothing," I said. "I'll figure it out."

"Okay. And Riley?" she said, her voice low and serious. "Come by the newsroom before you go. I have something I'm supposed to give you."

A little over a month ago, Flick told me that he left a file for me with Kay that I was to ask for should anything "happen to him." I closed my eyes against the possibility that that time had come.

"He's not going to die." My denial sounded so foolish, so childish, but I didn't care. I needed to believe that Flick was going to be okay, and if I had to say it out loud a